Praise for Returning to Adelaide

'Fun, flirty and full of laughs! Written with style and substance. I fell in love with the characters and was taken on a ride through their highs and lows while being transported to an exotic Greek Island,' *Nicole O'Brian, Montrose, Victoria.*

'I devoured this book! From a bleak season in London I was magically transported to the warm, balmy nights of Greece to follow Adelaide's adventure of spontaneity, love, lust, resilience and self-belief. Fun, inspiring and complete escapism!' *Lisa Kelly, London, UK.*

'Never a dull moment, nor a dull character. I was completely invested in the life of Adelaide Jones from the very first page. Every twist and turn had me captivated and some of the characters had me laughing out loud. This novel is an absolute joy to read, and at the same time grapples with very real and challenging themes that people, and especially mothers of young children, cannot avoid and must find a way through. Sometimes those challenges make us lose something of ourselves and sometimes they help us return to ourselves. I thoroughly recommend,' *Marion Osmond, Eltham, Victoria.*

'This book came at a time when I really needed a chance to get away from it all but clearly couldn't—thanks COVID-19! It was amazing and also a not too subtle reminder to love yourself first. Here's to all of us finding a tanned, brilliant person to whisk us away and devour us on a Greek Island. Loved it,' *Brooke Adair, Northcote, Victoria.*

'I was hooked from the beginning. The writing was impressive and the story touched on so many big themes, for women especially. It was the perfect distraction. I can't wait to read whatever Anne writes next. Amazing,' *Valentina Smith, Kensington, Victoria.*

'I loved going on this ride with Adelaide. I wish I had her courage to tip life upside down to find something better,' *Andrea Maher, Croydon, Victoria.*

Praise for Returning to Adelaide

'The characters are so vibrant and full of life. I didn't know how invested I was until I realised I'd read the second half of the book in one sitting! I didn't want Adelaide's story to end but I couldn't stop reading,' *David Bowley, Caulfield North, Victoria.*

'I read this in a day and a half. An incredible novel! The characters were wonderful and the images of Greece were evocative. I loved escaping into this story. Enjoyable and totally addictive!' *Bronwyn White, St Kilda, Victoria.*

'Adelaide is a character that grabs hold of your hand and pulls you along through page after page. I found myself thinking of her during my day, questioning what I would do, how I would respond if I was in her situation. A story littered with shades of pain that give way to the bright light of hope and joy. I look forward to reading more by the wonderful wordsmith that is Anne Freeman,' *Andrea Dato, Melbourne, Victoria.*

'The writing style is refreshing. I was absorbed in every detail of this story of courage, quest for self, love and adventure,' *Carly Ruggeri, Geelong, Victoria.*

'Glorious! This book is a beautiful celebration of strong women, and of the power of reconnecting with our passions and remembering who we were before the metamorphosis of motherhood. There's delicious romance, a breathtaking setting, and heart-warming friendships. I laughed, I cried, I raged and I cheered! And thank you to Anne Freeman for taking me to Ikaria—what an escape!' *Brooke Crawford, Altona North, Victoria.*

'This was an easy read—entertaining, engaging and peppered with deep emotion. The characters were so well drawn, particularly Adelaide. You could literally feel her pain as she navigated the sudden difficulty of managing the end of her relationship. Her journey to a new life is uplifting, her bravery and sense of positivity shines through. Thoroughly recommended,' *Christine Kelly, London, UK.*

RETURNING TO ADELAIDE

ANNE FREEMAN

HAWKEYE

PUBLISHING

First published in Australia in 2022 by Hawkeye Publishing.

Copyright © Anne Freeman

Cover Design by Ellen Milligan and Anne Freeman

Proudly printed in Australia.

ISBN 9780645309942

 NATIONAL LIBRARY OF AUSTRALIA

A catalogue record of this book is available from the National Library of Australia.

www.hawkeyepublishing.com.au
www.hawkeyebooks.com.au

For Paul, the sun around whom I spin.

PROLOGUE

'MAKE your nipple into a burger shape and shove it in his mouth.'

Adelaide Jones tried to focus on what the midwife was saying but the halitosis wafting out with each stern word was making her queasy. After a twenty-three hour labour and two largely sleepless nights, her head swam with exhaustion as she tried to focus her wandering mind.

'A burger! Shape it into a burger! That's not a burger!'

The stench reminded Adelaide of the liquid which inexplicably formed in the bottom of the kitchen bin sometimes and she turned her head slightly to stifle a gag.

'Shape into a burger,' Adelaide repeated, wincing as she gingerly manipulated her flesh, raw as it was from her previous failed breastfeeding attempts.

'Wake up, little man! Wake up!' trilled the midwife, rubbing Darcy vigorously on the back. He curled his little body tighter into Adelaide's embrace.

'Shouldn't we let him sleep?' asked Adelaide, her eyes falling on Estée, asleep in the Perspex bassinette by her side.

'Do you want them losing weight? You're out of here today and I can't discharge you if you don't know how to feed them,' barked the midwife. 'Things can go very wrong, very quickly, when they're this little.' Her eyes darted up with each "very".

Adelaide nodded.

On the other side of the room, Joe stood amongst a swarm of relatives and family friends, most of whom Adelaide had met for the first time today. She stared intently at him, hoping to catch his attention. Instead, it was Joe's father, Tony, who looked over and Adelaide blushed with embarrassment over her partial nudity, lifting Darcy higher to conceal the engorged orb of her left breast. Feeling overwhelmed and bullied by her matronly companion, she opened her mouth to call out to Joe but her words caught in her throat as the midwife seized her nipple and clamped Darcy's mouth to it, manipulating his head like a sock puppet. His eyes snapped open momentarily before settling into a languid suckle.

Adelaide's eyes filled with tears just as she heard Joe insisting that everyone follow them home for lunch.

AN hour later, once the capsules containing their sleeping newborns had been installed in the car, Adelaide turned to Joe. 'I don't think I can do this…' she began, searching for words in the thick fog which engulfed her mind. 'Lunch I mean, having everyone to the house. Well, it just feels a bit too…'

'Yeah, it's fine. You don't have to cook. I've ordered platters from the kebab place,' he said, giving her a reassuring pat on the leg.

Defeated, Adelaide shifted in her seat, trying in vain to find a comfortable position as Joe maneuvered the car out of the gloomy carpark and into the bright midday sunshine. Resting her head against the doorframe, she drifted in and out of consciousness until she was jolted awake by Joe's mother, Lienna, opening one of the rear doors. She cooed loudly at her grandchildren, jiggling the handle of Estée's capsule and exclaiming, 'How does this work? How do I get her out?' She turned to address the cluster of relatives standing by the front door. 'New-fangled technology! I held Ġużeppi on my lap, home from the hospital.'

'Mum,' grumbled Joe, 'don't call me that.'

Lienna clicked her tongue and rolled her eyes theatrically for the benefit of her audience.

Adelaide stood on shaky legs. 'Here, I can…'

She slid past Lienna and extracted the capsule, taking care not to wake Estée who grimaced at the disturbance.

'I'll take her,' said Lienna, swatting at Adelaide's hand until she relinquished her possession of the infant. She watched as the babies who, just days ago, had been cocooned within her body, rode a wave of strangers into the house.

'Mixed shish platters?'

Adelaide turned slowly to find that a stack of aluminium trays was being thrust at her.

'Thanks,' she muttered at the retreating delivery boy, before shuffling into the house.

'Tony! Come and get the food,' Lienna yelled at her ex-husband from where she sat on the sofa, proudly showing off her granddaughter. Next to her, Joe twitched Darcy's lower lip with his index finger, so it looked like the baby was talking. 'I have the best dad in the world,' he said, in a cartoonish voice.

'I'll go,' said Joe's stepmother, Valerie, halting Tony's trajectory as she scowled at an oblivious Lienna.

Relieving Adelaide of the food trays, Valerie offered an insipid smile before hissing at her daughters to come and help.

Adelaide watched in surreal detachment as the women spread her prized possession—a newly restored South Sumatran ceremonial cloth—across the dining table and set down the food. Orange oil stains sprang from the base of the trays like an aura through the fine fabric, and Adelaide looked down at her still-outstretched arms to realise her sleeves bore the same stamp.

Standing motionless in the throng, Adelaide vaguely registered that one of her babies was crying.

1

ADELAIDE stood at her Caesarstone island bench, assembling pinwheel sandwiches. The secret to the perfect pinwheel sandwich was in the even distribution of fillings. She smeared on a modest layer of her famous guacamole before arranging the paper-thin slices of chicken she had poached especially the night before, taking care to avoid one guacamole laden edge. Next, came a light scattering of chopped coriander and parsley—coriander on its own seemed, to her mind, too severe a flavour for five-year olds—and a barely-there grind of Himalayan salt and black pepper. Then, with the expertise of a Cuban *torcedor*, she rolled the wrap firmly, sealing the cigar-like creation by running her index finger down the outside edge. The final step was to cut the cylinders into two-centimetre-wide segments before arranging them two-high in the four-centimetre-deep bento lunch boxes which sat on the bench, brimming with mixed berries, cubes of waxy Jarlsberg cheese and uniformly cut veggie sticks.

Adelaide hurried around the house collecting kindergarten essentials (backpacks, water bottles, beanies, coats, mittens) all while Darcy shadowed her demanding, 'Cuddle! Cuddle me, Mumma!' She leant down several times to give him a quick squeeze, which she knew would not satiate him, before continuing her well-worn circuit of the house. Estée meanwhile sat, body hunched over her train set, her rosy lips agape in a display of immersed concentration.

From upstairs, the sound of flowing water signified the commencement of Joe's morning ablutions. Wriggling free of Darcy's advances, she padded her bare feet up the stairs in search of shoes.

'Morning,' she greeted her husband as he emerged, partially sodden, from their ensuite.

'I didn't know the circus was in town,' he replied, eyes dancing.

Adelaide raised a hand to the brightly coloured scarf she had tied around her head and forced a weak laugh. 'It was a rough one last night, I chose extra sleep instead of hair washing,' she said, sliding the fabric off and slipping past him and into the ensuite where she stared at her exhausted reflection in the mirror.

In the early hours of the morning, Adelaide had responded, yet again, to Darcy's distressed cries. He was prone to night terrors which left him shaken and unable to separate from her. His shrill cries and thrashing would rouse Estée, so the three would end up in Darcy's single bed, where Adelaide would remain, listening to the measured breathing of her sleeping children, trying not to move. "The night shift" as she begrudgingly thought of it, had begun the moment the twins were brought home from the hospital and was yet to draw to a close.

Adelaide administered a generous spray of dry shampoo to her dark hair and grimaced at the ashy film it left behind. She forced a smile and emerged from the bathroom still wearing it.

'I better run, have a good day,' she called to Joe who was buttoning his shirt, framed in the walk-in wardrobe.

'Hey! Don't forget, I've got that thing with the buyers tonight!' he yelled down the stairs after her.

ENCUMBERED as a pack mule, Adelaide unlatched the kindergarten gate and ushered her dawdling children into the courtyard. As they were swept away by their classmates, Adelaide spied her best friend Rosemary chatting amiably with one of the dads. As she turned, her glorious red curls caught the early morning sunshine, momentarily giving her an otherworldly, haloed effect. Rosemary broke off from her conversation and strode over, her face blossoming into an impish grin as she relieved Adelaide of her burdens. Adelaide exhaled and greeted her friend with a clipped, 'Good morning, Rosie.'

'Working today?' asked Rosemary.

'Yeah. We're expecting a big delivery from a deceased estate and Ivy just can't handle it on her own. I'm really starting to worry about her, she's always been so...' Adelaide trailed off into her own exhaustion before catching herself and continuing with her under-developed thought. 'So, competent… I don't know.'

'She must be getting on in age,' offered Rosemary.

'Yeah, you're right,' said Adelaide, checking her phone for the time. 'And on that note,' she said with a dramatic flourish of her hand, 'I will bid you *adieu*.'

SETTLED back into her car, Adelaide thought back over the past five years since the twins were born. In these rare quiet moments alone, she marvelled at how profoundly the direction of her life had pivoted. She remembered so clearly the day she was told she may not be able to have children.

It was an unseasonably cool November morning as she shuffled into her year twelve English exam with her peers and a somber mood descended upon the usually jovial teenagers. Adelaide, although prepared for the exam, had been struck with the unfortunate arrival of her period that morning. She was afflicted with terrible cramps but, without any real benchmark for what was considered normal, had simply assumed that everyone suffered as she did. The reluctant *thump, thump, thump* of hundreds of scuffed brogues and T-bars echoed in her head and abdomen as she was carried forward by the wave of students. Relieved to arrive at her desk, she fell heavily into her seat and rested her face briefly in her hands. Somewhere in the distance the teacher droned through the particulars of the exam. Adelaide tried to focus on the old woman's monotone voice as silver flickered the outer edges of her vision. The pain became so intense that it felt like she was being turned inside out, like socks being paired. She did not hear the scrape of metal against the polished floorboards as her chair slid from beneath her, or the dense thud as the right side of her body connected with the floor, or the nervous giggles which rang out through the otherwise tomb-like space. The next thing she remembered was being roused by her frantic mother in the school's sickbay and being bundled into their Landcruiser. Adelaide would later joke to her classmates that the fifteen-minute wait in the unforgivably gaudy waiting room of the local bulk bill medical clinic was by far the most traumatic element of the whole ordeal. As she curiously regarded a gold mesh sculpture, placed atop a turquoise, marble-painted column, she heard her name called with detached indifference in a gruff eastern European accent.

'Edilad Jonz? Edilad Jonz?'

Once inside the consulting room, Adelaide was subjected to the doctor's intimate inquisitions before being instructed to remove her underwear and arrange herself, legs akimbo, atop the paper-covered examination table. What struck Adelaide as strange was not the intense pain and discomfort she felt, or even the sheer embarrassment that a woman she'd never met before was knuckle-deep inside her, but rather the sound of the doctor chewing gum as she conducted the examination. *Squelch, squelch, squelch* went the bovine mastication of the doctor's rubbery wad. *Squelch, squelch, squelch* as she fished around inside Adelaide's cervix as if looking for car keys in the depths of a disorganised handbag. Once the doctor's latex gloves were discarded and Adelaide's nether regions were cloaked in the comforting cotton sheath of her underwear, they sat opposite each other to discuss the findings of the expedition.

'You have heard of the condition called endometriosis?'

Adelaide nodded numbly as the doctor explained that she would need to submit to an ultrasound which would determine if surgery was required. The older woman, who had at first come across as abrasive, put a comforting hand on Adelaide's arm before confessing in an uncharacteristically caring tone that, 'This might mean you can have no babies.'

As the years passed and the surgeries tallied, Adelaide forgot that there was once a time when she had envisaged motherhood in her future and instead began to concentrate on the other ways she intended to enrich her life. By the time Adelaide was in her twenties she proclaimed boldly and often that she didn't want to have children and, perhaps most remarkably, she believed it.

ADELAIDE pulled into her parking spot at Retrograde Mid-Century Salvage, gathered up her belongings from the front seat and slid out of the car. Squinting up at the former office building's 1960s facade, she imagined the fresh-faced people arriving for work each morning, when the building had first opened. Men dressed in close-cut wool flannel suits and trilby hats, a crisp edition of *The Melbourne Herald* tucked neatly under one arm. Women in A-line shift dresses and coordinating coats with Peter Pan collars, handbags swinging elegantly from the crooks of their arms. She pushed open the brass-framed glass door and entered. The familiar smell of timber and leather polish greeted her like a friend.

'Good morning, darling,' crooned Ivy, from some as yet unknown vantage point.

The swish of Ivy's palazzo pants announced her descent down the floating staircase. At just over five feet tall, Ivy was one of those compact entities who, by sheer credit to their ostentatiousness, seemed much larger. Her silvery hair fell in soft waves around her deeply lined face, heavy tortoise spectacles framing her avian eyes. She reached the foot of the stairs and peered up at Adelaide.

'Oh, darling,' she said, taking in Adelaide's pallor.

Adelaide gave a small, resigned shrug and lowered herself into a nearby armchair. Ivy sat on the coffee table opposite her and leant forward.

'It feels like forever when they're little,' Ivy began knowingly, 'but then one day it all changes and they don't need you as much anymore. And as crazy as it may seem, you will look back fondly at this time.'

Adelaide nodded. It did sound crazy.

'I'm certainly pining for the old days this morning,' said Ivy, straightening. 'I just got off the phone with my daughter. On and on and on she goes about my selling this place. Says she's worried about me. "You're not as young as you used to be, Mum. One day those mountains of old junk are going to crush you to death,"' Ivy said, affecting her most irritating tone of voice, the one reserved for impersonations of Amy. 'Charming!' complained Ivy.

Adelaide smirked at her old friend with eyebrows raised, her head tilted to one side, and waited. Suddenly aware that she was ranting, Ivy swatted the air in front of her, shooing away the bad *juju* Amy's phone call had conjured.

'Celeste not in today?' asked Adelaide.

'No. Tomorrow. Says she's got a huge home staging assignment due for her interior design course. Whatever that means!' she laughed. 'Anyway,' she declared, 'the boys will be here with the truck soon.'

THE deceased estate had come in from Park Orchards, a suburb in Melbourne's outer northeast, and contained some of the best mid-century modern furniture that Adelaide had seen in her sixteen years working at

Retrograde. Teak bookcases and room dividers that possessed such a lustrous depth of shine, one had to wonder if they'd been used at all in the sixty years since they were crafted. A pair of Arne Jacobsen egg chairs posed such a delectable temptation to Adelaide that she immediately fell into one. George Nelson pendant lights and lamps, a Kai Kristiansen extendable dining table, leather upholstered Z-chairs, silk dupion curtains that seemed to weigh a tonne and a bespoke modular bar. All of them needed to be catalogued and priced. Adelaide retrieved her phone from her handbag and logged into the Catalogus App Joe had developed.

WHEN she was newly pregnant with the twins, Adelaide had returned home one evening, exhausted from an intake. She was bone-tired and frustrated by the inefficiency of Ivy's archaic processes. It had taken her the entire day to catalogue less than a quarter of what they had received. Identifying each piece by year, designer and manufacturer, describing the form and condition, cross referencing against client requests and pricing each item. All the information was meticulously handwritten into Ivy's heavy ledger, a satisfying strikethrough would eventually signify an item's sale or, as Ivy liked to put it, its "re-homing". When Joe arrived home, he was uncharacteristically inquisitive about her complaints. He normally ignored her into a sheepish self-awareness of her own rambling, at which point, still dissatisfied, she stopped. On this night however, he listened attentively, questioning her for more and more detail. She smiled, remembering the feeling of being *interesting* to him. At the time, he was working as a junior developer at a digital agency, specialising in Apps. But it wasn't until the following morning, when he told her about some of his preliminary ideas, that she realised what his questioning had been about. A few days later he presented her with his first prototype—a simple program to streamline the processes she had complained about. Adelaide was thrilled by the romanticism of the gesture. He had *made* something for her. Perhaps not in the traditional sense, but she received it with the appreciation of someone being gifted a sculpture or a sonnet, for which they were the inspiration. Then came the day when Joe revealed that he had been working on a more sophisticated version of the App, utilising artificially intelligent image recognition. He explained that not only would the App be able to identify a piece of furniture as, say, a coffee table, but it would also be able to pinpoint the designer, country of origin, condition and market value. To Adelaide's analogue mind, this sounded like a science fiction fantasy.

ADELAIDE thought of herself and Joe as inextricably linked. So much of their shared history was laced with a kind of serendipitous magic. A preordained chain of events that bound them together. And now here he was in the midst of selling the company they'd created together in their garage, with Catalogus as the cornerstone. Adelaide thought back over the past six years with Joe. During this time, she'd felt like a kite being tossed about in the wind. Trying to elegantly ride the current but not in control of the direction she was moving. Motherhood had been thrust upon her so unexpectedly, and had been so all-consuming, that she felt as though she was only just emerging from a thick and disorienting haze. Those early, heady days of being a human food source to her absurdly vulnerable babies, of being unable to distinguish where they stopped and she began, of nocturnal disturbances that were so frequent she felt trapped in a cruel experiment designed to push a person to the brink. The soul-splitting eruptions of raw, primal love that flooded her body in visceral waves. The complete awe and wonder that someone as ordinary as she could produce not one, but two, perfect specimens of human life. Not to mention the way those two divine entities could drive her to the verge of utter despair, making her question not only herself but the very bedrock on which she was built. But the fog was clearing now. Even Darcy's plethora of needs seemed to be simmering down to a manageable volume. With the sale of Grasp Digital almost complete, Adelaide hoped that she and Joe were about to embark on the springtime of their relationship. They'd never even dated. It was her housemate, Mae, who Joe had been dating.

One cold Sunday morning, she'd shuffled into her kitchen wearing just a nightshirt, expecting to find Mae causing the clatter that had roused her, but instead she found the hunched figure of a man rummaging in the far reaches of her cupboards. The sound of her approach made him start, bumping his head on the shelf above. He let out a groan and stood, rubbing the back of his head. He looked at her with one eye scrunched tight.

'Hello?' she enquired.

'I'm Joe Spiteri. You must be Adelaide,' he said, straightening.

As she shook his hand, she had a sudden involuntary vision of him touching her all over. She dropped his hand, and his gaze, and felt her neck grow warm. 'Nice to meet you,' she muttered, moving towards the sink.

She was suddenly very aware of her current state of undress, that was somehow magnified by the juxtaposition of his fully clothed form.

'You couldn't point me towards the coffee, could you?' he asked.

'Oh,' she said, 'of course.'

She squeezed past him, retrieved the canister from the shelf above and handed it over, her bare feet grazing his heavy boots in the process.

'I'd better get dressed. It was nice to meet you,' she said again, silently chastising herself for her social ineptitude.

Once back in the safety of her bedroom, she face-palmed herself and silently hoped that Joe Spiteri would go the way of so many of Mae's gentlemen callers and she'd never have to see him again. But fate had other plans and, after months of decreasingly mortifying encounters with Joe, he moved in. His presence in the house drove her to distraction in those early weeks. He made her so nervous, so unsure of herself and, she feared, so transparent. He constantly teased her about her outlandish attire, accusing her of falling into a thrift shop donation bin or some other such brotherly taunt.

'I think you'll find that this is a pristine vintage Pucci dress,' she would retort, punching his arm while feeling inwardly wounded. Then, when she finally completed her arts doctorate on the traditional textile crafts of primitive societies, he irritatingly began referring to her as "Doc". But the infuriating teasing was peppered with bright gleaming moments of raw authenticity.

One rainy night when Mae was at work, they'd sat at the kitchen table drinking cheap wine and he'd spoken of his parents' divorce. He described how his life had been split in two. Two bedrooms, two sets of clothes, two sets of toys, and parents using him to get back at each other. She'd reached out for him then, reached across the cold, scuffed Formica and taken his hands in hers because she too had been split down the middle by her own parents' divorce. He'd laughed self-consciously as he reclaimed his hands from her grasp, and she could almost see him resurrect the wall that had only briefly fallen.

RETURNING TO ADELAIDE

After that night, she knew. She realised with inconvenient clarity that she was in love with this man. This man who belonged to someone else. So, she did what any self-respecting love fool would do—she dodged him like an overdue credit card bill.

2

'THANKS for getting Charlie, I'm right in the thick of something here,' said Rosemary, flinging open the door before Adelaide had a chance to knock.

She leant down to address the three children. 'I have chocolate biccies, why don't you take some out to the cubby house?'

Adelaide grimaced, imagining the post sugar-high comedown that was undoubtedly in her future. *Something must be going on for Rosemary to be distracting the children with refined sugar.*

When the two women were alone, seated with cups of tea in the kitchen overlooking the backyard, Rosemary began. 'After I saw you this morning, I went to do a quick shop. Well, the milk and bread run turned into a stock-up so big you'd think I was bunkering down for Armageddon, you know. So, I get to the register and my card doesn't work. I think, *that's weird*, and hand over a different one. Same thing again. This goes on until I'm out of cards. My full deck gone!'

'What?' Adelaide exclaimed.

'Right?' replied Rosemary. 'So, I make some dumb, half-hearted joke about it to the cashier and the people staring at me in line, and rush out of the supermarket like I'm on fire. I get home and go looking for our statements. I'm thinking, *someone's stolen our identities or something.*'

'Oh my God! No!' exclaimed Adelaide, enthralled.

'So I'm looking through the filing cabinet and I can't find a single statement since, like, November last year—Adam is the worst at filing. I go online and bring up the statements and there're all these weird charges. Small ones. Pages and pages of them to somewhere called Camnation.'

'Camnation?' Adelaide repeated, perplexed.

'Then I get to the more recent statements,' Rosemary went on, 'and there's bigger charges—hundreds and thousands—to something called Direct Sauce.'

'Direct Source?' queried Adelaide.

'Sauce, as in tomato. So I Googled the companies...' Rosemary paused for effect. 'And they're porn sites!' She burst out laughing. 'Someone's stolen our credit card information to get their freak on!'

Adelaide gasped salaciously before echoing her friend's laughter.

'Yeah!' said Rosemary, clearly pleased with the captivation level of her audience. 'Camnation is one of those webcam-girl sites—creepy old men live-chatting young girls to take off their undies and stuff—but that's not the best bit,' she said. 'Direct Sauce is a made-to-order porn service!'

Adelaide gasped. 'Bespoke porn!'

The two friends belly laughed, struggling for breath.

At length they regained their composure.

'Anyway, I just got off the phone with the bank. They've put a stop on our cards and are investigating the transaction. It's a giant pain in the arse though. All our accounts are drained! But these things get sorted out quite quickly these days, they're very good.'

Rosemary leaned back in her chair and sipped her tea. Her phone rang. 'Ha!' she said triumphantly, 'That'll be them now.'

ADELAIDE nursed her tea, watching the three children playing. They were rugged up in their coats and beanies, making them look like miniature adults. They had an assortment of variously dismembered and overly loved plastic dolls—the "outside dolls" as Rosemary referred to them—and were bathing them in the sandpit to the left of the cubby house. In turn Estée would bring over a doll to Darcy. He would place it in the tub—a large terracotta plant pot they'd acquisitioned from somewhere—then Charlie would pour copious amounts of sand over it from an old enamel tea pot. She laughed to herself at the sight of Darcy vigorously scrubbing the poor doll before placing it gingerly to the side. She glanced over her shoulder at Rosemary, talking on the phone, perfectly framed in the doorway to the lounge room. Her mouth was slack, her head nodding slowly. Adelaide turned back to the children.

After a minute or so, Rosemary returned and lowered herself slowly onto a chair, her narrowed eyes fixed on the scene outside.

Adelaide placed a hand on her friend's arm. 'Rosie?'

Rosemary's gaze remained on the children, her lips parted as if willing words to come. 'They came from here,' she finally said. 'All the transactions came from here.'

Adelaide opened her mouth to speak but the sound of heavy footsteps made her stop.

'Hello, Adelaide!' Adam boomed. 'Honey,' he said, before kissing his wife on the cheek.

He deposited his keys on the kitchen table and ventured out to the backyard to greet the children. Rosemary continued staring as Adelaide gathered up her belongings and strode to the open sliding door calling, 'Estée! Darcy! We're leaving!'

The obligatory groans ensued as they dropped their toys and shuffled towards her.

Adelaide placed a hand on Rosemary's shoulder who turned, unseeing, to face her.

'Call me if you need me,' said Adelaide, eyes stern, before ushering her children down the long hallway and out the front door.

3

ADELAIDE was trapped under her sleeping children when she heard Joe come in late from his dinner with the buyers of Grasp. She made a futile attempt to extract herself but was halted by the catapult of a tiny arm across her face. Whose it was remained unclear. When Joe finally emerged mid-morning, Adelaide was practically bursting with the news of yesterday afternoon's surreal happenings at Rosemary's house. He plodded downstairs, crease-faced, as she was constructing a playdough mermaid garden with Darcy and Estée. 'How'd it go last night?' she asked, joining him in the kitchen.

'Yeah, great. I mean, the dinner was a bit of a snooze-fest, but yesterday afternoon we got some exciting news about operations after the acquisition. They want me to stay on in a GM role. Should be pretty flexible too, which will be a change of pace from the last few years.'

'Oh, perfect,' said Adelaide.

Unable to contain herself any longer, Adelaide launched into a blow-by-blow account of all that had transpired at Rosemary's the day before.

'Jeez,' exclaimed Joe when the tale had come to an end, 'I didn't think Adam had it in him.'

THE following morning brought another kindergarten drop-off and Adelaide felt nervous as she approached the gate. Rosemary hadn't replied to any of her texts and Adelaide couldn't help but wonder what her friend had been through since she'd beat a hasty retreat from her kitchen.

Walking into the courtyard, she scanned the familiar faces of kids, parents and grandparents for Rosemary's but came up short. She lingered, making cliché-ridden small talk with other parents. They stood in a

16

semicircle, watching their children play and delivering their lines without a trace of irony.

'Cold enough for you?'

'I'm going to need two more coffees to get going today.'

'Forget coffee. Is it wine time yet?'

Adelaide heard the gate unlatch and turned to see Rosemary and Charlie shuffling in. She strode the short distance to meet them.

'Hi, baby girl,' she greeted Charlie, cupping her cheek briefly before the child skipped away.

'Hi, baby girl,' she repeated, this time to Rosemary.

Rosemary's face was usually luminous but today it was waxy and grey. Her eyes were bloodshot and deep indigo circles shadowed her lower lashes, giving her a hollow appearance. She met Adelaide's gaze with the defeated look of the battle-weary.

'Sorry I didn't reply to your texts, beauty. Got time for a coffee?' she asked.

BACK at Rosemary's house, they sat once more at the kitchen table.

'All our savings are gone,' she said. 'He spent every last cent on getting himself off. The crazy thing is, when I actually confronted him about it that night, he was *relieved*.' She paused to sip her coffee. 'He tells me he's addicted. Wants me to help him work through it.'

'Do you think you can do that?' asked Adelaide, trying to keep her tone even.

'I don't know. I'm just raging. Every time I look at him, I want to slap that goddamn pitiful look of self-loathing and remorse off his face. Like, "YOU caused this shit-storm buddy! I'm the victim here, so stop feeling sorry for yourself!" you know?'

'God, it must be so hard,' said Adelaide. 'What will you do?'

'I've agreed to go to counselling but, I mean, is porn addiction even a thing? Or is it just some made-up bullshit to get guys off the hook for being selfish pricks? And it's not even that, you know? I'm not a prude! It's the betrayal that's got me. The lies, the deception, the goddamn duplicity of it all.'

'This is going to sound like a strange question,' prefaced Adelaide, 'but where did he get the *time* for all this?'

'Oh! Tell me about it!' said Rosemary, her voice soaring several octaves higher than normal. 'Like, excuse me while I raise our child and work and keep the house from falling apart! Sure, you go skulk off and jerk it to your smartphone every chance you get! Do you know how long it's been since I've had time to fucking masturbate?'

Adelaide tried to suppress a smirk. Catching the look, Rosemary smiled too before letting out a half laugh, half sob, and burying her face in her hands.

STRIDING across Retrograde's showroom, Adelaide greeted a customer who was running an appreciative hand across the back of a leather chaise. She poked her head into various warrens looking for Ivy, finally finding her looking resplendent in a gloriously tall, wicker peacock chair. Celeste was perched, in comical contrast, by her side on a miniscule Swedish telephone desk, uploading listings to their website from her phone.

'Darling!' Ivy exclaimed, her face brightening.

'Hey Adelaide,' said Celeste.

'Ladies,' Adelaide greeted with pomp, doffing her invisible cap.

'Sorry I'm late, Ivy, you'll never guess what's going on with poor old Rosemary!'

At length, Adelaide regaled the two women with the whole sordid story, Ivy compulsively shaking her head in disbelief for the entire duration.

'It's a real problem,' said Celeste, 'half the guys that my friends and I hook up with have literally been watching porn since they were kids and can barely even get it up for a real girl.'

Adelaide's eyes widened at this revelation. 'It just makes me appreciate Joe all the more, you know? He really is a decent husband. And the way he loves Darcy and Estée. I mean, you go to the park on a Saturday morning and all you see is dads on their phones. Meanwhile, there's Joe coming down the slide.'

The three women laughed in unison.

'You're so lucky, Adelaide. To have someone who loves you,' said Celeste.

Adelaide felt her cheeks grow warm. 'Shall we get into it then, ladies?' she said, turning away.

4

AN icy wind blew through the market, sending tablecloths flapping. Adelaide flipped up her coat collar and scanned the sea of would-be bargain hunters for Ivy.

'I'm cold, Mumma,' said Darcy, peering up at her.

'It'll warm up soon,' Adelaide said, pulling his beanie down over his ears. 'The sun is trying to come out.'

She thought back over countless mornings spent at Camberwell Markets with Ivy. In the beginning, this Sunday morning ritual had been part of her job, something she was paid to do. She and Ivy would arrive before dawn, torches at the ready, hoping to score décor and small pieces of furniture to resell in the store. Adelaide had a sixth sense when it came to the rummage. As a teenager, she would pick through the bins at thrift stores, seeking out unusual garments to resurrect. Sometimes her mother would tag along, shadowing her and lamenting, 'It smells here. Why do you want to wear these old clothes when I'm happy to buy you new ones?' Adelaide knew that her mother had been deeply ashamed of the second-hand clothing she had worn as a young migrant in Australia, and couldn't understand Adelaide's fascination with all things vintage. But with Ivy it was different. Ivy could tell immediately that Adelaide had an intuition when it came to unearthing things of beauty and value. And for the first time in her life, Adelaide felt understood.

'Cold enough for you, darlings?' Ivy said, appearing at her side.

She wore a heavy, black lamb-fur coat and a white fluffy hat which, being the same colour as her hair, gave her an unhinged, startled appearance. She removed one of her gloves and produced two five-dollar bills from her handbag. Crouching down to meet the twins, she declared,

'One for you, Estée, and one for you, Darcy. Now go forth and find your treasure.'

She rose, holding onto Adelaide for support and kissed the younger woman on the cheek, before rubbing away the lipstick she had left behind.

'It's not what it used to be,' Ivy said, indicating their surrounds.

'Well, it stopped being about the chase a long time ago,' said Adelaide, taking up her friend's arm as they fell into step behind the children.

They strolled in amiable silence, pausing occasionally at items of interest. Darcy crouched over a timber-framed suitcase full of old black and white photos, as Estée extracted a die-cast dump truck that she promptly exchanged for her money. She held it up for Ivy's approval.

'Let me see here,' said Ivy, taking the object and turning it over in her hands as if it were a precious artefact. 'Yes. What a find. Well-loved for certain but a treasure of the highest order nonetheless,' she decreed, handing it back to a beaming Estée.

Darcy abandoned the photos and walked on, looking as though the money he clutched was a burden.

'Roses, three for thirty dollars!' a man's voice bellowed.

'I want these ones, Mumma,' said Darcy, eyeing a bunch of flowers almost as tall as him.

'Are you sure, baby? They're very big, they might be awkward to carry,' said Adelaide.

'I don't mind,' he said, eyes solemn.

'I'll get some too. Birds of paradise have always been one of my favourites,' said Ivy.

Darcy puffed out his chest.

The sun broke through at intervals, warming their backs as they strolled. Ivy gave Adelaide a gentle shove, indicating a pair of 1970s block-heeled, gold boots. 'Didn't you have some like those?' she asked.

'God, you've got a memory,' said Adelaide.

Ivy exhaled deeply and stopped walking.

'What is it?' Adelaide asked, raising an eyebrow.

'There's something I've been meaning to tell you,' said Ivy, turning to face Adelaide. 'Somehow my telling you this just makes it all a bit too real for my liking.'

'Makes what too real?' asked Adelaide.

'Argh! It's such an old lady thing to say! I have Alzheimer's! They've gone and told me I have Alzheimer's!' she blurted.

'Oh, Ivy,' said Adelaide, placing a hand on Ivy's arm, 'what a total load of fuckery.'

Ivy laughed, tears squeezing from the edges of her eyes.

'What have they said?' asked Adelaide.

'Oh, if I'm a good girl and take my pills, we may be able to keep the beast at bay for a while yet,' said Ivy. 'I can keep working—in fact, it may actually help—but I wanted to talk to you about taking on more. With the twins starting school next year, I was hoping you might consider increasing your hours.'

'Well, of course, whatever you need,' said Adelaide, without hesitation. 'So, how did all this come about?'

Ivy looked wistful. 'When you get to my age, they're practically champing at the bit to find something wrong with you. But it was Roger, really, who told Dr Harris about a few "episodes" as he likes to call them. I told them that everyone gets forgetful at my age, but I suppose I knew deep down it was more than that.'

Adelaide nodded.

'Roger was all in a tizz about my taking, shall we say, an impromptu evening stroll the other week. There I was in my nightgown, halfway down Fulham Road by the time he caught up with me. One of the kids from that hideous new apartment block was asking if I was alright and where I lived,' she trailed off. 'To tell you the truth, darling, that snippet of information had completely escaped me.'

'Oh, Ivy,' Adelaide said again, tucking a stray lock of hair under Ivy's hat as the first fat drops of rain coloured the bitumen around them.

Ivy let her eyes follow the tide of marketgoers beginning to flee. 'It's just the most disconcerting thing when you've completely forgotten who you are.'

BACK in the car, Adelaide let the news of her friend's diagnosis absorb. Of course, she would help Ivy in any way she could, but increasing her hours at Retrograde went against what she'd been privately hoping for her and Joe.

'I know you're excited about your flowers, Darcy, but when they poke into Mummy's neck, they make it dangerous for her to drive.'

'But why, Mumma?' he asked, fumbling with the birds of paradise once more, causing them to peck her.

'*Broom! Broom, broom, broom!*' Estée bellowed, spinning the wheels on her dump truck.

Adelaide took a deep breath.

'Shall we call Si Si?' she asked, desperate to distract them so that she could think for a minute.

'Yeah!'

Adelaide pulled up at a red light and dialled her mother's number. The ringtone gave way to Sia's voicemail, and the twins groaned.

'I want to talk to Si Si,' whined Estée.

'Why did you tell us we could talk to Si Si, Mumma?' Darcy complained.

Adelaide ended the call and rested her head on the steering wheel. The car behind her tooted, telling her to move on.

ADELAIDE had just finished bathing Darcy and Estée, and was halfway through her fluffy towel-monster routine, when Joe's voice cut through the waves of giggles and delighted squeals.

'What do we have here?' he asked, with booming affection.

'Daddy! A monster is trying to eat us!' Estée screamed, throwing her hands up to her cheeks for extra effect.

'Get it, Dadda! Get it!' pleaded Darcy.

Adelaide continued to growl and snatch the little bodies up in the towel, in turn.

'Never fear. I will save you!' cried Joe, gathering Adelaide up and throwing her over his shoulder.

He swept her from the bathroom and down the hall, two naked little bottoms bouncing after him. Throwing her onto their bed, he implored the excited children to 'Tickle her!'

Now it was Adelaide's turn to squeal. She tried to fight back, softly pinching doughy flesh in retaliation. They were all laughing now, then panting in a heap, then silent.

'Hi, Dadda,' said Darcy, craning his head like a meerkat.

'Hi, precious,' replied Joe, chest heaving from his exertions.

'Can you do story time tonight?' asked Estée.

'You know I can. Let's get your 'jamms on.'

'WHAT'S all this?' asked Joe, taking in the candles and wine as he returned from putting the children to bed.

'Well, nothing,' said Adelaide, suddenly self-conscious, 'I just *miss* you, that's all.'

She put deliberate emphasis on the word 'miss' to let him know where she intended the evening to go. Rosemary's situation had reminded Adelaide that marriages needed tending in order to thrive.

He smiled, the subtlety not lost on him.

As they ate, Joe talked through the terms of sale for Grasp Digital. While they would be expected to adhere to their parent company's overarching strategy, they were largely free to govern themselves. This meant that the entire team, with the exception of Accounts and HR, would stay.

'It can't really be helped, it doesn't make sense to be paying for those departments when they have more than enough of their own resources,' he reasoned. 'Barb has made no secret of the fact that she's planning to retire at sixty and she's just turned fifty-nine. She'll be happy to get the pay-out, I think.'

Adelaide nodded. She was the one who had hired Barb when the accounts had become too much to manage herself.

'It's kind of a shame about Kim though,' he went on, 'she's only been with us about six months.'

'Kim?'

'Yeah, the HR manager. I told you about her.'

Adelaide didn't think so and was just about to point this out, when Joe pushed their empty plates away. He raised an eyebrow and, sliding his hand around the back of her neck, drew her in for a long kiss. He stood and she lifted her gaze, lips parting in anticipation. *How long has it been?* She wondered. She stood to meet him, and he leant down, scooping her up onto the table in one fluid movement before positioning himself between her knees. He ran his hands up her thighs and tugged at her underwear until she lifted her bottom obligingly.

'So helpful,' he muttered, lowering himself to the ground and pushing her legs apart. She closed her eyes and reclined onto her elbows, feeling his hot breath creep up her inner thighs.

The next cries she heard were not of pleasure, but rather the distressed cries of Darcy, emanating from the baby monitor in the kitchen. Adelaide and Joe stood up like a couple of school kids caught making out behind the shelter sheds. Adelaide pulled down her dress and fled, taking the stairs two at a time. If she got there quick, it might be a swift resolution.

FORTY-FIVE minutes later Adelaide descended the stairs, willing herself to shapeshift from mother back to woman. She was determined to pick up where they had left off.

'Kids are such cock blocks,' she called out, trying to make light of the situation.

She walked through the kitchen to the dining room, where their discarded dishes lay abandoned and congealing in the darkness. She approached the living room sofa.

'Joe?'

His snores confirmed what she already knew. The moment had been extinguished along with the candles.

5

A raucously twangy folk track resounded through the packed café, accentuating the bustling atmosphere as Adelaide sat at a shared table, waiting for Rosemary. The café at the end of Adelaide's street had reopened recently, after being closed for renovations, and she couldn't help thinking that it was a little too cool for her now. The polished concrete floor rose in an abrupt wave to create the counter, behind which the barista stood making matcha lattes—whatever they were. Next to her, two girls in their late teens (or were they early twenties?) sat pulling out and reviewing their recent clothing purchases, occasionally swishing fabric across Adelaide's arm. She wondered if she was completely invisible to them. Adelaide had a persistent theory that once you became a mother, you became invisible to whole segments of the population, and she had a suspicion that teenage girls were one such segment. The girls hastened to pack away their purchases as their brunches arrived, looking more decorative than edible. *Quick*, thought Adelaide, *get it on Instagram before your flowers sink into your chia!* She lowered her face to hide a smile as the girls simultaneously pulled out their phones.

'Hey, what can I get you?'

A waiter had appeared at her side, and she was momentarily dazzled by his teeth. They had a fantastic plastic sheen to them and she was just pondering their authenticity when he narrowed his gaze and enquired, 'Do you need a couple of minutes to decide?'

'Oh, sorry. I'll just have a latte. I'm waiting for a friend,' she said indicating the seat next to her which was currently occupied by her handbag and coat. The waiter nodded and turned, almost bumping into Rosemary who hastily added, 'Make that two, please.'

'Sorry I'm late,' she said, as Adelaide made space for her to sit.

IT had been weeks since the friends had caught up properly and it occurred to Adelaide that she hadn't had the chance to tell Rosemary about Ivy's Alzheimer's diagnosis, with everything else that was going on.

Rosemary peeled off her coat and scarf, and settled herself before beginning. 'I've just come from another counselling session with Adam,' she said.

'How's it going?'

'Surprisingly well actually. I mean, it's early days but we seem to be getting somewhere. The first session, I walked in there all furious and self-righteous. I guess on some level I wanted the psychologist to take my side and, I don't know, give Adam a lecture about what a jerk he is.'

Adelaide smiled.

'I walked in there and wanted to introduce us like, "Hello, I'm the saint and this is the arsehole," but she pretty quickly got us to see that the porn thing is a symptom of some bigger underlying problems in our marriage. There's no way we could get through this without help. We were totally stuck—me in my anger and him in his shame and guilt. She's helping us look at the situation from different angles, so we can understand where things went wrong, and try to reconnect with one another. She helped me to see that his behaviour wasn't a "go-to-hell" to me, it was about him and how he was feeling. That he was lonely and depressed and trying to escape, which just magnified all the negative stuff he was feeling about himself. That's why he was so relieved when it all came out; the shame was consuming him. He's going to see someone separately to address the addiction side of things, so we can focus our joint sessions on the marriage.'

'Well, it sounds very promising,' said Adelaide, nodding briefly to the waiter as he set down their coffees.

'There's a long way to go. I'm still so mad, especially about our savings, and it's going to take a lot for me to trust him again, but I'm starting to understand that I had a part to play in it too. It's so cliché but you get busy and tired and lazy. You think it's easier to just sit on the couch watching Netflix every night, but the psych' has really helped us to see that the words you leave unsaid pile up like bricks, until all you have between you is a wall.'

'Yep,' said Adelaide, 'marriage sometimes feels like the most unnatural social experiment, doesn't it?'

'Seriously,' Rosemary agreed. She sipped her coffee before going on. 'So the porn thing totally spiralled out of control. You know it's linked to sexual dysfunction? So on the off chance that we *would* try to get our sexy on—which hasn't been often, if I'm honest—he couldn't get it up. So I put that on myself, thinking he doesn't find me attractive anymore. Big. Fat. Mess,' she concluded.

'Can I ask you something? And you don't have to answer if you don't want to,' said Adelaide, her voice low.

Rosemary leant in, indicating her assent.

'Did you ever find out what the bespoke porn was about?'

'Yes!' exclaimed Rosemary. 'I asked him to show me. They all feature the same woman. A redhead.' Rosemary motioned to her own curls for effect.

'Doing what?' Adelaide asked tentatively, her nose involuntarily crinkling.

'Lots of different stuff, in various stages of undress. But normal stuff like painting her toenails, brushing her hair, putting lotion on her body. There's one where she's putting cat food into a dish and when she bends down to put it on the ground you see she doesn't have any undies on.'

'Did the pussy come into view?' Adelaide asked, bursting into raucous laughter at her own double entendre.

The two women howled with laughter, dabbing at their eyes to contain tears. Once Adelaide was able to compose herself, she asked, 'So, is the redhead meant to be you, or what?'

'Yeah, I think that's part of it,' said Rosemary, taking a sip of her coffee. 'The psych' seems to think this whole thing stemmed from him feeling isolated from me and "undeserving", I think was the word she used. Ever since Charlie was born, he's had me up on some divine mother pedestal, which isn't exactly conducive for sexual intimacy.'

'Maybe if things work out you can jump down off your pedestal and make his dreams come true?' Adelaide offered.

'Adelaide Jones, I like the way you think,' said Rosemary. 'How have you been though? I've been over here in my crazy bubble and have no idea what's happening in your world.'

Adelaide brought Rosemary up to speed regarding Ivy's diagnosis and what it would mean for her.

'But it's not just you, right? There's… is it, Celeste?' asked Rosemary. Adelaide nodded.

'So, can she take on more hours, at least share some of the load with you?'

'Yeah, she can. She wants to, in fact, and she'll be finishing her interior design course in a few months anyway. She's pretty keen on getting involved with the TV and real estate clients too, which is great. It'll certainly be easier to show her the ropes, rather than start from scratch with someone new. She's a great kid, really bright and enthusiastic. All she lacks is a bit of confidence in herself, but she'll get there.'

'Okay,' said Rosemary, getting into full problem-solving mode now. 'So, you spend the next few months mentoring her and training her up, and then you can take a step back without feeling like you're letting Ivy down. Then you and Joe can, I don't know, ride off into the sunset together with your big bag of money from the sale of the business,' said Rosemary, laughing.

'Speaking of riding off into the sunset with Joe,' said Adelaide, grinning, 'he's arranged for the twins to have a sleepover at his mum's house tonight. He's dropping them off over there now.'

'Ooh la la!' cooed Rosemary, approvingly.

ADELAIDE returned home to an empty house and immediately busied herself with laundry and tidying up. She had such a good feeling about this weekend. It was so rare that she and Joe had any quality time alone and she felt touched that he had made the arrangements unprompted. Darcy and Estée loved visiting with Nanna, she had a sprawling backyard with fruit trees and a veggie patch, and the most exciting of all things—chickens. They would share a cosy queen size bed together in the room that had once belonged to Joe, and Adelaide knew that if either of the kids needed comforting during the night, Nanna would be only too happy to oblige.

Adelaide wondered if Joe might have some further surprises in store for her this weekend. It was all so clandestine, so unexpected. She was just considering whether she should prepare lunch for them when she heard the front door click open and Joe appeared in the doorway.

'All okay?' she enquired.

'They didn't even look up when I left. They were feeding the chickens.'

'Ha, perfect,' she said.

'Perfect,' he repeated quietly.

Adelaide started talking excitedly, 'So, what shall we do today? Maybe we can go out for a boozy lunch somewhere? Or see that new movie? You know, that one with what's her face who used to be married to the guy from that show we liked?'

He was beside her now.

'Adelaide,' he said, his voice soft, 'I've fallen in love with someone else.'

'Good one,' she said, laughing awkwardly at the joke she didn't fully understand.

She reached for the dishcloth and wiped down the already clean countertop. He placed a hand over hers, halting her.

'Adelaide,' he tried again. 'I've fallen in love with someone. I'm leaving you.'

She felt it then. Felt it as if it were a physical thing that erupted inside her. The dam that had held in her greatest fears and self-doubts was finally bursting. The carefully suppressed knowledge that he had never really loved her, came bobbing up to the surface as she drowned. The silence of every unreciprocated 'I love you' pounded in her eardrums, deafening her. She had known he wasn't in love with her back then, but he had been so sad, so vulnerable when Mae had walked out on him. So out of place in their share-house without her. So, she kissed him until he kissed her back and before she knew it their clothes were strewn all over the lounge room, and she was straddling him where he sat, on the sofa. It had been over so quickly, was so awkward in the days and weeks that followed. He had told her he was looking for somewhere else to live, but then she realised she was pregnant. She hadn't meant for that to change things. She told him as a courtesy, that she would be keeping the baby. It wasn't supposed to alter anything, but then he was saying that they should get married, give the baby the type of family that they themselves were cheated out of. His reaction was so unexpected, so... exhilarating. She was terrified of the prospect of being a single mother, and wasn't entirely sure how she would do it. He had offered her an idyllic picture of familial domesticity, so she said yes.

He had been there with her at the twelve-week scan—dutifully held her hand as the sonographer traced the curve of her swelling belly with the transducer probe and proclaimed they were having twins. He had held her hand as they stood together at the Marriage Registry office, making their vows. And now, here he was in their kitchen, holding her hand, telling her he had fallen in love with someone that was not her.

'How could you do this to our family?' she asked in disbelief.

'I'm not leaving our family, Adelaide. I'm leaving our marriage,' he clarified.

'Who is she?' Adelaide demanded in a guttural voice that was not her own.

'It doesn't matter who she is,' he said, eyes cast down.

'It sounds like she matters a lot,' she countered. 'Where would you even meet someone, Joe?'

She looked at him, her eyes keen, and saw guilt flash across his face.

'Work,' she concluded.

He averted his eyes.

'It's that HR woman, isn't it?' she said with sudden, surprising clarity.

'Kim,' he confirmed.

He pulled out a barstool and sat, motioning for her to do the same.

'I will always love you—you are the mother of my children—but I'm not *in love* with you. Have never been in love with you. I think on some level you've known that. I thought that everything we had was enough for me. I had honestly intended for this to be my forever. But when you find the one...'

'The one?'

She was yelling now, despite herself.

'The one? I did find the one, Joe! I found you!'

Hot tears streaked her face and she felt as though she was falling. He reached out for her, and she tried to shrug him away, but he folded her into his arms. She sobbed and gasped, allowing herself to go limp. She was Darcy, awoken into a nightmare, unable to find her footing, to lift herself out, clinging to this human anchor, terrified that the real world would cease to exist if she let go.

Adelaide wasn't sure how long she and Joe sat there clinging to each other, but she was suddenly overcome by profound exhaustion. She stood wordlessly and walked out of the kitchen. She needed to put her head down for a minute, to make the unbearable throbbing in her temples stop. She scaled the stairs as if she was an alien-being inhabiting a human's body, unsure of how to move it naturally. Once in their bedroom—*their* bedroom—she climbed into bed fully clothed and fell into a deep sleep.

WHEN Adelaide awoke, all around her was dark and silent. *What time is it?* She wandered from room to room in a fog. The house, normally a place of warmth and activity at any hour, was as devoid of life as a corpse washed up on a shore, barely even resembling the thing it once was.

Where are my children? she wondered. *Where is my husband?* But she knew where her husband was, didn't she? He was with her.

She located her handbag on the hall table by the front door and rifled through it until she found her phone. There were three text messages. The most recent one was from Joe simply saying, "I'll be back in the morning so we can talk." The second was from Joe's mother Lienna and contained a video of the twins. They were smiling unnaturally and looking off camera. Presumably on Lienna's cue, they began chorusing, "We miss you, Mummy and Dadda! We're having such a fun time at Nanna's. Love you."

Adelaide's head throbbed anew.

The last message was from Rosemary. "Thanks for this morning, beauty. Time with you is the best therapy. Hope your weekend is wild. Can't wait to hear about all the things Joe surprises you with."

That was this morning, Adelaide thought numbly. Coffee with Rosemary was mere hours ago, not the lightyears she felt it to be. She thought suddenly of the teenage girls who had been sitting beside her and hated them for... what? Existing? For having their whole lives ahead of them instead of falling apart around them?

Adelaide walked into the kitchen, poured herself a big glass of cooking wine and carried it upstairs. She set it down on the bathroom vanity unit, sloshing its scarlet contents onto the white ceramic as she opened the bathroom cabinet. Pulling out Joe's toiletry bag, she located a crumpled blister pack of Temazepam, extracted two and washed them down with the entire contents of her glass.

THE early morning sun spliced across the pillows like a painful shard, rousing Adelaide from her drug-induced slumber. Her mouth was dry, with a rancid red wine tang. Sleep and salt and mascara crusted her eyes partially closed. Sitting up, she wiped drool from her chapped lips.

Adelaide shuffled to the ensuite, turned on the hot tap and, after discarding her clothes in a wretched heap, stepped into the scalding water. She took to her body with a loofah and scrubbed until red blotches plumed all over her skin, pausing briefly to throw up in the toilet bowl. Next, she filled her shaking palm with shampoo and scrubbed her scalp with a ferocity she hoped would cleanse her mind. When she finally emerged, the bathroom was filled with thick steam, heavy drops of condensation cutting through her mirrored reflection in violent slashes.

Once dressed, she made her way to the kitchen, seeking coffee. She missed her children. She ached for their little bodies, their sing-song voices, their unwavering love. The front door clicked, and she felt her body tense in anticipation of Joe's presence.

'Hi, Adelaide,' he said, appearing in the doorway.

The "hi" sounded somehow crass to her ears, so she didn't return it, choosing instead to gaze at him momentarily, before placing the moka pot on the stovetop. He dropped his keys on the bench and retrieved their two espresso cups from the drying rack by the sink, setting them down next to her before seating himself at the island bench. Adelaide had always enjoyed the thick gurgling sound that emanated from the little aluminium espresso maker, signalling the perfect brew, but today it sounded sinister and hellish. She poured the contents, perfectly filling the two cups and slid one across the bench to him, wincing inwardly at the memory of her pitiful figure collapsed into him yesterday.

They eyed each other, taking small bitter sips, waiting for the other to speak.

'We'll have to tell the children,' he began.

'Tell the children?' she said, incredulous. 'Don't you think it's a little early for that?'

'Adelaide, I'm moving out. They're going to notice that their dad's not here.'

Panic rose in her chest, the way the coffee had erupted into the top chamber of the pot just moments before.

'Wait…' she said, beginning the sentence without knowing how to end it. 'Maybe we can… tell the kids that you're going on a business trip for a week, just until we figure some things out.'

'Adelaide,' he said, already shaking his head.

'Joe,' she said with more force, 'you have just dumped this shit on me out of the blue and I need a little bit of time to process it, before I can be a goddamn rock for our children.'

The corners of his mouth puckered downwards, and she knew he would concede.

'Okay,' he said, running with the idea, 'so I'll pick up the kids, then I'll pack a bag and tell them I'm heading out on a flight this afternoon.'

Adelaide nodded. She couldn't decide whether she would feel better or worse if she asked the next question. 'Where will you be?' she asked.

'Don't,' he said.

JOE had offered to pick the twins up from his mother's house, but Adelaide wanted to do it herself. It felt like a lifetime since she had bundled them off to their Nanna's house, excitedly awaiting her romantic weekend with Joe. She felt ashamed of her naivety. How could she have been so stupid? Pulling into Lienna's driveway, she turned the engine off and sat for a moment trying to compose herself. There was a very high possibility that she would have a complete meltdown when she saw them. She rested her head on the steering wheel and took a deep breath.

'Mummy!'

'Mumma!'

The twins tore across the lawn and jumped up and down at her window. She laughed, opening the door, taking care not to knock them over in the process.

'Babies!'

She crouched in the driveway, with an arm curled tightly around each of her children. She nuzzled into their warmth, wishing she could disappear into it, never to emerge.

'Hello, love,' her mother-in-law greeted her, making her way across the lawn.

Adelaide stood. 'Hi, Lienna, thanks so much for having them.'

'Oh, I love having them,' she said, waving away the thanks. 'You'll come in for a cup of tea?'

'Sure, thanks,' Adelaide replied.

She was in no great hurry to return home.

ADELAIDE sat at the table in Lienna's large kitchen, a child on each knee.

'Did you two have a nice weekend?' Lienna enquired.

'I certainly got a lot of sleep,' Adelaide replied, ambiguously.

'Good,' said Lienna.

'We'd better get going soon. Joe just found out he has to head out to a conference. With that and client meetings afterwards he'll be gone a whole week.'

Adelaide had decided to address this news to Lienna. She wasn't sure she could deliver the lies directly to her children's trusting faces.

'Oh no,' exclaimed Estée.

'I don't want Dadda to go,' whined Darcy.

'I know, you guys, I was really sad too when Daddy told me he was leaving,' Adelaide said in earnest.

'Why does he have to go?' Estée asked.

Something shattered inside Adelaide.

ADELAIDE and the children returned from Lienna's, laden with vegetables from her garden. As they walked into the hallway, Adelaide noted not one but two large suitcases by the stairs.

'Daddy! Dadda!' the twins chorused, trying to draw out Joe.

He met them in the kitchen and exclaimed, 'What's all this?'

'We harvested them with Nanna,' Estée explained.

'This one is… What is it, Mummy?' asked Darcy.

'Swiss chard, baby.'

'Yep, and these are potatoes,' Estée concluded.

'I dug the potatoes with a big fork,' said Darcy, proudly brandishing a badly impaled example.

'What good farmers you are,' said Joe.

'What time are you heading to the airport? Adelaide asked, trying to keep her tone even.'

'I'll need to head off in an hour or so,' said Joe.

'The kids will need lunch. I'm going to have a bath,' said Adelaide, climbing the stairs.

'Oh, ah... okay,' he said, slightly taken aback. 'What should I get them?' he asked her back, and received no reply.

AN hour later, Adelaide made her way downstairs. In the almost six years she had lived in this house, that was the first time she'd ever used the bath herself. She marvelled at how time could manifest so easily with a little distribution of responsibility.

Joe was on his hands and knees picking up crusts and crumbs from underneath the play table. Darcy was chanting, 'Dadda, my water is finished. Dadda, my water is finished.' Estée chimed in with, 'I want an apple! An apple please!'

Adelaide noted, with no small amount of satisfaction, that Joe looked frazzled.

A little while later, the four assembled at the foot of the stairs to farewell Joe, as they had for countless business trips. Adelaide felt like an actress playing a part she had never auditioned for. Joe crouched down, saying goodbye to the children, tears glistening in the corners of his eyes. The twins hastily brainstormed what they would like their business trip presents to be.

'I want a snow globe,' said Estée, ever the decisive one.

'I want a fridge magnet! No, a book! No, one of those aeroplanes!' said Darcy, a ball of nervous energy.

After several rounds of hugs and kisses, Joe opened the door to leave.

'Wait!' cried Darcy, aghast. 'You forgot to kiss Mumma!'

Adelaide and Joe stared at each other, the moment lasting an eternity. Finally, Joe stepped forward, an awkward half-smile across his face. He slid his hand tentatively around her waist and leant in towards her lips. She turned, offering him her cheek at the last moment. She breathed in his familiar scent and her heart broke all over again.

6

'ARE you actually bloody kidding me?' Rosemary blurted.

After dropping off their kids at kinder, Adelaide had followed Rosemary back to her house. Now, they sat, nursing cups of coffee, as Adelaide gave a full account of what had transpired after they departed from the café.

'I wish I was, Rosie,' said Adelaide, taking a sip from her mug.

'So, he's obviously going through some kind of midlife crisis bullshit,' said Rosemary, outraged.

ADELAIDE and Rosemary had met at mother's group when their babies were almost two months old. They sat next to each other on the first day, and were listening as each of the mothers introduced themselves in turn and told the group a little about themselves. Much like beauty pageant contestants claiming their greatest wish is "world peace" the women had gushed about how "being a mummy" was the greatest gift, they were so besotted with their babies, who were feeding and sleeping well, and they were just so *blessed.*

Adelaide felt particularly out of place, not just because she was the only one with twins, but because all these women seemed so put together, so capable, so completely different to how she felt. Then, the introductions progressed to Rosemary.

'I'm Rosemary, I don't know what the hell I'm doing. I never even held a baby before Charlie was born and I'm just trying to get through today.'

There was nervous laughter, and a few shocked expressions from the other women, but Adelaide had loved Rosemary from that moment on.

'YOU know what it is?' said Rosemary. 'That man doesn't know how good he's got it. He completely takes you for granted and has no clue that you are the linchpin of his whole existence.'

Adelaide frowned. 'If that's true, Rosie, what can I do about it?'

'It seems to me that this week is going to be a bloody Club Med shag fest for him and *Kimmy*,' said Rosemary. 'What he needs is a preview of what being a single parent will be like for him. He tells you that he's not leaving the family, he's leaving you? Well, my friend, you *are* the family. You're the one that provides this charmed life for him. You're the one who put your own dreams on hold to help him build his. And you're the one that can make him realise what he's losing for the sake of a cliché midlife meltdown.'

'Well, what are you suggesting? That I leave him to look after the kids on his own? I've never been away from them for more than a night, Rosie.'

'I know, my love,' said Rosemary, gently. 'But they're not babies anymore and what we're talking about here is you leaving them with their dad, not at a kennel.'

Adelaide grinned and rolled her eyes.

'And if you really are splitting up, there will be a lot of nights that they're not with you, especially if he goes for joint custody.'

Something gripped Adelaide's heart and squeezed. 'I don't know, Rosie.'

'Just think about it. You may not want him back after what he's done, but he needs to understand exactly what he's losing by walking away from your marriage.'

7

SHUFFLING into Retrograde with her shoulders slumped, Adelaide felt a heaviness in her body that emanated from the depths of her bone marrow.

'Morning, Adelaide,' said Celeste, cheerily. 'Gosh, are you okay? It looks like you might be coming down with something. There're some nasty colds going around at the moment. My housemate had this virus thing, and it lasted a whole month. Although, she did keep having all-nighters, so maybe that's why she didn't get better for so long...' Celeste trailed off, having forgotten that she had asked Adelaide a question at all.

'Where's Ivy?' Adelaide asked.

'Oh, she's not coming in today. That's why I'm here, she said she needed the day off. I don't know why.'

'Oh,' said Adelaide, disappointed.

She realised how much she wanted to share her troubles with Ivy. Adelaide's relationship with her mother had always been complicated, and Ivy had stepped into a maternal role in the sixteen years they had worked together. A weight lifted when she'd talked with Rosemary earlier, and Adelaide hoped the catharsis would continue with Ivy. She looked over at Celeste who was writing out price tags.

'Do we have any appointments today?' Adelaide asked.

'Yes, but not until midday,' replied Celeste. 'It's those TV people, you know the ones?'

'Televisual?'

'Yeah. They're doing something set in the seventies.'

'Do you want to take the lead this time?' said Adelaide.

'Yeah, I mean, I'll try. Are you sure?'

Celeste's eyes were wide.

'You can handle it,' assured Adelaide, 'and I'll be here if anything unexpected comes up.'

Adelaide paused before continuing. 'So, how was your weekend?'

'Oh, you know, pretty good. Saturday night Cass and I went to this house party in Thornbury. Do you know Cass? She's been in here a couple of times. Anyway, we went to this party and her ex-boyfriend shows up with some other girl. They only just broke up a few days ago and he's already hooked up with some random. There was this *whoooooole* situation. It got super awkward because the chick didn't even know about Cass being his girlfriend and she stormed off and he ran after her, but we stayed and had MDMA caps and danced till 5:00 am. The music was awesome. Some guy brought decks and was DJing in the kitchen.'

'Well, that certainly sounds action-packed,' said Adelaide.

The younger woman nodded in agreement.

Then Adelaide heard herself say, 'Something kind of similar happened to me on the weekend. My husband told me that he's fallen in love with someone else.'

Celeste stopped what she was doing and turned to face Adelaide. Her mouth hung open giving her a strange, amphibian quality. Adelaide had a vision of her tongue darting out to snatch up a fly.

'Yep, I got home from coffee with Rosie on Saturday afternoon and boom! "Adelaide, I'm leaving you."'

Adelaide wasn't sure why, but she felt mildly amused at the younger woman's shock. Finally, Celeste found her voice. 'Shit, Adelaide, I mean… Shit.'

'Yeah, shit,' Adelaide agreed. 'Rosie thinks Joe's going through a midlife crisis and will come crawling back.'

'Do you want him to crawl back? Like, he's gone and cheated on you. Could you really stay married to that?'

Adelaide thought about the black and white world that Celeste inhabited. When Adelaide was Celeste's age, she would have asked the same question. Hell, she would have flat-out branded Joe a love-rat and he'd be dead to her. But things were different now. She and Joe had a life together, children, a home and friends. The idea of disentangling themselves from one another seemed way more insurmountable than the idea of forgiveness and rebuilding.

'Don't get me wrong, I am hurt, and I am angry. But the thought of telling Darcy and Estée that their parents are splitting up is enough for me to get over anything. The inconvenient truth in all this mess is that I still love him. Even after he shattered me, I still love him.'

Adelaide lowered herself into a chair and cried.

'Oh man,' said Celeste. She walked over and rubbed the centre of Adelaide's back as if she were suffering from hypothermia. 'Bloody men. You might still love him, but I think he's a selfish prick.'

Adelaide laughed and sniffed loudly. 'Oh, I agree with you there!'

JANE from Televisual was scheduled to arrive at noon so when a tall, salt and pepper haired man walked in at five minutes to, Adelaide assumed he was a customer browsing. She sidled up next to him as he was running a hand across a teak sideboard.

'She's a beaut' isn't she?'

'She certainly is,' said the man, turning to address Adelaide squarely, the corner of his mouth turned up in a poorly suppressed smile. 'I'm Michael Laine, from Televisual,' he said, offering his hand.

'Oh,' said Adelaide, slightly taken aback, 'we were expecting Jane. I'm Adelaide, Adelaide Jones, it's lovely to meet you.'

Celeste, overhearing the exchange, joined them and introduced herself.

'Jane's under the weather today, she sends her apologies,' Michael explained.

'I hope it's nothing too serious. Can I get you anything before we begin? A coffee perhaps?' said Celeste, trying on a professional persona for the occasion.

'I'm fine, thanks,' said Michael, addressing Adelaide.

'Could you tell us a little about the new show?' asked Adelaide.

'It's a six-part, drama mini-series called West Gate which follows the lead up to the 1970 West Gate Bridge collapse, and goes right through to the outcome of the Royal Commission investigation,' Michael said.

'Oh yes, didn't that kill a number of people?' asked Adelaide.

'Yes,' said Michael, nodding, 'Thirty-five construction workers died. It's still considered Victoria's worst industrial disaster.'

'Crazy,' said Celeste reverting back to herself. 'I've never even heard of it.'

Adelaide and Michael exchanged an almost imperceptible glance.

'We're looking to furnish around a dozen sets in the mid-century style. Mainly houses belonging to key characters, but also the Melbourne headquarters of the British designers, and the Victoria-based construction company. There's a particularly pivotal scene that takes place at the Winston Charles Discotheque in Toorak which I'm really excited about. I have some storyboards I can show you. It's going to be a fairly large undertaking. Obviously, most of the bridge stuff will be CGI but everything else is up to us.'

'Well, you're in luck. We have a particularly extensive inventory at the moment. As you can imagine, this type of business can be quite cyclical,' said Adelaide.

'Cyclical,' echoed Celeste, looking between the two.

Again, the barely perceptible smile.

Adelaide took her leave after that. She wanted to give Celeste the opportunity to manage the project without feeling as though Adelaide was looking over her shoulder. She busied herself updating the online store and responding to customer queries. If Celeste hit a roadblock, she could just seek her advice.

CELESTE emerged almost two hours later with a tablet full of notes and a satisfied smile.

'How'd it go?' asked Adelaide.

'Awesome actually. It's kind of a rush, building an entire make-believe world. I think we've got most of what we need in inventory, but it'll take a bit of work piecing it all together. I might just run it by you once I've done a bit more on it. If that's cool?'

'Yeah, sounds like a great plan,' said Adelaide, flashing Celeste an encouraging smile.

'But before we go any further, can we please take a moment to acknowledge how much that dude was vibing on you?' said Celeste

'Vibing on me?' said Adelaide, her eyebrows darting up.

'Vibe-ing,' confirmed Celeste.

'Don't be silly. You're imagining it.'

'Oh, am I? Why did he ask about your "situation" then?'

'He did not!' exclaimed Adelaide, through a poorly suppressed smile.

'Ya-ha he did.'

'What did you say?'

'I said I wasn't sure but that I'd pass his number on to you,' she said, waving a scrap of paper in the air.

Adelaide gasped, sending Celeste into a frenzy of giggles and clapping.

'Look, I know you've got your heart set on winning back "Husband of the Year" but if it doesn't work out maybe you can cry on Mr Laine's pillow. All I know is that you're a stone-cold fox and you don't need to settle for shit.'

Celeste placed the paper scrap next to Adelaide's hand where it rested on the mouse, and walked away.

Adelaide looked at it in disbelief. Life was weird.

THAT evening, after she had put the twins to bed, after she had fed them, bathed them, read them 'Just one more story, Mummy', after she had cleared away the dinner plates, stacked the dishwasher, folded laundry, picked up toys and planned out tomorrow's meals, Adelaide sat on the sofa with a cup of tea. She thought of Joe, wondered what he was doing right now. Then she scrunched her eyes shut, banishing the unwelcome vision that came to her. She thought about what Rosemary had said that morning, about Joe being on a week-long shag-fest, and felt tired. But when did she not feel tired? Even their family holidays weren't a holiday for her. She was like a solitary stagehand frantically creating the perfect backdrop for the egocentric actors of a play. Joe and the children sat in their dressing rooms, while she moved mountains, waiting to emerge at the moment when everything was perfect. They came out to deliver their lines before retreating into their ignorance. Blissfully unaware of what it took to create their stage. She quietly cursed herself for providing Joe with such a pampered existence, the perfect breeding ground for him to take her for granted. She had tried to make herself indispensable but, in a twist of cruel irony, had made herself invisible instead. Perhaps Rosemary was right. Maybe she did need to give Joe a taste of what life would be like as a single father. But paradoxically, though she craved a break, the idea of being away from her children, especially now, made her heart ache. She knew that Joe would seek some form of custody. How on earth would she cope with that? She picked up her phone and texted Joe.

"I've been thinking. I'm just not ready to tell the twins about what's going on with us. I need a little more time, I hope you'll understand. After you return from your "business trip" I'd like to go on one of my own. I'll call you tomorrow to discuss."

THE next morning, after Adelaide dropped the twins off at kindergarten, she phoned Joe on her drive to work. She explained to him that she needed to mentally prepare herself for guiding the children through, what would surely be, a tremendously difficult time for them. She would arrange to have some time off work and speak to her mother about staying with her for the week. He reluctantly agreed to the disruption in his work schedule, taking on board Adelaide's suggestion that Lienna would gladly take the twins on the days they didn't have kindergarten.

As Adelaide dialled her mother's number, she was overcome by a feeling of foreboding. Why did she feel so ashamed? Surely, if anyone would understand what she was going through, it was her mum. She would certainly understand the need for headspace. It had been Sia's idea to send a teenaged Adelaide to stay with her own mother for a Greek summer vacation, when she and Niall were attempting to work through the marriage troubles that would ultimately culminate in their divorce.

At the time, Adelaide's parents had tried to sell it to her as an exotic beach adventure, but she had accused them of shipping her off. Staying in a sleepy seaside village with her *yiayia*, who spoke no more than a dozen words of English, when Adelaide spoke no Greek, was hardly the glamorous Mediterranean jaunt that her parents made it out to be. Adelaide was sixteen at the time and hadn't even seen her *yiayia* since she'd moved back to Greece, more than ten years earlier. Once Adelaide had given her parents one final scowl at the departure gate, she boarded the plane and sobbed. Thankfully, the air hostess was kind, bringing her extra snacks and drinks, and she had binge watched movies and listened to music. After the tempest of her recent home life, the flight had provided a welcome respite.

She disembarked in Athens, feeling groggy and stale, and boarded a bus to make the one-hour journey to Loutraki. She dozed on the way, having strange fitful dreams that her teeth were crumbling away to gravel in her mouth. The bus driver was a kindly moustached man who, remembering her intended destination, gently shook her awake when they arrived. Adelaide had gathered up her backpacks and stumbled down the stairs, running right into *yiayia* Vaso, before ricocheting off her and landing in the dirt. *Yiayia* Vaso was a stern-faced block of a woman dressed entirely in black, owing to the perpetual mourning of a husband who had died before Adelaide was born. Adelaide looked up at the stout woman from her vantage point on the ground and offered a half-smiled greeting.

'You come,' *Yiayia* barked, before turning on her heel and marching towards town.

Adelaide frantically collected herself, and her belongings, and set off in pursuit.

When Adelaide arrived at *Yiayia's* apartment, the smell of chlorine overwhelmed her. She would soon learn that her grandmother began each day by mopping the entire apartment with bleach, at dawn. After a largely sleepless, jetlagged first night, she was woken by the *swish, swish, thwack* of the saturated string mop, making its way around the sofa bed on which she lay, in the living area. Adelaide covered her head with the lumpy pillow and groaned. This could not be happening. All her friends were back in Melbourne on school holidays, and she was on the other side of the world being held prisoner by a crazy woman. When the sun rose on the already stifling day, Adelaide walked two blocks to the pebble beach. She submerged herself in the cool water and felt her tension wash away with each gentle lap. After a swim, she laid down on her towel, turned on her Discman and drifted off to sleep. The next thing she knew, she was being shaken awake by the silhouetted figure of *Yiayia*. Adelaide may have been impressed by the small woman's strength if she wasn't so completely mortified at being dragged to her feet on the now-crowded beach. Unsure of her misdemeanour, Adelaide was goose-stepped back to the apartment under a machine gun fire of *tsks*, headshakes and unintelligible mutterings. Once inside, Adelaide was pushed towards the kitchen table, laden as it was with lamb and bean stew, crusty bread and white cheese. Although Adelaide didn't feel hungry—it was the middle of the night back home— she sat down to eat in order to placate the old woman. The lamb, having cooked for hours in tomato and red wine sauce, fell apart on her tongue. It was salty and tangy with an underlying garlic sweetness. Seeing a flush of pleasure cross Adelaide's face, *yiayia* Vaso's own face spontaneously contorted into a complex synoptic chart of lines—she was smiling.

After lunch, there was a knock at the door. *Yiayia* blurted something before getting to her feet and hurrying towards the door. A young woman, around Adelaide's age, entered the kitchen behind *yiayia* Vaso. She had a kind smile and a blunt fringe framed her beetle-black eyes.

'Hi, I'm Penny Leventis. I live in the apartment upstairs,' she said in perfect, prettily-accented English.

'WELL, look who figured out how a phone works,' said Sia, answering Adelaide's phone call.

Adelaide grimaced. 'Hi Mum, sorry it's been a while. Busy busy, you know.'

'Oh yes, I know, sweetheart. To what do I owe the pleasure now?'

Adelaide took a deep breath. 'I was actually hoping you could do me a favour. Joe and I are having some… issues. We're having a little time apart and I was wondering if I might be able to come and stay with you next week,' she said.

'Trouble in paradise, is there?'

Adelaide gritted her teeth and recalled the countless times she'd been told, 'I would have made something of my life if your father hadn't knocked me up and my parents forced me to marry him.'

'Look, Mum, if you're going to be smarmy about it, I can just go stay in a hotel.'

'Now now, there's no need to be so sensitive, of course you can come and stay. It'll be lovely to have you.'

'Okay, thanks,' said Adelaide, half regretting asking her in the first place.

'So, that husband of yours still hasn't figured out that he hit the jackpot with you, hmm?'

'That fact does seem to have escaped him of late,' Adelaide laughed.

Why was it that at the exact moment Adelaide had decided her mother was the absolute worst, she would redeem herself?

'Does this mean you can forgive me now, for sending you to stay with *Yiayia* in Greece?' Sia asked in a mocking tone.

'I forgave you for that a long time ago, Mum.'

'Well, it wasn't all bad was it. Are you still in contact with the Leventis kids?'

'They're hardly kids anymore, Mum. They're pushing forty now. I had an email from Penny at Christmas and I'm not sure when I last heard from Alec…' she trailed off. 'I think the last I heard he was working at a chalet in Whistler. When was that though?'

Adelaide was frequently astounded to find that motherhood had her living in a kind of vacuum. She thanked her mother again for letting her stay and hung up the phone.

Adelaide pulled into the carpark at Retrograde, retrieved her phone from the holder and sent two identical emails to Penny and Alec.

"Can you believe it's been twenty years since we met? Might be time for you to visit my side of the world! How are you? What's been happening? Tell me everything!"

It had been far too long since she had checked in on her old friends, but she didn't much feel like bombarding them with the catastrophe that was her life at the moment.

ADELAIDE was half-way through a furniture rental proposal when her phone lit up, showing an email from Penny. She said she was doing well and, having worked as a nurse anaesthetist for many years, had finally completed further studies to become an anaesthesiologist. She joked that all the men in Greece were defective and maybe she should come to Melbourne to find a nice Australian husband. Adelaide was laughing out loud as Ivy wandered over.

'I hope you're going to let me in on the joke, darling,' said Ivy, eyes sparkling through her spectacles.

'Oh, it's nothing, just an email from an old friend in Greece,' she said, replacing her phone on the desk where she was working.

'Oh, the artist? What was his name?' asked Ivy.

Her Bakelite beads emitted a rhythmic, mah-jong-click as she fingered them absentmindedly.

'No, not Alec. His sister, Penny.'

Ivy, not having heard, went on, 'What was it, sculpture? I remember when you first started working here, you were always going on about "my friend told me about this band or that film or this book". What was his name?' Ivy asked, beginning to show signs of frustration.

'You're thinking of Alec. He was the artist, although he's never really been able to make a living from it that I know of,' Adelaide explained.

'Darling, you just described exactly what an artist is—struggling!' said Ivy, laughing.

Adelaide, seeing her point, joined in.

'No, I mean, he's always done other things to support himself. He's spent most of his adult life travelling, following the work.'

'A nomad,' said Ivy, nodding wistfully, her voice full of romance.

ADELAIDE hadn't even met Penny's older brother for the first few days. He was at a water polo training camp. She and Penny were helping Mrs Leventis make *dolmades*. The three of them sat in a semicircle around the kitchen table, scooping the aromatic rice mixture into the middle of vine leaves before rolling them into firm parcels. Mrs Leventis, who had insisted that she be called *Theia*—Aunty in Greek—found Adelaide's clumsy ineptitude for the task endlessly hilarious. She kept bursting into spontaneous fits of laughter. She teased and jibed Adelaide, through Penny's giggled translations, that her Australian father's side must have completely ruined her otherwise superior Greek lineage. Adelaide was feigning being deeply wounded by her insults when a clatter of door locks, dropped baggage, and heavy footsteps halted her mimed act. In strode a tall, lanky boy who scooped his mother into the air, where she dangled momentarily before being gingerly set down. Excited conversation burst like fireworks and, although Adelaide couldn't understand a word of it, she grinned along with them, looking from one face to another, swept up in their good cheer. Noticing Adelaide for the first time, the boy froze, stunned to find a stranger sitting in his kitchen. Mrs Leventis placed a proud hand on his shoulder and stated in heavily accented English, 'Alexandros, my son.'

Adelaide regarded him for a moment. He was tall and broad, his shoulders jutting out so sharply it gave the appearance that his t-shirt was still on the hanger. His glossy black hair was caught in an interminable loop of falling into his eyes and being swept back by his fingers. He stepped forward and offered her his hand.

'Alec,' he simplified.

'This is Adelaide, she's *theia* Vaso's granddaughter, from Australia,' Penny explained.

His eyes were deep green, the length of his eyelashes lending a feminine quality to an otherwise angular face. His hand was warm and strong and enveloped hers, making it all but disappear. When he pulled her into a kiss on each cheek, he smelled like salt and mastic.

'Adelaide,' he repeated, trying the word out. Somehow the syllables multiplied within the embrace of his accent.

'Or perhaps it's Adele,' she said, instantly wondering why she said it. She had never been known as Adele in her life.

'Adele,' he said, his eyes sparkling down at her.

8

THE week progressed in a strange state of limbo. Adelaide's days were so full that she could fool herself into believing that Joe really was on a business trip and that, upon his return, life would return to normal. It was in the evening, after the children were in bed and all her tasks for the day were complete, that the illusion shattered. When the house was dark and quiet and felt uninhabited, her fears for the future crept up from the ground like vines wrapping around her ankles, slowly pulling her down.

Now, she sat at the kitchen bench drinking a glass of tempranillo, tracing the lip with her index finger and enjoying the haunted lullaby it created. *Friday night drinks are different these days,* she thought, emitting a quiet yet audible laugh before beginning to cry.

This had become her nightly ritual. Get everyone and everything sorted, leaving nothing whatsoever unfinished, then sit alone and cry. For some reason, the fact that it was Friday night made it more pitiful. Her breath became short, and her problems sat on her chest with their full weight. Her life was falling apart and what was she doing about it? Running back to her mother and hiding? She texted Rosemary. "Hey, Rosie, are you up? I'm having a bit of a freak out. Got time for a chat?"

A second later her phone rang.

'Hi, Rosie, sorry to bother you. I think I'm having a panic attack!' she blurted, answering the call.

'I mean, of course you are. This whole situation is a complete disaster. Any rational person would have a bloody panic attack,' said Rosemary, evenly.

Adelaide felt better already. Rosemary had a way of making Adelaide feel heard and validated that no one else could match. She was never made to feel foolish, and Rosemary didn't sugar coat or diminish the gravity of a situation with inane positive spin.

'Oh, Rosie, I just feel like an idiot. Leaving the kids with Joe to go and stay with my mother? I mean, what the hell is that?'

'So, we talked about this. You need to show Joe exactly what he's getting himself into. I'm not saying that this is going to be an easy week for you. You're going to miss your kids like crazy and your mum is probably going to do your head in, but it's not about that. This is about Joe realising what an arsehole he's being. To make him come crawling back on his knees, begging your forgiveness.'

In true Rosemary style, she quickly finished giving empathetic support and had now progressed to a cold, hard reality sermon.

'Is it going to be awkward as shit when he comes back home on Monday morning? Yes. Is it going to rip your heart out to say goodbye to the twins and leave? Yes. Will you get through it like the strong warrior that you are? Hell yes.'

Adelaide laughed in sad resignation. It could be no other way.

'You're right, you're always right,' she agreed, silent tears streaking her cheeks.

'I'll tell you what, why don't I come over on Sunday night after our kids are all in bed? We can eat all the chocolate in the house and binge watch some deplorable television.'

Adelaide sniffed loudly and laughed. 'Now that's a plan I can get behind,' she said, patting her cheeks with her sleeve. 'Thanks, Rosie.'

ADELAIDE did her best to make the weekend fun and to keep her thoughts from dwelling on the ticking clock in her mind. She and the twins went to the zoo on Saturday and Adelaide resisted the urge to pack them their usual nutrient-dense lunch boxes, opting instead to purchase that most coveted of cuisines—hot chips. On Sunday morning, they visited the plant nursery and spent the remainder of the day covered in dirt from head to toe. As Adelaide shepherded the children through their bath and bedtime routine, she was more and more thankful that Rosemary would soon arrive to cast her luminescence on all of Adelaide's shadows.

Adelaide had just finished packing her suitcase when a text alerted her that Rosemary was at the front door. She zipped the case, lugged it downstairs and threw open the door to behold her friend's beaming face.

'Belgian chocolates and French champagne,' she announced, holding up the delicacies for approval.

'A life without you, Rosie, would be no life at all,' said Adelaide, making way for her friend to enter.

Rosemary headed into the kitchen and retrieved two champagne flutes from the cupboard. She poured, handed a glass to Adelaide and clinked. Then, gathering up the bottle and the chocolates, made her way to the sofa with Adelaide following dutifully.

They both knew that the promise of trash television had been a ruse to affect normalcy. In fact, they huddled together like storm-weathered castaways on the life raft of the sofa, talking in detail about all they had endured. As the champagne diminished and the confessions tallied, both women began to understand themselves, and each other, that much deeper. It was well into the second bottle of wine that Rosemary texted Adam to tell him she couldn't be bothered stumbling home, and that she'd stay at Adelaide's for the night. As their words became slurred and their conversation evolved into ostentatious declarations of love for one another, Adelaide's phone chimed with a new email.

She could do nothing to conceal her excitement when his name flashed up on her screen: Alec Leventis.

9

THE twins woke around 7:00 a.m. and, having found their parents' bed unoccupied, plodded downstairs. There they found Adelaide and Rosemary asleep, fully clothed, at opposite ends of the large modular sofa.

'Mumma,' cried Darcy, aghast, 'you forgot to go to bed.'

'Rosie, is Charlie here too?' Estée asked, poking Rosemary in the arm.

The two women groaned in unison as they attempted to extract themselves from the padded embrace of the upholstery.

They exchanged a glance.

'No honey, Charlie is at home with her daddy. I came over last night to keep your mummy company and we got so tired we fell asleep on the couch. That's funny, isn't it?' said Rosemary, in a sing-song lilt.

Dear Lord, Adelaide thought, *Joe will be arriving in an hour.* Rosemary, reading her thoughts, immediately took charge.

'Come on, kids, you get to watch TV during breakfast today,' said Rosemary, ushering them onto the sofa before shoving a dumbstruck Adelaide towards the stairs. She then showered the twins with a selection of packaged snack foods and headed up to the bathroom to administer Berocca and Panadol to Adelaide.

By the time the doorbell chimed an hour later, the two women each wore a convincing veneer of composure. Adelaide looked at Rosemary, drawing courage from her friend's confident single nod, and opened the door.

'Good morning, madame,' said the middle-aged Bangladeshi man on the front step. 'Ready to go?'

Adelaide looked at Rosemary, who shrugged.

'I'm sorry, I think you must have the wrong address,' said Adelaide, her head pounding despite the Panadol's best attempts.

'Adelaide Jones?' he enquired, his smile never faltering.

'I *am* Adelaide Jones,' said Adelaide, slowly.

'I will take you to the airport now,' he said, motioning towards the Audi parked out front.

'The airport?' asked Adelaide, frowning.

Rosemary raised her hand to her mouth and gasped.

'What?' Adelaide asked, impatiently.

'You're going to Greece,' Rosemary blurted.

Adelaide laughed nervously.

'You're going to Greece,' Rosemary repeated, more forcefully.

'This is your bag? I will put it in the car?' the driver asked, stepping towards Adelaide's suitcase at the foot of the stairs.

Adelaide's mouth was hanging open now, her eyes wide with disbelief as fragments of last night emerged in her mind.

'She just needs to pack a few more things,' said Rosemary, sporting a forced smile. 'Would you mind waiting in the car for five minutes?'

The driver looked from Rosemary to Adelaide and back again. His mouth was set into a smile, but his eyes belied a mild wariness.

'Thank you so much,' Rosemary added, placing a guiding hand on the man's arm as she gently pushed him out and closed the door.

Adelaide's eyes searched Rosemary's face for confirmation of what she already knew was true.

'So, your friend Alec emailed you last night. He's managing a little hotel in the Greek Islands. You told him you needed a break from your life, and he told you he's just had a cancelation. The accommodation is pre-paid, Adelaide. You booked flights last night. You should go.'

'I can't go to the other side of the world, Rosie, what about the children?' Adelaide shrieked.

'The twins are taken care of. What difference does it make if you're in Mornington or Ikaria?' Rosemary challenged.

'There is no way…' Adelaide began, but there was a knock at the door.

She opened it, this time revealing Joe.

He barely looked up from his phone to acknowledge her as he entered. 'Hey, I'm going to need you to come and look after the kids a couple of times this week. I've got a dinner on Wednesday, and this drinks thing on Friday that I can't get out of, you don't mind, do you?'

Without waiting for an answer, he strode into the house in search of the children.

Rosemary looked at Adelaide with intense eyes, her jaw set. Adelaide met her friend's gaze and called after Joe. 'That's not going to work for me. I've decided to take a trip this week. In fact, I might be a little longer than a week,' Adelaide said gathering up her suitcase and heading upstairs with Rosemary at her heels.

ONCE in the Audi, Adelaide commenced freaking out. What the hell was she doing? As if on cue, she received a text message from Joe asking, "What the hell are you doing?" This was followed immediately by another demanding, "What kind of mother are you?"

Adelaide's whole body seethed. What kind of mother was she? What kind of mother was she? The kind who spent twenty-three hours in labour, the kind who breastfed not one but two babies twenty-four hours a day for fifteen months, the kind that changed every nappy, wiped every runny nose, made every meal, dried every tear, for more than five years, without so much as a break. That's what kind of mother she was. Joe was a good father, but he was a good-time guy only. He made sure he was present for all the fun, all the cheer and none of the work. She placed her hands over her face and squeezed her eyes tight, trying to focus on her breathing.

'Madame, is everything alright?' the driver asked tentatively.

Absurdly, she had forgotten that he was there.

'Oh. Yes, I'm fine,' she lied. 'It's just that this is the first time I've ever gone on holiday without my children.'

'I see,' he said, nodding.

They sat in silence for a while, Adelaide looking mournfully out of the passenger window at the crawling traffic.

'You know, when a mother attends to her own happiness, it is not at the expense of her children. It is to their benefit also,' he said, sagely.

10

THE breeze whipped at Adelaide's unwashed hair as she stood on the top deck of the ferry. She raised her chin to receive the restorative rays of the bright Mediterranean sun, breathing in the sea air, allowing it to cleanse the furthest corners within her. It was the twins' bedtime back home. Something deep within her ached for her children, their soap scented skin, their still-damp hair, the way their five-year-old faces regressed back into infancy when sleep laid its soft veil upon them. She thought too of the relief she felt each night when they were finally asleep. Thought of the sudden absence of their ceaseless demands, creating a silence so foreign to her, it sometimes seemed deafening. Now, here she was on the other side of the world, on her way to meet a man, who was once a boy she used to know.

The ferry ride was long, and Adelaide cursed herself for not purchasing something to read. It had been so long since she had travelled alone—hell, it had been so long since she *was* alone—that she had forgotten how to… be. She looked around at the other passengers. A pair of elderly Greek women were preparing their lunch. She couldn't help smiling to herself as one of the women extracted a Tupperware container of hard-boiled eggs from her cavernous handbag and peeled them on her lap. Meanwhile, her companion produced a sizable cucumber, which she expertly peeled and chopped with a paring knife, before placing the glistening chunks on the lid of her friend's container. The first woman, having completed her eggs, fished around in her bag and withdrew a crusty quarter-loaf of bread. She tore off a hunk and silently handed it to her friend whose open-mouthed cucumber crunches could be heard even above the ceaseless hum of the ferry's labouring engine. The two women sat in comfortable silence, intuitively passing the food between them, just one in a lifetime of shared meals together. Adelaide wondered if they were sisters, so easy was their manner with one another. They reminded her of her *yiayia* Vaso, who had passed away when the twins were only a few months old.

She remembered inexplicably waking in the middle of the night, at home in Melbourne, at the exact time that *Yiayia's* funeral service was being held in Loutraki. She felt wounded and heartsick, not only for the loss of her grandmother, but for the loss of herself. She felt so incredibly tethered by her children, by their insatiable need for the sustenance and comfort of her body. A body that no longer seemed to belong to her. She remembered the silent tears that fell down her cheeks as she looked at the faces of her babies, willing them to remain sleeping for just a little longer, so she could fully experience her moment of grief.

ALEC had said, in one of the many quick-fire emails they had exchanged, that he would send someone to pick her up from the port at Evdilos. She was more than a little relieved that he wouldn't be picking her up himself. She had gone from drunk, to hungover, to jetlagged in the last forty hours and it showed. The last time Alec had seen her, she was a fresh-faced sixteen-year-old with her whole life ahead of her. At this moment in time, she felt decades older than her thirty-six years, with her whole life crumbling down around her.

When a gruff voice announced over the loudspeaker that they would soon be arriving at Ikaria, Adelaide had already situated herself and her luggage close to the exit in the vehicle deck. Motorists who'd brought their cars along for the voyage readied themselves to disembark. As more and more passengers arrived, Adelaide was lightly jostled. The ramp lowered like a medieval drawbridge, providing tantalising glimpses of the island as the vessel bobbed. Crystalline waters glittered and sparkled like sequins on a flapper's hemline and gave way to rows of chalky white buildings, which glowed luminescent in the bright sunshine. The excited anticipation of the passengers was palpable, and Adelaide was squeezed in the front line by the overzealous throng.

The ramp had barely kissed the pier when the wave of eager passengers swept forward. Adelaide was almost knocked down by a boisterous group of American teenagers. She pressed herself close to the rail, unable to grasp it to steady herself, laden as she was with her handbag, vanity case and suitcase. Then, at the precise moment the wheels of her suitcase were traversing the ridge between ferry and ramp, Adelaide was flung sideways like a bowling pin by a tank of a woman who was waving her arms madly about her head, in greeting to someone awaiting her. Adelaide's ankle gave way. Dropping her belongings, she grabbed for the rail, watching as her suitcase slipped neatly through a narrow gap in the railing. It bounced off the rudder with a sickening crack and Adelaide watched in horror as all her clothes burst forth and were tossed about in the breeze like carnival bunting. It occurred to her in that moment that she detested all those clothes, all those colourless, shapeless clothes she had accumulated to make herself blend in, go unnoticed. She dressed how she thought a wife and a mother should, and she hated it. There were a few gasps from passengers who were close enough to witness the mishap, and a kind Swedish couple helped Adelaide steady herself and retrieve the bags that had fallen at her feet. She shuffled forward feeling deflated and ridiculous. Picking her way through the seagull-like squawks of hotel hustlers, she spied a familiar name emblazoned on the side of a retro VW Kombi van. It was Ilios Choros, the name of Alec's hotel.

As Adelaide rounded the vehicle, she saw a long pair of intricately tattooed legs, partially encased in black, cut-off jean shorts, protruding from the side door. The owner of the legs straightened at the sight of Adelaide.

Her hair hung about her face in choppy defiance and mirrored sunglasses concealed her eyes. She took one last drag of her cigarette before throwing it to the ground and crushing it with her Dr. Martens.

'*Ya*,' she said, using the Greek informal greeting. 'You are Adele, right? I am Xena,' she said, her voice like a straight shot of whiskey.

Adelaide took the hand being offered and was surprised at the strength of Xena's handshake. Her own hand felt weak by comparison.

'But where are your bags? Did you leave something on board?'

'Something like that,' said Adelaide, before blurting out the catastrophe that had befallen her possessions. She was surprised to find that Xena was laughing, and Adelaide couldn't help but join in.

'Okay, so you would like to shop?' Xena asked.

'Can I? I mean, is there somewhere I can get a few clothes? All I have in this one is toiletries,' Adelaide said, holding up her vanity case.

'Sure. I know a shop in town—very *fashionistic*. I can take you now, I have time,' said Xena, unaware that she had invented a new English word.

'Now? Isn't Alec expecting me?' Adelaide asked.

'You didn't get his text? Alec was called away to Athens yesterday, something unexpected came up. He will return tomorrow.'

Adelaide felt a strange combination of disappointment and relief at hearing this. In that moment, she realised she had spent the entire ferry journey psyching herself up for their reunion, yet she was pleased that his first impression of her wouldn't be this bedraggled shell of herself.

'Well, in that case. I guess we go shopping,' said Adelaide.

THE store was blissfully cool after the stifling heat of the Kombi van and Adelaide was soothed by the nonchalance of Peggy Lee crooning about *Waitin' for the train to come in*. Adelaide gazed around the store. It had been a long time since she had shopped anywhere like this. The stores she found herself in these days were at the very minimal end of the spectrum. White cavernous cubes with the type of racks that seemed to be miraculously suspended mid-air, displaying clothing that Ivy would disdainfully describe as "aggressive neutrals". Here, she found a carefully curated selection of luxury resort wear, set against the backdrop of a black and white chequerboard floor and lavender pink walls.

Adelaide instinctively ran a hand across the garments as she wove her way around the perimeter of gold racks, which glittered under the galaxy of lights overhead. Silk, linen, cotton, her expert fingertips identified the fine fabrics sending electric jolts of pleasure up to her brain. She wanted it all.

A sales assistant emerged from behind a velvet curtain. She sported a twist turban and fringed earrings, her red lips parted to reveal an endearing, crooked-toothed smile. '*Yassas*. Welcome,' she said warmly.

'*Yassas*, this is Adele. All of her clothes have gone to Atlantis,' said Xena cryptically, before erupting into a fit of husky giggles that Adelaide could not resist echoing.

After the unfortunate tale had been repeated, the sales assistant asked, 'So, do you see anything you will like to try?'

IT was late afternoon by the time Adelaide climbed back into the Kombi van, utterly depleted.

'I could really use a drink,' she said.

'Well, my friend, you're in luck, because I am a bartender at Ilios Choros,' said Xena, her eyes sparkling mischievously in the rear vision mirror.

'You are?' asked Adelaide in surprise. 'Then why did you pick me up?'

'Because you are an old friend of Alec and he wanted to make sure you were well looked after. Me and Alec have known each other for years. He felt terrible that he couldn't collect you himself.'

'Thank you, Xena, for everything. I mean it, you turned a day that was horrible into something magical,' said Adelaide, indicating the shopping bags surrounding her.

Xena winked before refocusing her attention on the hairpin bends she navigated at breakneck speed.

As the town's sprawl gave way to a scorched-earth landscape, dotted with the occasional scrawny goat, Adelaide asked Xena where the hotel was located.

'It's a little more secluded than the more touristic parts of the island. It means we can make more noise.'

Adelaide wondered what kind of noise but didn't ask, she was beginning to succumb to the van's rhythmic vibration and was trying to focus all her energy on not falling asleep and embarrassing herself. They rounded a bend and Adelaide had a bird's-eye view of a sprawling expanse of terracotta-roofed, chalk white buildings skirting a picturesque inlet below.

'What is that town?' Adelaide asked, stifling a yawn.

'That's not a town, it's Ilios Choros,' said Xena.

Adelaide was dumbstruck. In all the frantic happenings it hadn't occurred to her to look up Ilios Choros on the internet. She simply assumed that Alec was managing a quaint pensione. What she beheld now was a luxury resort of the highest order, complete with its own lagoon-style swimming pool and...

'That's not a helipad, is it?' Adelaide asked.

Xena emitted a contralto laugh as Adelaide's eyes widened. The view of Ilios Choros grew larger in the Kombi's split windscreen as they approached.

Coming to the end of the road, Adelaide noticed a giant illustrated black and white dismembered hand pointing a single finger toward a narrow gravel path. Xena turned right and they journeyed onward through closely planted olive trees whose boughs seemed strained under the weight of their ripening fruit. Finally, they came to a large circular driveway with a small unassuming gate at its centre.

After they parked, Xena wordlessly gathered up Adelaide's newly acquired hatbox and most of her shopping bags and disappeared through the narrow entrance. Adelaide, fatigued and disoriented, felt like Alice trying desperately to keep up with the White Rabbit. The rambling path gave way to a modest reception area where a dark-haired boy with a Salvador Dali moustache sat painting his fingernails.

'Yassou, Xena,' he said lazily, setting his pot of nail polish to one side and blowing on his fingertips.

'Ya, Stephan. This is Adele.'

Adelaide straightened and offered an apologetic smile to the beautiful, glossy boy. She felt unforgivably unkempt.

'Adele!' he exclaimed, his whole disinterested body suddenly coming alive.

'Yassas,' he said, eyes fixed on her. 'We are having your room ready for you.'

'Oh. Lovely. Thank you,' she replied haltingly, chastising herself for her lack of sophistication.

Adelaide, hyper-aware of how much of Xena's time she had sapped already, felt self-conscious as she was led through the maze-like warren of accommodations. Somewhere in the distance a low bass beat marked the passage of time. Finally, Xena came to a semicircle archway, overhanging with lush vines, a wrought iron "eighty-eight" confirmed they had arrived at their intended destination. Xena handed Adelaide the key—a weighty relic that seemed to have been forged in the bronze age. A satisfying click announced her admission into the space beyond.

The low, exposed-beam ceiling in the matte black room created a comforting, womb-like environment in which the occupant was given no clue as to what time of the day or night it was. Clocks stopped in here and all was completely silent. Above the excessively pillowed bed, a pink neon sign implored guests to "Trouble the Darkness".

Adelaide turned to Xena who had deposited her bags on the luggage rack and was now waiting in the archway.

'I honestly don't know how to thank you, Xena,' said Adelaide, shaking her head.

'No need. Come by Tazo Bar after you've rested, I'll make you that drink you need,' she said, before disappearing back through the vines.

Adelaide sent a text to Joe letting him know she had arrived safely before stepping into the ensuite which looked like it was designed by M.C. Escher. After her long and arduous journey, the hot shower cleansed more than her exterior and she climbed into bed naked, luxuriating in the thread count of the brushed cotton sheets.

11

ADELAIDE ran down a long passageway, opening door after door, searching for something. Finally, she opened the last door and fell into her own rippled reflection. She awoke with a start, gasping for air. She wondered aloud what time it was, but her room remained silent on the subject. Her phone however, confirmed it was just after 8:00 p.m. and her stomach confirmed she was ravenous. When had she last eaten?

Adelaide began unwrapping the countless tissue paper bundles, each revealing a garment she could barely remember selecting, the whole experience having been conducted in a haze. She laid them out on the bed and marvelled at how absurdly beautiful everything was. She thought of her boring and practical "mum clothes" each selected for such tiresome attributes as "hides stains well" and "doesn't need ironing". Imagining them in their watery grave made her laugh out loud. She thought of the rashie swimsuit and baseball cap she had hastily packed into her suitcase after removing the winter clothes that had been intended for a visit to her mother's house. She held up a sleek, black strapless one-piece swimsuit with an onyx-rhinestone encrusted belt and a sisal hat whose sweeping brim was so immense she might have trouble passing through narrow doorways. *I won't be building any sandcastles in this.*

Adelaide left her hotel room feeling like a world-travelling sophisticate in a chic, silk-linen shift dress, but after getting hopelessly lost several times over, she was ready to go back to her room and cry herself to sleep. She had all but given up when she rounded an unassuming corner and found herself in a quiet alcove where an antique taxidermy zebra, wearing Elton John sunglasses, held a sign in its mouth which read "Tazo".

Xena stood behind the bar looking bored, the smattering of patrons clearly not enough to hold her interest. She wore a sequined military jacket with fringed epaulettes, her mouth a red lipstick slash across her disinterested face. Feeling Adelaide's eyes on her, she looked up, her face instantly brightening. 'You made it,' she said.

'Just barely,' Adelaide confessed, seating herself. 'How does anyone find their way around in this place?'

'You'll get used to it,' said Xena, shrugging. 'So, what are you drinking?'

'I normally drink wine,' said Adelaide.

'No wine for you,' said Xena, matter-of-factly. 'I'll make you something.'

Xena swiftly added ingredients into a cocktail shaker, her beaded jacket providing a percussive soundtrack to her movements as she vigorously muddled the herbs. She poured the yellow liquid into a martini glass, garnished it with a sprig and slid it over to Adelaide.

'What is this?' Adelaide asked before taking a sip.

'I call it About Thyme,' she said.

Adelaide let the lemon and honey compete on her tongue, while the gin went to work uncoiling the inhibitions and self-doubt that bound her. By the time she wet her lips with the last drop, she was confessing the entire sordid story of how she found herself on this side of the world, on this island and in this bar.

Adelaide had met people like Xena before. The type whose faces gave so little away, you found yourself talking incessantly in order to fill the silence and distract from the penetration of their gaze. Feeling suddenly sheepish at the depth of her confessions to this woman, whom she'd known only a few hours, Adelaide laughed nervously and said, 'God, what a lightweight I am. I really need to eat something.'

Xena assembled a simple assortment of *mezethes* in quiet contemplation and slid the plate across the bar.

'Okay, so he doesn't love you, and doesn't respect you, and your plan is to get him back, right?' Xena asked, her eyes stern.

'Well...' Adelaide began, but couldn't finish the thought.

12

THE mid-morning sun flirted with the deep blue Aegean, its glittering surface giving the effect that it was being tantalised and tickled. Adelaide sat in the pebble-mosaic floored pergola sipping a frappe, the ice emitting a satisfying clink as she twizzled the narrow straw. She thought of Joe. Was it possible to love and hate someone at the same time? He hadn't even replied to any of her texts since she left. Thank goodness Rosemary had Skyped her last night. It had been kindergarten drop-off time back home and Adelaide cried happy tears at the sight of her pink-nosed children, perfectly framed on her phone. She was both heartbroken and relieved to find that they were totally fine without her. The question was, could she be fine without them? She resolved to follow their example and try to have a good time. This was paradise, for goodness' sake.

Alec would be on the ferry coming back from Athens now. She blushed under her giant tortoise-shell sunglasses, remembering the crush she had on him when they were kids.

She must have seemed like a child to him then. He was nineteen-years-old, and about to embark on his compulsory military service, and she was just some scrawny kid from Melbourne who hung around like a lost kitten. But he had been so sweet to her, not like the older brothers of her friends back home, and she was thankful for that kindness. She remembered the first time she tagged along with Penny and Alec to the beach. He threw down his towel and removed his shirt, revealing a soft trail of hair that started above his belly button and disappeared into his swimming shorts. Her cheeks burned hot when she realised she was staring, imagining herself tracing the line with her fingertip. That day was the most fun she'd had in ages. Alec had good-naturedly picked up and thrown her and Penny into the water, over and over, amid a chorus of their delighted squeals. Adelaide relished their contact, feeling his glistening skin and the lithe power of his body. Her longing would peak just before he thrust her into the air. The sting of her bare skin slapping the water's surface would break the spell, before she was swallowed by a flurry of her own bubbles.

When they returned home that afternoon, Mrs Leventis handed them a huge container of Neapolitan ice-cream and three spoons, and sent them, still dripping in their swimsuits, up to the roof of the apartment block. They ate and talked, Alec confessing trepidation about his impending conscription, Adelaide voicing for the first time that she thought her parents would divorce, and Penny admitting that she may not earn the grades required for her further study. Adelaide still wasn't sure who threw the first blob of ice-cream, but the three of them were soon locked in a giddy, dairy-based combat. When the ice-cream container was empty and their delirious laughter had finally petered out, they sat in a heap with chests heaving. Frothy clouds rolled in over the pastel-coloured sky, bathing everything in an otherworldly tint. The first fat raindrops fell with a distinct splat creating a miniscule secondary spray to fly up on impact. They turned their faces and palms skyward as the heavens opened and saturated them in a type of baptism. Even in that moment, sixteen-year-old Adelaide knew she would never forget this for as long as she lived.

ADELAIDE meandered back to her room and felt a surge of anxiety as if she had forgotten something. Where were her children? Where did she need to be? Was she late for something? What should she be doing right now? Over and over, she reminded herself that she had no responsibilities here. She made an effort to breathe deeply and try to get out of her head. To be present in the moment. This shift felt as forced as cogs being turned in the opposite direction. She could almost hear her brain creaking under the strain of it. *Perhaps a swim will help*, she thought as she arrived back at her room.

Standing in front of the full-length mirror, Adelaide regarded her unclothed figure. Since becoming a mother, she found that she was kinder to herself. She would often hear her peers talk about their bodies as if they were a disappointment or inconvenience to them. Since giving birth to the twins, Adelaide had a newfound respect for her body, for what it could do. She felt that it would be ungrateful to lament the imperfections when her body had proven itself to be a tool of divine creation and boundless strength. Who was she to accuse it of not being decorative enough after all it had done for her? She could not quite persuade her internal monologue to sing her praises, but she had been able to silence the negative self-talk that plagued her in her youth. Now, in its place she used a simple phrase that she mentally uttered anytime she was confronted with her reflection. She would turn this way and that, running her eyes over the elements she admired and skimming over any that she didn't, saying to herself, 'Not too shabby. Not too shabby at all.' She never admitted this to anyone, not even Rosemary, but this simple technique had allowed her to make a modest sort of peace with herself. Stepping into her new swimsuit, Adelaide employed this technique, even going so far as to offer herself a broad and confident smile.

'Okay,' she said aloud, 'let's do this.'

Strolling along the winding path in her ostentatiously large hat and dark sunglasses, Adelaide could've been anyone. She smiled demurely at her fellow hotel guests, enjoying the fact that here she was not "Joe's wife" or "Darcy and Estée's mum".

A familiar figure flitted up the path towards her, sporting a delighted smile.

'Adele!' Stephan exclaimed grabbing her hand and lifting it high in the air to examine her. 'You look glorious!'

Adelaide threw her head back and laughed, placing a hand on her crown to keep from losing her hat.

'So, you'll be attending the party on Saturday? DJ Allora is arriving from Ibiza this afternoon, she's staying with us for a few days beforehand,' he blurted, excitedly.

'Party?' she asked.

'Yes. Electric Blue,' he said, dropping her hand, presumably in disgust at her ignorance.

'Oh, I didn't know about it. This was kind of a last-minute trip for me,' she said.

'It is the massive party of the season and DJ Allora is headlining, I'm having no idea how Alec convinced her to play here,' he said, clearly impressed.

'Sounds unmissable,' said Adelaide, feigning a suitable level of excitement to match Stephan's.

'Well, I better run. I'm late,' he said, before scurrying away.

AT the pool, news of DJ Allora's impending arrival had everyone twittering excitedly. Adelaide had befriended Cora and Dave, a couple who had driven from Manchester in the 1970s Aston Martin Vantage they restored together, timing the trip to align with Electric Blue.

'We're buzzing to see DJ Allora again,' said Cora, her thick accent unable to retain the "g" on the end of any word.

'We saw her play Glastonbury two years ago, it were sound,' said Dave, nodding keenly.

Adelaide kept the saga of her life out of the conversation, and enjoyed the reprise from thinking about it.

'Can I get you a drink, love?' Dave asked after a while. 'You must be gagging in this heat.'

Adelaide tried not to let her delighted fascination in her new friends' broad accents show, but she suspected her face was set into an amused smirk which could not be suppressed.

As Dave returned with a round of iced tea that Adelaide suspected originated more in Long Island than in Ceylon, an all-mighty roar rumbled from the heavens. Pool goers collectively searched the sky for the source of the disturbance, most rising to their feet as a gleaming helicopter approached the helipad. Adelaide stood beside Dave and Cora, holding her hat as the aircraft whipped up the atmosphere. Sensing someone beside her, she turned to see Alec smiling down at her. They stood, transfixed for a moment, as everyone else at the hotel stared at the figure of DJ Allora running from the chopper.

Alec took Adelaide's hand and guided her to sit beside him on a nearby sun lounger.

'Adele,' he said.

The smooth face of the boy she had known was now covered by a kempt, close-cropped beard. His dark eyebrows framed the same deep-green eyes, embellished with fine lines that radiated like sun rays. She was the sixteen-year-old girl again who had just realised she was staring at him.

'Alec,' she said, chiding herself for how breathlessly the word came out. She began again, 'Alec, this is… I mean, all this is so wonderful,' she said, indicating their surroundings.

He smiled broadly, making the rays around his eyes shine brighter.

'What is wonderful, is that you are here. When I got your email…'

Alec's phone rang in his shirt pocket and he smiled apologetically. 'Forgive me,' he said, rising to answer the call. Adelaide could see him nodding and rubbing the back of his neck as he walked to the edge of the pool. She looked over at Cora and Dave who gave her a thumbs up in acknowledgment. When he had ended the call, Alec returned, took her hands in his and said, 'I must go but let's have dinner tonight and we can catch up properly, without distractions. I'll come to get you at nine?'

'Perfect,' she said, privately amused at the contrast between this and her regular 5:00 p.m. dinner time.

He kissed her on each cheek and strode away.

HOLDING up various new outfits and regarding her reflection, Adelaide was having fun pretending she was getting ready for a date. She knew it wasn't a date, of course. She may not be a geeky kid to Alec anymore, but she wasn't sure that her evolution into a frumpy mother was any better. Besides, there was a lot of speculation around the pool this afternoon about why DJ Allora had chosen to come here. Cora and Dave had enlightened her that the Italian musician was one of the most sought-after House acts in the world and a party at Ilios Choros wasn't exactly her usual calibre of event. Adelaide listened, thinking of Stephan's comment about how Alec had managed to book her. It seemed pretty obvious to her but she wasn't about to sacrifice her dear old friend as fodder for the rumour mill. No, the part she was enjoying was that she had a dinner date to get glamorous for and could do it at a luxurious pace. She shook her head thinking of the time she had gone along with Joe to a client dinner with only one leg shaved because Darcy had a meltdown over taco fillings and she'd run out of time.

Adelaide was stepping into a black, wide-leg jumpsuit when there was a knock at the door. *He's early*, she thought, as she grabbed madly for the zipper at her back. She opened the door to reveal Xena, who let out a loud whistle. 'Look at you! Greece suits you, I think.'

Adelaide smiled broadly before turning this way and that, making the silk swish. 'All thanks to you,' she said. 'What's up?'

'I just finished work and I don't want to go home. Do you want to go for a drink?'

'Oh, that sounds so fun but I'm having dinner with...' Just then Alec appeared. 'This guy,' said Adelaide, throwing a thumb towards him.

'This guy?' he asked, coming within earshot.

'Xena came to ask me out, but I'm already spoken for tonight,' Adelaide explained.

Alec raised his eyebrows. 'Did she? Avoiding going home again?' Alec asked.

Xena rolled her eyes.

'That's what you get for living with your parents,' he teased.

Xena punched him in the arm and received mock smarts in return.

'You live with your parents?' Adelaide asked.

'Unfortunately,' said Xena.

'I think it's sweet,' said Adelaide.

'That's because you haven't met them,' said Xena.

They all laughed.

'Are you ready, Adele?' Alec asked.

'Yes, let me get my shoes on.'

'Okay, so you two are no help,' said Xena and walked away.

'Ya,' said Alec

'Maybe we'll see you later,' Adelaide called after her.

ADELAIDE and Alec were seated at the same terrace where she'd had breakfast that morning, but the space was transformed by night. Brightly coloured Ottoman lanterns swayed gently overhead, and the neat breakfast tables had been replaced by brocade-cushioned daybeds and low tables. Adelaide began the conversation by asking Alec how he had come to be here in Ikaria. She was curious, of course, but part of her wanted to delay any questions about her own life. She realised, to her dismay, that she was more than a little embarrassed about her husband finding it so easy to walk away from her.

To her surprise, Alec admitted that it had been through Adelaide's encouragement that he had first discovered, and fallen in love with, Ikaria.

'You remember I was stationed in Samos for my military service, right?'

'Of course,' she said.

'Your letters were the only thing that got me through that year. When it was finally over, I was ready to go straight home and never look back.'

'That's right,' said Adelaide, beginning to recall. 'Your mates were going to tour the islands together before heading home.'

Alec nodded, smiling.

'You told me to "suck it and go!"'

Adelaide laughed loudly before correcting him, 'Suck it up and go!'

Alec laughed. 'That is when I fell in love with Ikaria. It's probably when I fell in love with travelling.'

'But all these years, I kind of thought you were just chasing the sun.'

'And the snow,' he added, nodding, 'I was in a way, but I was also... how do you say it? "Climbing the latter?"'

'Ladder.'

'Right. All the hotels and resorts I worked at are owned by Eden Group.'

Realising she had underestimated him, Adelaide experienced a pang of guilt.

'So when this position came up a couple of years ago, I rushed on it. It's been years since I've lived in Greece and this place needed some sparking. That's why we started the parties. You'll come on Saturday, yes?'

'Oh, I'd love to. Everyone is talking about it. Especially about how you booked DJ Allora.'

Adelaide knew she was fishing for information but couldn't help it.

Alec smiled to himself. 'Let's just say there's something to be said for a personal connection,' he said, as the waiter arrived with their food.

ADELAIDE had forgotten how easy it was to talk to Alec, how he listened. His attentive face was like truth serum and she found herself telling him everything. She realised that, although she and Alec had corresponded for the last twenty years—first in letters and then via email—details about Joe and the twins had been skimmed over. She supposed it was because Alec represented a place that was only for her, somewhere

Adelaide Jones could be Adele. Alec provided a window into a different world. A world that she once believed she would be a citizen of herself.

So she told him everything, even the parts she was most ashamed of. She spoke of the twins' unlikely conception, how afraid she was to be a single mother, how she hoped that Joe would grow to love her, how she thought he had. In the telling of it, she realised she had been surviving on crumbs from Joe and, now that the spell had been broken, she wasn't sure she could go back to that, even if it was an option.

Alec listened, his eyes never leaving hers.

Finally, he said, 'You want to hold your family together because you are a good mother, because you think that is what your children need?'

She nodded.

'But, Adele, if it is not meant to be, you can still give your children a great gift,' he said.

'How?' she asked, feeling hopeless.

'You can teach them how to overcome adversity with grace and courage. You can show them they can be their own heroes. How to create their own happiness,' he said, placing his hand on hers.

'I'm not sure I'm that strong,' she said.

'You're stronger than you know.'

AFTER that, the conversation turned to the passions of their youth.

It had been years since Alec had sculpted but he still sketched. He admitted that it was during these moments that he felt like the most authentic version of himself. He asked her what had become of her passion for textiles, and she told him how she had discovered she was pregnant just after completing her PhD.

'Let's face it, my studies didn't provide me with a whole lot of commercial value,' she laughed. 'I did make a list of museums and galleries around the world who specialise in textiles though and had been making some promising contacts. A museum in Canada invited me to interview for a curatorship but then I found out I was pregnant. Gosh, I haven't thought about that in years,' she said, almost to herself.

Adelaide's phone sounded in her bag. It was a text from Rosemary saying that she was just about to take Charlie to kindergarten if Adelaide wanted to Skype the twins. Adelaide realised that she and Alec had been talking for more than four hours.

'Alec, I'm so sorry but I'm going to have to turn back into a pumpkin,' she said.

Alec gave her a look of complete bewilderment.

'I'm sorry,' she said, laughing. 'I mean, I think it's time for me to go. It's the morning in Melbourne and I'm going to Skype Darcy and Estée.'

'Of course,' he said, standing immediately and indicating to the waiter that they were leaving.

He offered Adelaide his hand. 'Let's get you back to your *pethakia*.'

SEATED at the end of her bed waiting, Adelaide was giddy with excitement. She answered Rosemary's call at the first tone and greeted her friend, 'Hello, you.'

'Hello yourself. I'll put them on. We can talk after,' said Rosemary, her face becoming a blurred streak.

'Mummy! Mumma!' the twins chorused.

'Babies! Oh, how I miss you. It's so good to see you,' she said, wanting to gather them up in her arms and breathe them in.

'Mumma, we have been having so much fun,' said Darcy.

Estée nodded vigorously.

'Daddy had to go out last night, so he got us this amazing babysitter. She let us have ice-cream for dinner and then we watched Harry Potter. Darcy cried because there was a scary dog with three heads, but I didn't cry, Mummy,' said Estée, proudly.

It took Adelaide a moment to process what she heard. Ice-cream for dinner, scary movies, what was going on?

'And the best part was that she had a sleepover at our house!' said Darcy, his eyes wide.

Adelaide felt swallowed by a dark and menacing ocean. 'Who had a sleepover?'

'Kim,' said Estée.

'Yeah, Kim,' Darcy echoed.

Adelaide couldn't speak.

'We have to go in now, Mummy,' said Estée.

'Bye, Mumma!' yelled Darcy and they were gone.

Rosemary's face appeared, asking if she was okay, but Adelaide's head was pounding so intensely that the question seemed muffled.

Finally, she said, 'Rosie?'

'I know, babe, I just heard it too.'

The two women stood at opposite ends of the earth, staring mutely at one another.

ADELAIDE'S ribcage threatened to burst under the strain of her hammering heart as she dialled Joe's phone number.

'Hello, Adelaide,' he said, sounding impatient.

'How could you bring that woman into my home? Leave her alone with our children?'

She could almost hear his eyes rolling.

'I told you there were some things I had to go to this week. You're overreacting, as usual,' he said, as if addressing a child.

'How could you? How could you do this to me, to them?'

'They *loved* her,' he said, baiting her with the word. 'And you're the one who left them alone to go gallivanting on the other side of the bloody world.'

Adelaide darkened. 'I didn't leave them alone. I left them with their father, not with his mistress,' she said, through clenched teeth.

'Look, I have to go. If you don't like it, you can come home,' he said, ending the call.

Adelaide felt lightheaded, robbed of oxygen. She placed a hand on her chest and tried to practise the mindfulness breathing she had been teaching to Darcy and Estée. The walls of her room, once comforting, closed around her. She staggered the few steps to the door and burst out into the cool night air. Walking towards the sound of the ocean, she replayed the conversations in her head, focusing in on the most soul-destroying moments.

Adelaide walked through a leafy passageway to the beach and saw Alec sitting on an outdoor settee, illuminated by the glow of a tiki bar. She quickened her pace, relieved to find a friendly face. As she drew nearer a woman with short, cropped hair and a filigree neck tattoo came into view. She leant in close to whisper something in his ear, causing him to throw his head back and laugh. Adelaide made to retreat unnoticed, when Alec spotted her.

'Adele! Come and join us,' he called.

She resolved to say a quick hello before leaving the pair alone.

'Hi,' she said, forcing a smile and walking over with her shoulders square. 'Hi,' she said again, surprised to see that Xena was seated caddy-corner to Alec.

'This is Alessia, also known as DJ Allora,' said Alec. 'Adele is an old friend of mine,' he explained.

Alessia rose and extended an elegant hand in greeting. *She must be as tall as Alec*, Adelaide thought.

'*Ciao*, you will join us?' asked Alessia.

'*Ella tho*, come sit,' said Xena, motioning to the place beside her.

Seeing that she wasn't a third wheel, Adelaide took a seat.

'You spoke to your children?' Alec asked.

Adelaide nodded.

Seeming to sense that she didn't want to elaborate, Alec changed tack. 'Alessia was just telling us about her summer.'

'I've played sixty-seven shows in the last three months,' she explained to Adelaide. 'I really needed this vacation,' said added, her gaze settling back on Alec.

As Alessia spoke of the rigorous schedule she'd just come from, Adelaide found she was staring. The musician had an enigmatic quality that seemed to be the result of contradictory traits. Her frame was almost ethereal but seemed to pulse with a raw sinewy strength. She appeared boy-like in her physique and mannerisms, yet her face was endowed with full cupid's bow lips and disproportionately large eyes. The entire effect was compelling. Adelaide was transfixed.

Adelaide looked over at Alec. He hung on Alessia's every word. Adelaide frowned slightly to herself. Why should she care that Alessia was so magnetic?

'Adele?'

Adelaide snapped back into consciousness to find three pairs of eyes staring at her.

'I'm sorry, I must have zoned out for a second. Jetlag I guess,' she lied. 'What were you saying?'

'Alessia was just saying that she has invested in a friend's fashion label,' Alec began again.

'She has just graduated from the *Istituto Marangoni* in *Milano*,' added Alessia.

'The style is very… what was it Alessia?' Alec asked.

'Boho.'

'Boho, right. I was telling her about your PhD.'

'Oh,' said Adelaide, blushing. 'Yes, well. My area of interest was the role that textile folk arts played in primitive societies. Not quite as glamorous as your friend's fashion label.'

'Perhaps not glamorous, but extremely interesting, in any case,' said Alec.

'Interesting to a textile nerd like me,' she said.

Alec nodded expectantly, so she went on. 'You see, the production of textiles has always been a vocation that's acceptable for women, unlike many others of course, but textiles have extremely significant implications when it comes to cultural ceremony and tradition, and even the economic success of entire communities.'

'You are a professor or something?' asked Alessia.

'Oh, nothing like that,' said Adelaide.

'That sounds like my village,' said Xena, before taking a deep drag of her cigarette.

'Your village?' Adelaide asked, realising with shame that she knew little about her new friend while Xena knew *everything* about her.

'Most of the men in my village lost their jobs when the machinery factory closed down after the financial crisis,' she said.

Alec nodded knowingly.

'My mother and the other women began selling their embroidered linens to tourists. Before that they had only embroidered for themselves, for dowries and stuff. Their husbands are proud men, very old fashioned. They would never allow their wives to work but this kind of trade, they close their eyes. It puts food in their bellies, but they don't even acknowledge it. It makes me crazy, this kind of small-town chauvinistic mentality.'

'Women are resilient, no?' said Alessia.

'Xena, that's fascinating. I'd love to see their work sometime, buy some things to take home,' said Adelaide.

'Sure,' said Xena, extinguishing her cigarette along with the conversation.

'It's getting late. I need to get up early tomorrow,' said Alec.

'Tomorrow!' exclaimed Adelaide. 'I'm meant to go on a hike tomorrow!'

Adelaide couldn't believe that her promise to join Cora and Dave had slipped her mind.

'You hike?' said Alec, his eyes dancing with amusement.

Adelaide scowled at him in mock offence.

'I made friends with this couple from England, it was their idea to go hiking and, let's just say that after a very strong cocktail by the pool, I thought it was a *great* idea,' said Adelaide, waving her hand with a sarcastic flourish.

'Just text them and say you can't go,' Xena offered.

'I don't have their number. They're picking me up in…' she checked her phone, 'four hours!'

They all laughed, and Adelaide couldn't help joining in.

'I'll walk you back,' said Alec, getting to his feet and offering her his hand. Adelaide placed her hand in his and watched it being enveloped. Her pulse quickened as he pulled her to her feet, and she looked up at him forgetting momentarily about everything else. Feeling Alessia's eyes on her she quickly dropped his hand. *I am not about to "do a Kim"* she thought and declined his offer.

13

ADELAIDE lay awake in her bed calculating how much sleep she would get if she could only fall asleep *now, now, now.*

She wondered if she should return home to the twins. She felt lost without them. In her mind, all the daily struggles and maddening frustrations of caring for pre-schoolers had faded away. In their place, recollections of foraged dandelions, sleepy confessions and grazed-knee sobs seized her heart, wringing it like a dishcloth. She could hear Rosemary's voice in her head telling her that she deserved this break, that Joe needed a good healthy dose of reality, that the twins were fine. Hadn't this whole hare-brained scheme been concocted to make him come crawling back? She wasn't sure she wanted that anymore. She felt wretched.

A knock at the door broke Adelaide's short and fitful slumber. *Damn! I've slept through the bloody alarm*! She grabbed for her robe, tripping on the belt and bumping into the wall with a *thud.*

She flung open the door to reveal the enthusiastic faces of Cora and Dave.

'I overslept!' Adelaide shrieked by way of a greeting. 'I think you'd better go on without me today.'

'You're not getting out of it that easily,' said Cora, teasing.

'We'll just wait 'til you're ready, it's no *mither,*' said Dave.

Seeing that there was no backing out, Adelaide grabbed the tangle of sportswear being offered from Cora's outstretched hands.

'Give me five minutes,' she said.

Adelaide emerged, looking like every second mother back home who was off to do a school pick-up or grocery shop. She realised how much she had been enjoying the role-play that her new vacation wardrobe afforded her, and this utilitarian ensemble made her feel like a complete fraud. Maybe *this* was the real Adelaide Jones after all?

The three made their way to the carpark, talking excitedly.

'How was your reunion dinner last night?' Cora asked.

'It was… easy. You know those friends that are just so easy to talk to? It feels effortless, it felt effortless,' said Adelaide.

'There's nothing better,' Cora said, nodding.

As they walked out the front gate of Ilios Choros, Adelaide spotted a gleaming silver vintage car and turned to Dave. 'Is that it? It that the car you restored? Oh, guys, it's beautiful. I don't know anything about cars, but that is *beautiful*.'

Dave's chest swelled as he tried to suppress a prideful smile and he grew a couple of centimetres taller beside her.

'So, are we driving?' asked Adelaide.

'Not today, there's a minibus that'll take us to the beginning of the trail and pick us up at the end,' said Cora.

Adelaide looked longingly at the car. *They sure don't make them like they used to.*

A few minutes later a dinged-up minibus appeared on the horizon.

'That'll be us,' said Dave.

The driver pulled up, and gave the trio a nonchalant eyebrow raise but remained seated. Dave slid open the side door and Adelaide climbed in after Cora. They took their place at the back of the vehicle after greeting an excessively tanned blonde couple who appeared to have been slow baked over many years.

Once they were moving, Adelaide spoke. 'I have a confession to make. I had totally forgotten about our hike today, I only got to bed a few hours ago.'

'You what?' exclaimed Dave, laughing.

'You're not *hanging*, are you?' Cora asked, concerned.

'Hanging?' asked Adelaide.

'Hungover. Did you get on the *scoops* last night?' said Dave.

'Oh,' said Adelaide, smiling broadly, 'no *scoops*, just a late night of good conversation.'

She left out the part where her heart had been ripped out and stomped on by Joe. As far as Cora and Dave were concerned, there was no

Joe and she liked it that way.

'Still, you must be dead hungry, you didn't get breakfast,' said Cora, handing her a protein bar.

'Thanks,' said Adelaide, accepting the snack.

'Gotta get your strength up. We'll be at it for six hours today,' said Dave.

'Six hours?' said Adelaide.

Cora nodded. 'The hike will take us from the east to west of Ikaria, scaling the highest peak,' she said.

Adelaide was overwhelmed by a feeling of foreboding. She was a complete fraud, in borrowed clothes and the wrong shoes, about to scale a mountain. She wondered, in the ensuing silence, if she should just call the whole thing off. Surely, she could offer the driver a tip to take her back to the hotel, but what then? She would end up being alone with her thoughts all day. The idea of that emotional expenditure was far less appealing than the physical expenditure being offered. *Screw it*, she thought, *all I've been doing lately is climbing figurative mountains, maybe it's time for a literal one.*

They crept up the winding road, leaving the coastline behind. Coming to a small cluster of stone buildings, the minibus stopped abruptly and the driver leapt out. Adelaide and her fellow passengers looked at each other and shrugged, before the suntanned husband leant over and opened the sliding door, letting in the distinctive smell of tobacco. They assembled in front of the driver, who emitted thick plumes of cigarette smoke from his nostrils, giving him the appearance of a disinterested dragon.

'You take path to Kapsalino Castle. Then follow signs to Evdilos,' he croaked, throwing his spent cigarette to the ground. 'I pick you up one o'clock.'

With that, he climbed back into the vehicle and drove away in a cloud of dust.

The suntanned couple produced two telescopic hiking poles apiece and with a *click, clack, click,* extended them and strode off with a cheery, 'See you at ze other end!'

'Now or never,' said Dave, grinning.

'Now,' said Adelaide and Cora in unison.

They started off in the direction the suntanned couple had taken, crunching along the gravel path. The day was already promising to be a scorcher, but for now at least the air was fresh and cool, and Adelaide imagined it cleansing her from the inside out. At first, they chatted amiably, Cora telling Adelaide about her job as a call centre operator for a telecommunications company.

'It's the old ones that call you up that I like. The young ones are all impatient and angry, but the old ones are sweet. I have this one lady who I helped with a phone plan once. Now she calls me every week just to have a chat. Says I remind her of her daughter that died. Breaks your heart,' she said, shaking her head.

Dave broke in laughing, 'That's nicer than the old ones I meet in the chemists.'

'Dave's a sales rep,' Cora explained, grinning in anticipation.

'I'll be stood there, waiting to see the purchasing officer and an old one will come up to me and ask for some ointment for a fungal toe or something worse! They'll be bending down to take off their shoes to show me! I mean, do I look like the bloody pharmacist, love?' Dave bellowed.

The two women laughed.

They reached the site of an ancient castle that was no more than a ghostly outline of a cluster of simple buildings. The crumbling walls appeared flaky, reminding Adelaide of baklava. Just beyond, the expansive view of the bright blue Aegean glittered resplendently as they drank it in. Dave produced large water bottles from his backpack and handed them out. They sat on a low, weather-beaten wall, the occasional crackle of compressing plastic the only sound breaking the pristine silence.

'We better kick on,' said Dave, after a while. He gathered up the bottles, replaced them in his pack and drew out a dog-eared travel guide. 'No paths from here on out, but there're signs to follow.' He surveyed the area and pointed to a small hand-painted marker. 'There.'

They stared in the direction the sign indicated. There was no path, only a steep incline through sparse and thirsty-looking scrub.

As they climbed, Adelaide was dubious. The ground was gravelly underfoot causing her to slip in the ill-suited street shoes she wore. More than once, she slid backwards into the gnarled branches of thorny shrubs that bit into her skin, leaving a crosshatch of scratches and cuts. Even her friends, who were far better equipped, suffered the same fate, if less frequently.

The unforgiving flora gave way to a parched and craggy cliff face which, as they inched along it, seemed to work in unison with the sun to bake them from all sides. Adelaide felt gritty and hot. Her scalp was itchy under her borrowed cap and the occasional bead of sweat trickled down her brow, depositing sunscreen into her eyes and making them sting. The group was silent now, their pleasant stroll having turned into something they needed to overcome. Dave led the way, setting a pace that Adelaide struggled with. Sometimes Dave and Cora would disappear around a corner and Adelaide would experience a surreal and disconcerting alarm, as if they were figments of her imagination and she was really alone on this rock in the middle of the sea. She reminded herself that she was sleep deprived, an affliction she was only too familiar with. Just when she would get the feeling she was going mad, her friends would come into view, looking at her with encouraging smiles, waiting for her to catch up. Each time, as Adelaide arrived, they turned and resumed their ascent, making her feel like a donkey chasing a carrot. She began to seethe. She was exhausted and needed to rest for a minute but could never get close enough to Dave and Cora to tell them. She fantasised about screaming to them, but her lips were dry and her mouth claggy. The irony of her need for the water Dave carried was not lost on her. She paused briefly to pound on her burning quad muscles before trudging onward. As if in response to their unkind treatment, Adelaide's legs gave out momentarily and she placed a hand on the cliff face to steady herself. *Fuck this*, she thought, still holding on to the edge for support. She made her way around a large boulder and found herself on top of the world.

'How's this then?' said Cora, her arms open indicating the 360-degree view of the entire island.

Dave handed Adelaide her water. 'You must be gagging, here,' he said.

Adelaide could hardly believe it. She had climbed up to heaven.

'This is the highest point on the island,' said Cora, consulting the travel guide.

Adelaide looked around in wonder—she was a tiny speck on a rock in the middle of a vast blue expanse. She was ashamed of her imagined outbursts towards Dave and Cora. She was no better than the twins when they scrunched their little faces and stomped their feet in frustration at her.

They enjoyed a hearty meal of plastic-packaged snack foods which, due to the extremity of their hunger, were deeply satisfying. Recharged and refuelled, they continued on their way, following the hand-painted markers. Having sheepishly confided to her friends that she had found the pace a little gruelling, they took it slower.

Imposing boulders towered over them through this new stretch of terrain. Adelaide's heart beat hard as she inched along a narrow ledge, hugging the rock. *For God's sake*, she thought, *don't let me fall to my death and let my children be raised by bloody Kim.* Adelaide could see her friends' bodies relax, relieved smiles crossing their faces, as the path widened. She willed herself on, taking care to retain her diligence even in the face of her impending respite. Coming to the end, she breathed a sigh of relief and felt all her muscles loosen. She grinned at her friends who waited for her a few steps farther and, buoyed by their success, quickened her pace over to them.

She knew the moment she stepped onto the gravel-strewn boulder that she was going down. She felt like one of those TV henchmen skittering comically on ball bearings released by the escaping hero in a spy film. With nothing to grab for, she fell hard on her right side and let out a wail like a trapped animal. Her friends rushed over to find her sobbing. Hot tears fell in muddy rivulets down her dust-covered face as she brushed gravel from her palms and elbow.

She cried because of the unbearable pain in her hip. She cried because she missed her children. She cried because of what Joe had done. Her friends sat either side of her muttering soothing sentiments and handing over tissues, looking helplessly at one another. When her pitiful gasps and sobs petered out, she lifted the hem of her shorts to reveal the promise of a sinister looking bruise. Dave and Cora groaned.

'Argh, that is going to be rank,' said Dave.

Cora punched him in the arm.

'What? It'll be well gnarly by tomorrow,' he insisted.

'Do you want to see if you can walk on it, Adele?' Cora asked, rising and offering Adelaide her hands.

Adelaide took them and allowed herself to be pulled up. Leaning heavily on her left foot, she took a few timid steps.

A dull constant pain radiated from her hip, but it was no worse with each step.

'It's okay,' she said. 'I can go on.'

'Are you sure, love?' Dave asked, gently.

'We can rest longer,' added Cora.

Adelaide, not bothering to answer, marched onward.

The pain was white hot, and Adelaide found herself willing her mind to leave her body. Being a mother, she was well practised at it. She thought of being in labour with the twins. She had left her body then. Had escaped into some primitive quadrant of her mind. A place she had never been able to visit before or since. And when the twins were around six months old, teething and taking to her breasts with a ferocity that she had found frightening, she had left her body then too. Pain had shot through her nipples like a hot skewer piercing her breasts and her skin was worn down paper thin. She remembered Darcy smiling up from her breast, revealing two newly acquired teeth, his mouth tinted pink with her blood. Yes, she had left her body then and she could do it now. She scanned her memory for a happy place she could retreat to and found Alec. She thought of the look on his face as he sat across from her, listening attentively the night before. The way his green eyes never left hers for a second. She thought of his handsome, sun-kissed face and fantasised about gently stroking his beard. She thought of running a hand through his thick hair, of looking up into his sparkling eyes, of his lips parting in anticipation of meeting hers. On and on her physical body toiled, while her mind flitted on the outskirts of reality.

She led the pack, setting the pace with a dogged determination. Somewhere, in the farthest reaches of Adelaide's subconscious, finishing this hike was linked to her ability to take charge of her own life. She would live to tell this tale, even if it killed her.

CORA and Dave trailed after Adelaide whose pace, although slow, was ceaseless. Her trance-like state had them exchanging glances of concern.

'What should we do?' mouthed Cora.

Dave shrugged and shook his head, wide eyed. 'Adele, do you want to rest, love?' he called out.

Adelaide shook her head without turning and trudged on.

The views around them were breathtaking and Dave and Cora paused every now and then to take photos before hurrying to catch up with

Adelaide, who never broke her laboured stride.

Finally, the unobstructed views gave way to more scrubby vegetation and their goat's trail evolved into a path leading into a small village. They'd made it.

Cora spotted the suntanned couple sitting with the driver at an outdoor café on the edge of the town square and placed a guiding hand in the middle of Adelaide's back. Dave pulled out a chair for her at their table and she slumped into it, finally coming out of her trance.

'Ve vere vorried you got lost,' said the suntanned husband.

'Not lost,' said Cora. 'Adele took a tumble.'

'Show them, love. It's gnarly,' said Dave.

Adelaide obliged.

'*Mein Gott!*' exclaimed the suntanned wife

This made the perpetually bored-looking driver come to life and he scurried off. He returned with a tea towel filled with ice blocks and handed it to her. Adelaide winced as she gingerly pressed it to her hip.

'May I have some water please, Dave?' she asked, causing Dave to scramble in his pack and release a flurry of apologies for not having offered it.

'Shall we head back?' asked Adelaide, after draining the contents of the water bottle.

14

THE rumpled, unmade bed beckoned Adelaide as she peeled off her dusty clothes, but she ignored it, focusing instead on her almost primal desire to dip her weary body into the sea. The pain as she guided her swimsuit up and over her body was excruciating. She had to pause to catch her breath before wrapping a sarong around her waist, taking care to conceal her disfigured hip. Something had changed for Adelaide on that mountain top. She had been taken for granted and underestimated by Joe the whole time she'd known him. All the unique parts of her had been worn down by his scrutiny, like coloured glass made dull by the abrasive rhythm of the tide. Today, she was reminded of her grit. Today, she understood that no matter what, Adelaide Jones would prevail.

The first few steps into the cool saltwater angered Adelaide's grazes but she continued, dropping to her knees and submerging herself. This was the moment she had longed for. Her matted, sweaty hair came to life, floating in diaphanous waves around her field of vision. Her leaden body was weightless. She returned to the surface, smoothing her hair away from her face and reclined into a float. She was Amphitrite, goddess of the sea.

Adelaide emerged from the water reborn. Walking across the beach to retrieve her belongings she caught sight of Alec behind the tiki bar. She experienced a sudden rush of embarrassment, as though all her deepest fantasies were written across her face for him to read. As if every imagined caress, every exploratory kiss, every pleasure-filled exhalation were all plain as day on her flushed, pink face. Sensing her gaze, he looked towards her and smiled, but his brow furrowed, and he strode purposefully to her. Her initial confusion turned to understanding as he spoke.

'You've been hurt! This happened while hiking? Is anything broken?

How did you…?' he trailed off, his eyes searching hers for signs that she was alright.'

'I'm okay, it was silly really. I slipped. It looks far worse than it is.'

'Adele,' he said, his voice pained.

'I'm fine,' she insisted.

'You must come with me. Let me make you something to treat the bruising.'

Adelaide followed Alec through the gardens until they came to a small bungalow with a white hammock swaying on the verandah. He placed his hand near her lower back, barely touching it, to guide her up the steps. Once inside, he situated her in a cushioned, wicker armchair before bringing her a glass of iced lemon water which he placed on a metal coaster. The sweetness of this simple act of traditional Greek hospitality made her smile—it reminded her of visiting with his mother.

'Now, I will make you a tonic,' he said, disappearing out the back door before Adelaide could clarify what he meant.

Adelaide could see him through the breakfast bar when he re-entered the kitchen clutching a handful of small yellow flowers. He retrieved a *briki* from the drying rack, half filled it from a huge olive oil tin and set it to heat on the stove top. After a minute or so, he removed the tiny pot from the burner and stirred in the flowers before consulting his watch. He rejoined Adelaide in the lounge room.

'What kind of magic potion are you making in there?'

'The flower is *flomos*, I don't know how it is called in English,' he said, frowning. 'When you steep it in olive oil it produces a potent treatment for bruises. My mother used to make this for me when I was playing water polo. I was always coming home blue and black,' he said, grinning at the memory.

'You really don't need to go to so much trouble,' she said.

'You have been hurt,' he said simply before rising and walking to the kitchen.

He returned with a small bowl of oil, placed it on the coffee table and dragged over a leather ottoman. He sat down and leant forward. 'May I?' he asked, casting his eyes up to hers, his hand hovering above her ankle.

She nodded and he scooped her leg up onto his thigh. He dipped his fingers into the sweet-smelling oil as Adelaide peeled up her swimsuit, revealing the crimson bloom on her hip. Alec looked up at her, sadness crossing his handsome face. His large hands, now slick, gently circled her battered flesh and Adelaide feared she might cry in the face of his tenderness. She looked down at him and had an overwhelming urge to run her fingers through his hair, to cup his face and guide it up to hers. She could see the outline of his strong shoulders through his white linen shirt, the way his body gently pulsed as he rubbed oil into her skin. *How can someone so strong produce a touch so gentle?* Adelaide leant back in the chair and cast her eyes up to the ceiling, concerned about what she may do if she continued to look at him.

'I know what you need,' he said, interrupting her thoughts.

'Sorry?'

'Tomorrow morning, I will take you to the geothermal hot springs,' he said. When she didn't answer he added, 'I don't have to work tomorrow.'

'Oh, but wouldn't you rather be doing something else on your day off?' said Adelaide, thinking of Alessia.

'It would be my pleasure to take you.' He gave her a wry smile. 'Unless you already have some other extreme sports planned.'

ADELAIDE meandered through the lush grounds of the hotel heading back towards her room. A delicious veil of relaxation had settled over her body which she supposed was the product of Alec's healing touch, but was, in fact, just exhaustion. She replayed the entire encounter with him in her mind over and over on a loop, just as she had done when they were teenagers. She decided to let go of her guilt over fantasising about another woman's man, reasoning that it was harmless. He would never suspect that he was the object of such palpable desire in her, especially given that he probably saw her more as his sister. *His sister.* She would have to email Penny to let her know she was in Greece.

15

ADELAIDE was attempting to single-handedly devour the entire breakfast buffet. So far, it was going well. She had just finished her third plate of scrambled eggs and bacon and was pausing before turning her attention to pastries and fruit. She had intended to go in search of dinner last night but had instead fallen asleep after a long and intensely pleasurable shower. She woke ravenous after an uninterrupted, dreamless slumber. It had been years since she had slept like that and, although all her muscles felt stiff when she awoke, she was surprised to feel rested.

Alec appeared and seated himself opposite her as she was finishing a bowl of Greek yogurt and honey-poached quince. He looked at the dishes stacked neatly at the side of the table.

'Exactly how many people joined you for breakfast this morning?' he asked, unable to completely suppress his knowing smirk.

'It turns out mountaineering is hungry work,' she said, licking the last of the yogurt off her spoon with an exaggerated flourish.

He grinned at her and shook his head. 'You got me in trouble last night,' he said.

She raised her eyebrows at him, her mind leaping guiltily to Alessia.

'Penny,' he said.

'Penny! I emailed her,' said Adelaide.

'She called me this morning and accused me of trying to keep you all to myself.'

Adelaide laughed.

'In any case, she's coming here for the weekend. She will get the ferry from Piraeus tomorrow.'

'She will?' said Adelaide, clapping her hands.

'We're fully booked but she tells me she doesn't mind, she can stay at my place.' He laughed and shook his head. 'Now, let me see. What other messages do I have for you?' he said, stroking his beard in a caricature of seriousness. 'Oh yes. Your friend Xena told me that if you want to visit her this afternoon, she can show you her mother's linens. I can take you there after the hot springs if you like.'

'That would be wonderful.'

'*Endaxi!* If there are no more items of business, perhaps we can go,' he said, offering her his hand.

She placed her hand in his and stood, letting her eyes linger on him.

They strolled down the path towards the front entrance, talking and teasing one another as they had done when they were kids. When they arrived at the carpark, Adelaide scanned the vehicles trying to guess which car was his. He looked at her and smiled for a moment before throwing his leg over the quad bike they were standing closest to.

Adelaide tilted her head back and laughed. 'Nice wheels!' she said.

She placed a hand on his shoulder and carefully mounted the bike, thankful that she had opted for tailored shorts and a coordinating cami today.

'Hold on tight,' he said, turning around to her.

Oh God, she thought, putting her arms around his waist as the engine between her legs roared to life.

The Ikarian coastline zipped passed in a smudge of blue and beige. The sun's heat, so oppressive to her yesterday, was rendered almost imperceptible as they rode into the wind. Adelaide closed her eyes and breathed in the scent of saltwater, mingled with the wild oregano growing by the roadside. As they rounded a bend, she gripped Alec's waist a little firmer. Hyper-aware of his hips between her legs and her breasts pressed into his back, the firm warmth of his flesh through his grey, cotton-voile shirt made her flush. It took all her willpower not to slide her hands beneath the fabric.

Alec pulled the quad bike to the side of the road and came to a stop in front of a hand-painted sign "Hot Mineral Spring". Adelaide unclasped him, suddenly self-conscious without the veil of disconnectedness the whipping wind provided.

'So, do you have some hiking skills left over from yesterday?' he asked.

'You know it,' she said, trying to sound light.

The path was steep but short and deposited them on a red, rocky beach. Alec led her along the shore to a small alcove that, to Adelaide's delight, visibly steamed. Large rocks were arranged in a circle, creating a rust-coloured pool that kept the cooler water cordoned off.

'This is wild,' said Adelaide in disbelief.

Alec beamed. He threw their belongings on a boulder and unbuttoned his shirt.

The smooth, boyish chest of his youth was now endowed with a modest bloom of dark hair. The strength of his body obvious with every movement.

Adelaide's pulse quickened and she looked away under the pretense of taking in the view.

'What you are waiting for?' he teased.

She removed her top and threw it at him before stepping out of her shorts, as elegantly as possible with an injured hip, while standing on a pile of rocks in the sea.

Adelaide twisted her hair into a messy top-knot, watching Alec carefully position himself at the inner edge of the pool. He offered her his hand and said, 'Seeing as I know how slippery you are lately.'

Adelaide let out a hearty laugh.

'What? Is it the wrong language?' he asked self-consciously.

'It was the perfect description,' she said, taking his hand.

Adelaide, expecting to step into lukewarm water, was startled to find that it was hot. 'Yowza!' she exclaimed.

'Yowza?' Alec asked, following her in and sitting down on a rock.

'It's hot. Like, hot hot,' she said, wondering where her ability to construct sentences had gone to.

He laughed. 'Yowza,' he repeated quietly to himself.

Once Adelaide acclimatised to the temperature, her body began to unfurl. She closed her eyes and leant her head back, while her muscles melted. 'Darcy would love this,' she said, opening her eyes.

'He would?'

'He would think it was so cool. He's super into volcanoes at the moment. They made one at his kindergarten and ever since then he's been obsessed. So, this would blow his mind.'

Alec smiled. 'And Estée? What is she super into,' he asked, trying out her phrase.

'Anything with wheels,' said Adelaide, laughing.

'Your face lights up when you talk about them. Your love is so obvious,' Alec observed.

'Well…' she said, uncertain of how to respond with the absence of cliché.

They sat in comfortable silence, listening to the sound of the water lapping the rocks. Finally, Alec said, '*Endaxi*, unless we want to turn into *loukoumades* we'd better get out of here.'

When they were once again navigating the rocky path back up to the road Alec asked, 'So, do you want to eat lunch now?'

'Maybe if I hadn't had so many breakfasts,' she said.

'Oh yes,' he said, smiling at her and shaking his head slightly. 'So, in that case, I will take you to Xena's village.'

Adelaide mentally chastised herself—she had just inadvertently squandered her chance at more time with him. She arranged her face to mask her disappointment and nodded. 'You'll need to get back to Alessia,' she said, trying to keep her tone even.

'Yes, her sound check is this afternoon.'

A sombre mood settled over Adelaide as the quad bike took them away from the coast and towards the mountains. She sat behind Alec holding him as before but this time, instead of imagining their bodies coming together, she envisaged the inevitable moment, just days from now, when she would have to say goodbye. The precious few hours spent in Alec's company had recharged her. She felt interesting and worthy of his attention—even if it was platonic—intoxicated by her own feeling of vibrancy. She feared that without this place and without this man, the spell would be broken, and she would go back to being invisible and dull. She closed her eyes to quell the outpouring of emotion that threatened to liquefy her.

An ice-cold mist hit Adelaide's face, interrupting her thoughts. Her eyes snapped open. They were driving along a narrow, winding road under which rapid streams passed at almost every bend. Looking up, she saw lush vegetation and moss-covered cliffs, slick with trickling water. She opened her mouth and felt the moisture hit her tongue. She let out a delighted laugh. *If ever there was a reminder to live in the moment, it is this.*

The occasional white house gave way to clusters, leading them to the village and a picturesque town square. Alec pulled up in front of a storybook chapel, across from which a congress of dark-suited, grey gentlemen sat, presumably solving all the world's problems.

Getting off the bike, Alec raised a hand in salute to the men, some of them responding with an almost imperceptible lift of their heads. All eyes surveyed Adelaide. She climbed off the quad carefully and offered the group a tepid smile. They reminded Adelaide of a set of dusty old books, no doubt full of interesting information, that no one was interested in reading.

Alec guided Adelaide into a narrow, shaded alley. The path took them past cottages that seemed to have been placed one on top of another, after being carved from a giant block of feta cheese. Lacquered wooden windows opened to reveal lace curtains that fluttered as they passed. Adelaide was reminded of her *yiayia* Vaso, whose preponderance of lace doilies made her home look as though it had been snowing inside. One window ledge displayed three crusty loaves of bread next to a wooden slotted box for payment. Coming to the end of the lane, they were delivered to a small courtyard from which identical paths sprang like fingers from a palm. Adelaide turned to ask Alec for direction and, in doing so, caught sight of an open set of double doors. Within, three women sat hunched over the same length of white cloth.

Xena looked up from the middle of the group, gave a half smirk, eye-roll and greeted them with a simple, 'Ya.'

She extricated herself from between two women who, Adelaide noted with amusement, were like older, conservative versions of Xena herself. The two kind-faced women greeted Alec affectionately in Greek before waiting to be introduced to the newcomer.

'*Mana, Theia*, this is Adele. She is an old friend of Alexandros. Adele, my mother Eleni and my aunt Areti.'

'*Yassas, Theies*,' said Adelaide.

'*Yassas*, Adele,' said the younger woman, Eleni, who Adelaide took to be Xena's mother.

'*Eíste Ellinída*, Adele?' Areti enquired, squinting her dark eyes at Adelaide.

'My mother is Greek, but my father is Australian. I don't speak Greek unfortunately,' Adelaide replied.

Adelaide had been subjected to this question countless times in her life and always got the distinct feeling that her answer was a complete disappointment. She stepped forward to admire the women's work.

'May I?' she asked before picking up the edge closest to her and running her fingers over the stitching.

The fabric itself was a thick linen, weighty and rough. It was embellished with a primitive design depicting local flora and fauna, in a repeat pattern around the edge. The stitches were fine and even, and Adelaide felt a flush of appreciation for the quality and craftsmanship. She looked up at the women with a warm smile, her eyes sparkling. 'This is extraordinary,' she said. She had the oddest feeling that she may cry. The two older women beamed at her but remained silent. Xena nudged Adelaide with her shoulder and looked uncharacteristically sheepish. 'Come on, I'll show you the finished ones.'

'I will leave you ladies to it,' said Alec.

'I'll bring Adele back with me,' said Xena.

'*Yassas, Theíes*,' said Alec, crossing the threshold.

Adelaide's heart panged as she watched him stride down the narrow path.

A short time later, Adelaide followed Xena back down the narrow alleyway carrying a thick bundle of linens. Although she would never admit it, she had perhaps gone a little overboard, purchasing something for almost everyone she knew back home. But there was one tablecloth that depicted two-tailed sirens, amongst other small sea creatures and seaweed, that she would keep for herself. Adelaide had exclaimed the moment she saw it that she would make herself a dress out of it. Xena laughed loudly and shrieked, 'You wear tablecloths now?' But Adelaide didn't mind. It had been years since she had sewn for herself, and she revelled in creative inspiration that she hadn't realised was missing from her life until now. *Joe would hate this idea*, she thought with an odd sense of satisfaction. Joe would not be getting a say this time. As the two friends walked across the town square a low murmur rippled over the village men and Adelaide could have sworn that the persistent *click, clack, click* of their worry beads skipped several beats. Xena looked straight ahead and strode across the square with an air of determination that Adelaide wondered about.

Once they were past, Xena said, 'You didn't have to buy so much you know, it's not a charity.'

Adelaide was taken aback. She tried to match her friend's intensity, suspecting that Xena would disbelieve a weak response. 'It wasn't a pity purchase, Xena, I bought them because they're exceptional. They're art and frankly, I think you should be helping your family—hell, your whole village—to think bigger with this.' Adelaide surprised herself with this last statement but, hearing it said aloud, decided it rang true and went on, 'We should show these to Alessia, this style of embroidery would be perfect for the label she's starting.'

Xena didn't respond but Adelaide could tell that she was intrigued by the idea. In fact, the more Adelaide thought about it on the way back to Ilios Choros, the more convinced she became of its potential.

AS the two women crossed the hotel car park, Adelaide ventured a new topic of conversation with Xena.

'Those men in the town square looked like pretty serious characters,' she said, in a mildly sarcastic tone.

'Those men refuse to acknowledge that the world around them has changed, and they are no longer in charge,' said Xena, her face stern. 'They sit in the square all day long, blowing hot air. They have an opinion on everything and everyone. My father is the worst of them. Thinks it's time to marry me off to some promising young man so I will stop embarrassing the family,' she said bitterly.

'I'll never understand why some people are so obsessed with changing others... controlling them,' said Adelaide, thinking of Joe.

'I'm so sick of being his disappointment,' said Xena.

So am I, Adelaide thought, *so am I.*

ADELAIDE strolled the lush, meandering pathways, her freshly washed hair drying in soft waves around her face in the late afternoon heat. She thought of the twins' hair. When they were little, Darcy's hair had been white-blond while Estée's was a deep brown. But over the years, Darcy's had darkened, and Estée's had lightened, so they now shared the exact shade of luminous golden brown. She thought of how inseparable they were. When they were babies, they would reach for each other from their car capsules, never able to stretch far enough for their hands to meet. It broke Adelaide's heart as she looked back at them through her rearview mirror. She thought of their warm little bodies, sound asleep in their beds, on the other side of the world, and ached.

'There's our girl,' a man's voice bellowed behind Adelaide, making her jump.

She turned to see Dave and Cora, wrapped in beach towels. 'Hello, you two,' she said, grinning.

'We thought we broke you,' said Dave, laughing.

'You alright today, Adele?' Cora asked, her face concerned.

'Oh, I'm fine. A bit stiff this morning but I spent the morning at the hot springs with my friend, Alec. You'll be so impressed with my bruise though, Dave.'

'Show us.'

Adelaide gingerly lifted the hem of her shorts to reveal the deep aubergine colour that engulfed her hip.

'Deadly!' exclaimed Dave.

'The question is, can you dance on it?' asked Cora

'Countdown's on for Electric Blue,' added Dave.

'Definitely,' said Adelaide.

THE thud of bass pervaded the atmosphere as Adelaide approached the main pool. Alec had texted to invite her along to listen in on Alessia's sound check and, although Adelaide felt an irrational flush of jealousy at the prospect, she had sense enough to ignore it and accept his invitation. Alessia stood on a raised platform, behind a DJ booth, talking with a man who Adelaide supposed was the sound engineer. All eyes were on her, including Alec's, who sat on a tall stool by the bar, moving his body unconsciously to the beat. Adelaide stood for a moment, watching him move, trying to imprint the image in her memory. He turned to look in her direction, his face brightening at the sight of her, and returned his eyes to Alessia as Adelaide made her way over.

'She sounds amazing,' said Adelaide, climbing onto the barstool next to Alec.

'She's the best. We're lucky to have her,' he said.

'So they tell me.'

'Shall we have dinner tonight?' he asked.

Recalling her blunder with his lunch invitation, she quickly answered, 'Yes.'

'In any case, I guess all your breakfasts have worn off.'

She gave his arm a friendly push.

'What about Alessia?' she asked.

'She'll come. We can all go and bother Xena while she's working,' he said, sporting a cheeky grin which transformed his face back to his teens.

Twenty years, thought Adelaide sadly, *I've had a crush on you for twenty years*.

THE music stopped and the pool-goers applauded. Alessia didn't so much walk over, as stalk over to them. She wore a men's waistcoat and black skinny jeans with heavy black boots but, despite the heat, she looked impossibly cool.

'*Ciao*,' she said, leaning in to kiss Adelaide lightly on both cheeks. Her skin felt as smooth as Florentine marble.

'Tazo tonight?' Alessia asked, addressing them both.

'If you're sure I'm not imposing,' said Adelaide.

'You two haven't seen each other in twenty years, right? Maybe I'm imposing on you,' said Alessia.

'Let's go and impose on Xena,' said Alec, grinning.

16

AS she walked into Tazo with Alec and Alessia, Adelaide couldn't help but notice the other patrons pretending not to notice the world-famous DJ.

'*Yassas,*' said Xena, with sugary sarcasm from behind the bar.

Alec pulled out a barstool each for Alessia and Adelaide, before seating himself in the middle.

'*Veneziano?*' said Xena, addressing Alessia who nodded.

'What is that?' asked Adelaide.

'Aperol Spritz,' Xena replied.

'Oh, me too, please,' said Adelaide, feeling like a bogan.

'Also, me,' said Alec.

They watched as Xena prepared the drinks.

'So, how did you two meet?' said Adelaide, addressing Alec and Alessia.

'Xena and I met in Ibiza, when I was a resident and she was a bartender at Club Vertigo,' Alessia explained. 'I met Alec after Xena left to work here.'

'After my father lost his job, I came back home to help my family,' Xena explained.

'Speaking of Xena's family. I got to meet her mother and aunt today,' said Adelaide, identifying an easy segue to talk about the embroidery work. 'Xena and her family are producing some of the most exquisite embroidery I've ever seen. I thought of your friend's boho label when I saw it,' she said.

'Really?' said Alessia, looking at Xena.

'I took some photos in case you want to see.'

'*Prego,*' said Alessia.

Adelaide retrieved her phone and handed it to Alessia, whose eyes widened and settled on Xena for a moment before she spoke. 'You certainly have an eye, Adele. Do you mind if I text these to myself? I will forward to my business partner.'

'Please,' said Adelaide, gesturing with an open palm.

Xena finished mixing the drinks, lined them up on the bar, and everyone extended a hand to claim one.

'Should we toast?' Alec asked. He was interrupted by the text tone of Alessia's phone.

'Is Giovanna,' said Alessia, picking up the phone.

'What did she say?' Adelaide asked, more excited than the situation required.

Alessia laughed to herself before turning to Adelaide. 'She send me the sketch she works on right now.'

Adelaide's face bore a question mark until Alessia turned her phone around to reveal a work in progress, strewn with pencils. It depicted a stylised runway model wearing a flowing maxi dress with an ornately embroidered yoke

'Ha!' said Adelaide, a little too loud in Xena's direction.

Xena's face, usually steely, cracked open into a broad smile.

'The question is,' said Alessia to Xena, 'why was it Adele who came with this idea to me?'

Xena shrugged and sipped her drink.

'Write back to her and ask her to email us all her sketches and what kind of quantities she's looking at running. Oh, and her timeline for launch,' said Adelaide, counting out each point on a finger.

Alec smiled and shook his head. 'You haven't changed at all, Adele. You still see the world as one big opportunity, one giant puzzle for you to solve.'

Adelaide's eyes widened. She had an image of herself in her mind and it wasn't that. She saw herself as a disappointing version of the promising girl she had once been. She gave an imperceptible shake of her head and brought herself back on track. 'Xena, how do you price your work? Do you work from an hourly rate? A cost of goods?'

Xena frowned and looked worried.

'Don't stress, we can work it out together. It's really very easy once you have a formula.'

Adelaide smiled encouragingly, causing Xena's face to soften.

'*Endaxi*,' said Alec, 'so now can we toast?'

'To new possibilities,' said Adelaide, raising her glass, unable to persuade herself to look anywhere other than Alec's face.

'To new possibilities,' everyone repeated.

ADELAIDE'S face hurt from laughing. It seemed that between Alec and Alessia, every corner of the globe had been explored and they had the stories of hijinks and misadventure to prove it. When Xena's shift finally came to an end, Adelaide was beginning to feel that she should take her leave of Alec and Alessia, to allow them some time alone, but Xena seemed restless.

'Let's go to Ainigma,' she said, decisively.

Adelaide got the impression that Alessia would have preferred to call it a night, but Alec jumped on the idea.

'Ainigma?' Adelaide asked.

'It's the hotel nightclub, it's in the cellar,' Xena explained.

'In the cellar,' Adelaide repeated, following her friends out of the bar.

Alec led them towards the reception building and then continued around the perimeter until they came to a wide staircase, partially concealed by foliage. Adelaide could feel bass pumping like a pulse from underground. They descended the stairs and were greeted by a hulk of a man whose menacing face blossomed into a sweet, dimpled smile when he realised who they were. He opened the heavy door and the sound and humidity hit Adelaide in the face like a rousing slap. Alec let the three women enter before shaking the bouncer's hand and following them in. Xena led them past a woman wearing a neon pink wig, sitting at a small marble-topped brass desk, collecting an entry fee which didn't seem to apply to them.

The low, exposed-beam ceiling mirrored that of Adelaide's hotel room, but here the walls were an aged white stucco. A scruffy looking man—who would not have looked out of place drinking from a brown paper bag and asking passers-by for spare change—implored the crowd to raise the roof from behind the DJ booth. A large, mirrored disco ball reflected a thousand versions of the scene below.

Anxiety crept over Adelaide—afraid she was about to be exposed as the complete imposter that she was. It had been so long since she had been anywhere like this. All these people seemed effortlessly cool. *Where did they all come from?*

'Who's drinking, who's dancing, who's lounging?' Alec shouted over the music.

Adelaide decided to employ some false bravado. 'Dancing!' she called back enthusiastically as Xena and Alessia said in unison, 'Drinking!'

'*Endaxi!*' said Alec, his smile broad. He pointed at Adelaide. 'You and me, dance floor.' He pointed at Xena and Alessia next. 'You two are on drinks. We shall meet at the velvet lounges after, yes?'

Everybody nodded.

Alec took Adelaide's hand and led her towards the dance floor, which throbbed in hues of pink and purple. Adelaide stopped and leant towards him.

'Are you sure this is okay?' she asked, following Alessia with her eyes.

'Sure, it's okay, I come here all the time when I'm not working,' he said, misunderstanding the question.

Adelaide was just about to clarify her enquiry when he lifted her hand, twirled her around and drew her into him. Her body swooned in response. She tried to mask it by laughing and pounding him lightly in the chest, before extricating herself and leading him towards the throng.

Adelaide's earlier anxiety dissipated in the anonymity of the crowd. Here, she was a tiny organism of a much larger beast. Moving in time with the beat she was electrified—charged by the music. She closed her eyes, not trusting them to look at Alec without betraying her feelings for him. She could feel him close to her, feel the crowd conspiring to push them together. She let go of her thoughts and moved her body, riding the waves of sound. The music built to a climax, whipping the crowd into a palpable frenzy, before shimmering away into a pared-back interlude. Adelaide opened her eyes to see that the room was aglow with cool white lights and Alec's gaze was locked on her. She reflexively looked around for Alessia.

'Sorry,' he said, suddenly bashful. 'You're a really good dancer.'

'We'd better get back,' she said.

They wove their way through the crowd to the other side of the club, where configurations of velvet upholstered sofas and armchairs were arranged. Adelaide looked around for the women and spied Alessia sitting by herself.

'You head over, I'll be right back,' she said to Alec, indicating with a nod toward Alessia.

She wanted to give them some space to be alone. Adelaide scanned the room for Xena and found her locked in conversation with a beautiful, mocha-skinned man whose head was inclined towards her, nodding. She walked on, feeling alone and sorry for herself. As she headed for the door and climbed the stairs back into the freshness of the night, she texted Alec. "Heading back to Skype the twins, you kids have fun tonight."

ADELAIDE had dreaded speaking with Joe since their last bitter conversation, but it could hardly be put off any longer. She sat nervously at the end of her bed waiting for him to answer her video call. His face appeared on her screen, sitting in their dining room.

'Hi,' he said.

'Hi, Joe.'

'Are you having a good time over there?' he asked, in what she believed was earnest.

'I am, I think,' she said, really considering the question. She went on, 'I think it's been good for me. I think the distance is helping me come to terms with... this,' she said, unable to use the words "separation" or "divorce".

He nodded slowly. Or was it sadly?

'They'll be so pleased to talk to you,' he said and turned to call for the twins.

Adelaide heard what sounded like a stampede before her children came into view, having clambered onto Joe's lap.

'Hi, Mummy!' said Estée.

'Mumma, I caught a millipede!' said Darcy, holding up a jam jar containing the prized specimen.

Adelaide laughed. 'You're such a good entomologist,' she said.

'How is your holiday, Mummy? Is Si Si there too?' Estée asked.

'No, baby, Si Si's not here, I went on a little holiday by myself instead, remember? And you know what? I climbed a mountain yesterday,' she said, widening her eyes for maximum effect.

'Wow, cool!'

'And I went to hot springs. The water was so warm. Warmer than your bath. The water gets warm from the earth being hot in the middle. Just like volcanoes.'

'No way, that's amazing! Can you take us there too?' asked Darcy.

'Maybe one day,' said Adelaide, nodding.

'Mummy, when are you coming home?' Estée asked.

'Soon, baby.'

'Okay. But Daddy hurts when he brushes my hair.'

Adelaide tried not to smile.

'Okay, we'd better go. We're going to visit Nanna today,' said Joe.

'Okay, well. Thanks, Joe. Really,' she said, offering a smile. 'Goodbye, babies. Say hello to your Nanna for me please.'

'Okay, Mummy.'

'Bye, Mumma.'

'I love you, guys.'

A text had come through from Alec while she was on Skype. It read, "Okay, come back after?" She ignored his kind hospitality and got ready for bed.

ADELAIDE woke early, deciding she would take a walk on the beach before heading to breakfast. Penny would be arriving on the ferry today and she was looking forward to their reunion. Adelaide marvelled at how deep a bond you could form with certain people. She had only spent a four week holiday in Greece twenty years ago but had forged friendships that would last a lifetime.

At the end of that summer, before she had returned to Melbourne, Adelaide went upstairs to the Leventis' apartment and was smothered by an embrace from Mrs Leventis, while Adelaide, Penny and Alec made a solemn vow to be pen pals. And, although they had said their goodbyes, Alec had turned up at *yiayia* Vaso's doorstep a few minutes later. She was banging her way out of the front door and there he was, offering to walk her to the bus stop. He had always been so chivalrous, accompanying her and Penny every time they went out after dark even though Adelaide suspected he would have much rather been out with his own friends. She was a little embarrassed that Alec had devoted so much of his summer holidays to babysitting her, and she tried to insist that she would be fine to get to the bus stop alone, but then there was Penny's face, framed in the spiral staircase, calling down to them that she would come too. So together they had walked, Alec carrying her giant backpack, Penny carrying her small pack and Adelaide carrying nothing, feeling like a burden.

Adelaide knew from Penny's emails that her friend had not changed much over the years. She certainly hadn't lost her feisty determination and humour, and yet Adelaide still felt a slight trepidation about their impending reunion. What if they no longer had anything in common?

BY and large, the guests of Ilios Choros enjoyed a late morning start owing to their keeping of time at the opposite end of the hourglass. As she headed back up the beach at the end of her walk, Adelaide encountered only the occasional person. Even the overzealous Germans had not yet sequestered sun loungers by the main pool. As she rounded a corner of the rambling path towards the restaurant, she all but collided with Xena.

'Xena!' she exclaimed, surprised to see her friend so early in the day.

Xena's eyes darted around, and Adelaide got the strangest feeling that she had been spooked by their encounter. She hastened to go on. 'So, Alec said last night that you'll be picking up Penny this afternoon. Do you mind if I tag along?'

'Sure, sure, whatever,' said Xena in a hushed tone.

Adelaide realised that Xena was wearing the same clothes as the night before. She smiled broadly, remembering the conspiratorial conversation she had witnessed Xena having with the mystery man at Ainigma.

'Yes, yes, okay, you got me,' said Xena, noticing Adelaide's knowing look.

The two women laughed.

'You'll take the Kombi, right?' asked Adelaide.

'Yeah. I'll come back around midday and pick it up. I'll get you and we can go.'

'I was wondering if we could maybe go back to that boutique again? I need something special to wear to the party tonight.'

Xena perked up at this. 'Yes!' she said. 'Yes, yes, yes.'

WHEN Adelaide arrived at the restaurant, the energy was palpable. It seemed everybody was engaged in animated chatter about Electric Blue. Adelaide was swept up in the excitement. Last night, as she lost herself in the music, she realised that the only things out of place were her inhibitions. So they, she decided, had to go. She felt a hand on the back of her chair and turned to see Alec. He leant down to kiss her on each cheek, pulled out the chair next to her and sat.

'So, you are like Cinderella now?' he asked, eyes sparkling.

'Cinderella?'

'You run off from the party, leaving the prince in despair.'

Adelaide laughed. He always had such an uncanny way of making everyone around him feel like the centre of the universe.

'How is Alessia feeling about tonight?' Adelaide asked, blinking away a vision of them discussing her set as they lay in bed that morning.

'This is such a small party for her, I doubt she will even give it a second thought,' he said.

Adelaide felt a little silly for having asked the question, but she resisted the urge to chastise herself. 'I'm going with Xena to pick up Penny this afternoon. I can't wait to see her,' she said.

'Why do I get the feeling I'm about to become the odd man out, literally?' he asked, shaking his head and looking down at his clasped hands.

'You can be like our mascot,' said Adelaide, pinching his cheek lightly for effect. She couldn't help but notice the softness of his facial hair and momentarily lost the train of their conversation. She jolted back to reality only to realise that her hand was still on his cheek. His emerald eyes were fixed on her, his face set into a wry smile. She dropped her hand, knocking her empty coffee cup off its saucer with a clatter. He smiled.

'How was everything back home last night?' he asked.

'Good. I mean, I miss the twins so much, and then speaking to them only makes me miss them more. Being a mother is such an exercise in contradictions. You spend so much time wishing for a break and then when you finally get one, you spend the whole time wishing you were back with your children. It's like you're never really your whole self either way.'

He nodded, his face thoughtful.

'That probably doesn't make any sense,' she said.

'I think I understand. It's a little like travelling. The more you belong to the world, the less you belong at home. So you end up being a citizen of nowhere, a nomad. It is… I'm not sure how to say… *Paradoxos.*'

'Paradoxical. Yes! Gosh, yes,' she said, marvelling at him.

They sat for a few seconds in amicable silence.

'And Joe?' he asked tentatively.

'Joe,' she repeated the name as if it were foreign to her, then leant back in her chair, casting her eyes out into the blue. 'Joe is like a dream I've woken up from.'

AFTER Alec left, Adelaide lingered at the breakfast table long after her dishes had been cleared. She was so unaccustomed to being the mistress of her own schedule that she found herself faltering in the face of endless possibilities. She was busy having a heated internal debate, as to the various benefits of the pool versus the beach, when her phone announced an incoming text. "Giovanna has emailed me her designs. Do you want to take a look?" It was from Alessia.

ALESSIA gave Adelaide her room number and a brief description of how to find her. After going by her own room to collect some of the linens she had purchased, Adelaide made her way towards the beach, peeling off before the tiki bar as instructed. After walking for quite some time, Adelaide was beginning to think she should retrace her steps and try again when she came upon a tall gate set into a stone wall fence. She pressed the button on the intercom and waited.

'*Sì?*'

'Hi, Alessia, it's Adele.'

The intercom squawked her admission through the gate and Adelaide walked up the short path to see Alessia framed in the doorway, sipping an espresso.

'*Ciao,*' she said, leaning down to kiss Adelaide on each cheek.

Alessia turned and led the way into a sprawling open plan lounge overlooking a private lap pool and paved entertaining area with a recessed fire pit. Adelaide resisted the urge to comment on the luxuriousness of it all. *Pretend to be cool, pretend to be cool.*

'Would you like to have an espresso? I just made.'

'Oh, thanks.'

Alessia walked over to a minimalist kitchen that spanned the length of the space as Adelaide seated herself on the expansive modular lounge. She placed her bundle of linens next to Alessia's laptop, where it sat on a low marble slab, and looked out over the sundeck to the unspoiled view of the ocean beyond. She idly scanned the apartment and noticed a door slightly ajar, revealing a rumpled bed. A pang of jealousy rose in her chest as she thought of Alec and Alessia's entwined limbs, naked beneath the sheets.

Alessia rejoined her, placed a tiny cup on the table and gathered up the top piece of fabric before sitting down.

'Is really something, no?' said Alessia, fingering the stitching.

'It really is,' Adelaide agreed.

'Giovanna sent me all the finished sketches for her launch collection.'

Alessia opened her laptop, punched a few keys and turned the screen around to face Adelaide. When Alessia had used the word "boho" to describe Giovanna's label, Adelaide imagined garments that would be at home on the music festival circuit or perhaps the beach. What she beheld here was a sophisticated *haute couture* collection, showcasing clever tailoring accented with artisanal embroidery and dyeing techniques.

Adelaide looked over at Alessia with eyes sparkling. She nodded in response, a wordless conversation taking place between them over the quality of the designs.

'She said she had an idea to work with traditional makers but was having no luck to find contacts. She wants to know if you know someone who can do this type of dyeing,' said Alessia, pointing to trousers and jackets.

'It looks like wax resistant dyeing. This type of technique is usually practised in Japan and Indonesia, Africa too, but I don't actually *know* anyone who does it.'

'She said it's easier to find cheap knock-offs than the real thing.'

'She's right. You have fast fashion labels taking traditional designs and getting them reproduced cheaply. It's a form of plagiarism if you ask me. Meanwhile you have traditional techniques dying out, like lost languages. The women practising these techniques have to earn money elsewhere and the knowledge just doesn't get passed down to the younger generations.'

Adelaide, suddenly self-conscious about her overly passionate monologue, thought she should probably change the subject before she lost Alessia's interest altogether, but to her surprise found she had a captivated audience.

'So, what is needed? A museum or something?'

'Museums are for relics, these crafts need to be kept alive.' Adelaide thought for a moment. 'I read this article once about microloans given to women in Africa. It wasn't charity. They lent small amounts of money so that women could start their own businesses. They gave business advice and mentoring so the women could be empowered to support themselves and their families.'

Alessia nodded and sipped her coffee. '*Si*, I've heard of this.'

'Someone just needs to get the makers in contact with the designers,' said Adelaide.

'So, maybe that someone is you.'

Adelaide laughed, assuming Alessia was joking but the woman sat there, deadpan. 'Sometimes the most ridiculous ideas are the best, no?'

Adelaide didn't respond but her mind immediately jumped to Joe's Catalogus App. *A living database of traditional crafts*, she thought, *wouldn't that be something.*

'Did Giovanna send over the other things we asked for? Quantities and working drawings, dates?'

'*Si*, she has it. Here, you want to send it to yourself?' said Alessia, handing over her laptop.

She punched out her email address on the keyboard and said, 'I'm going with Xena later. To pick up Alec's sister. She's coming from Athens, she'll be here for the weekend. For the party tonight.'

Alessia nodded and looked bored.

Adelaide heard herself break out into nervous chatter. 'It must be so exciting, I mean... being up there. DJing in front of all those people. Commanding the crowd like that.'

Alessia shrugged. 'It's nothing new for me. It is my...' she searched for the word, 'routine. So many years, so many parties and nightclubs. I'm ready to finish and slow down. I'm tired of occupying the night. I want to be a part of the daylight. That's why I am investing in Giovanna's label and some other businesses. I'm ready to settle down,' she said, her gaze flitting towards the bedroom.

A feeling of loss washed over Adelaide at hearing the words "settle down".

THE heavy metal gate clicked behind Adelaide as she left Alessia's villa. She clutched the bundle of linens to her chest and fought back the urge to cry. What was wrong with her? It wasn't like she hadn't known that Alec and Alessia were an item, so why had this encounter pulled the rug out from under her? Maybe, up until this moment, she thought of his relationship with Alessia as transient, that there would someday be a chance for her? She had spent her entire time here fantasising about a man she knew was unattainable to distract herself from the fact that she would soon return home to a life in tatters. An inconvenient feeling nagged at her. One she had been trying to ignore, trying to daydream her way out of. Now she was looking into its ugly eyes—fear. It washed over her in visceral waves, forming a lump in her throat that choked her. It was the fear that she was unlovable, the fear of being alone, the fear of not being strong enough for her children, and it was the fear that she was that most fearsome of things—ordinary.

The threat of tears burned the edges of Adelaide's eyes and she quickened her pace, though she had no clear destination. She scanned her thoughts for something else to occupy her harrowed mind. She found the faces of her children, but this image only fuelled her distress. She blinked and found Xena and her family, their untapped potential, the beauty of their work. She conjured up images of other women just like them. Women with boundless talent but no means to create their own livelihoods from it. She thought of Alessia's words, *Maybe that someone is you.* When Alessia said it, Adelaide's first reaction was to reply, 'What would I know about setting up a company?' She stopped herself at the last moment when the rhetorical question was answered. *Me, that's who.* Hadn't it been Adelaide who spearheaded the setup of Grasp Digital when Joe was crippled by the alarmingly steep learning curve required? Hadn't it been she who created a business plan, managed all the required registrations and legalities, and secured the financing they needed? Hadn't it been she who strode into the unknown, and emerged having created something so successful that it was now being sold for an almost ungodly sum? She blinked the thought away along with her tears, choosing instead to focus on the decidedly more manageable task of helping Xena and Giovanna make a commercial connection.

Adelaide made her way to reception where she found Stephan talking on the phone. He twirled one end of his moustache, head cocked to the side, chanting an endless stream of languid *'endaxis'* and *'nais'* down the phone line. Noticing Adelaide, he winked an acknowledgement before rattling off a hurried succession of farewells, pressed the receiver and replaced it on his desk with a flourish. *'Ya,* Adele'

'Ya, Stephan. I was wondering if you could lend me some paper and a pen? Well, not lend the paper. Give me the paper and lend me the pen. I'll bring the pen back, but not the paper... is what I'm trying to say.'

He waited for her rambling to cease, face as blank as the paper she requested. Adelaide mentally kicked herself for her awkwardness before flashing a dazzling smile that she hoped would make up for it. Stephan opened the tray of the printer beside him, extracted a thick bundle of copy paper and set it on the desk. He laid a pen on top and slid them over to her, his eyes a mixture of suspicion and mild interest. If he had any desire to know what these were for, he didn't act on it. She thanked him quickly before offering up another smile and hurrying away, clutching her linens and newly acquired stationery.

In the shade of a large umbrella, Adelaide sat perched on a poolside sun lounger, scribbling feverishly on the stack of paper balanced on her knees. She inscribed a formula which would help Xena cost out not just Giovanna's current requirements, but any future work as well. She cursed herself for not bringing along her laptop. What was required here was a spreadsheet, but in the absence of that she would have to do it the old-fashioned way. When Adelaide was satisfied she had accounted for everything, she put her feet up and leant back, taking in her surrounds. The morning sun glittered on the pool's surface and tanned bodies, slick with sunscreen, fringed the perimeter. Everyone around her looked so outwardly carefree but Adelaide supposed, with a little probing, each of these people would have concealed pain to reveal. Adelaide thumbed back over the pages she had created, enjoying the autumn-leaf crackle they produced. She wondered again about the faceless crafters who could benefit from a kind of matchmaking service pairing them with designers. Fashion may be just the tip of the iceberg. Homewares, jewellery, accessories—her concept could weave its way through so many sectors. *Her concept.* In under an hour the idea had grown legs and ran around in her mind. In any other circumstance, Adelaide may have turned down the volume on the voice in her head. But this daydream provided a welcome respite from both her mess of a life back in Melbourne, and the fantasies she had just been forcibly evicted from here in Ikaria. She made a silent promise to herself that she would stop her mind from wandering ceaselessly toward Alec. She may even try residing in reality occasionally.

17

'I have been looking for you everywhere. We will be late!'

Adelaide felt a hand on her shoulder shaking her awake. She squinted one eye open to see Xena scowling down at her.

'Late?' Adelaide asked, rubbing her eyes and looking around confused. She was by the pool, the sun now high. 'We'll be late!' Adelaide echoed, springing up and scattering her pages.

Xena bent to pick them up. 'What is all this?' she asked, looking at the sheets of paper in her hand.

'It's for you, I guess. I mean... I went to see Alessia this morning and her business partner is keen to work with you—with you and your family that is—and she sent through designs and forecasts, and I just kind of started working on the costings. Well, not the costings exactly but some formulas for costings. You'd do the costings, obviously, but hopefully this will help,' said Adelaide thrusting more pages at Xena.

'You went to see Alessia?'

'Yeah, she sent me a text this morning. When Giovanna's email came through with her designs.'

'Come on,' said Xena sharply and strode away, forcing Adelaide to gather up her things and hurry after her.

Once they were seated in the Kombi, Adelaide placed a hand on Xena's arm, delaying their departure. 'Xena, are you okay? I mean, did I do something wrong?'

Xena frowned so fiercely that Adelaide flinched in anticipation of the tirade she was sure would follow. To her surprise, however, Xena rested her forehead on the steering wheel and sobbed. It took Adelaide a moment to know what to do, so unexpected was this behaviour from the sharp-edged woman. Adelaide placed a hand cautiously on Xena's back and rubbed in a slow circular motion. 'It's okay, just breathe,' she said in a soothing voice.

Xena complied, taking gulped breaths that became more measured and deliberate from where she remained hunched in the driver's seat. Finally, she lifted her head to reveal mascara-streaked eyes and a child-like pink nose. 'I'm sorry,' she said, attempting to wipe away the black streaks but somehow making them worse.

Adelaide shook her head, dismissing the apology.

'It's my father. When I snuck in this morning, he was sitting in my room waiting for me. He called me every name you can think of. Told me there is no place for me under his roof if I am bringing such shame to his name.'

'He's kicking you out?'

'My mother came in yelling, telling him to stop. That if I must go, she will go too.'

'Your mum is my kind of woman,' said Adelaide.

Xena let out a small, sad laugh.

They sat in silence, feeling a gentle breeze blowing through the Kombi's open windows, watching people come and go from the carpark.

'Maybe he just needs some time to cool down?' Adelaide offered.

'He's never going to approve of what I am,' said Xena, sadly.

'And what are you?'

'Something he doesn't understand,' said Xena, quietly.

'Didn't you return home because he lost his job? Aren't you helping keep the family afloat?'

'Float?' Xena asked.

'I mean, aren't you helping your family financially?'

Xena nodded.

'What you are, Xena, is the generous and kind daughter of an ungrateful prick.'

Xena laughed loudly and sniffed. She looked in the rearview mirror and exclaimed, 'O *thee mou*, what a face!'

Adelaide fished around in her handbag and produced a crumpled pack of baby wipes. She extracted one and, to her surprise, Xena lifted her chin and closed her eyes. Adelaide held Xena's chin with thumb and forefinger and wiped her streaked cheeks. When she was finished, she tapped Xena on the nose and pronounced her, 'Perfect'.

Xena smiled. '*Endaxi*, now we are really late,' she said, starting the engine.

To make up for the lost time, Xena manoeuvred the old van as if it was a race car. Adelaide, feeling queasy, gripped her seat and prayed to a God she didn't believe in to prevent them from crashing into the glittering ocean below. By the time the Kombi screeched to a halt in front of the port, the departing ferry was a dot on the horizon and Penny Leventis, leaning against a piling, was the only passenger remaining.

PENNY looked up from her phone to see Adelaide emerging from the Kombi. She sprang to her feet, threw her hands in the air and let out an excited squeal. Any nervousness Adelaide had been feeling dissolved. She ran the few remaining steps and was enveloped by Penny. Afterwards, the two held each other at arm's length laughing stupidly at the sight of one another.

'Of course, you look amazing,' said Penny, feigning annoyance. 'I look like a tired old hag compared to you.'

'As if,' said Adelaide.

'*Ya,* Penny,' said Xena, kissing Penny on each cheek.

Xena extended the handle on Penny's suitcase and wheeled it back to the van. Penny linked arms with Adelaide, and they followed.

'Did Alec tell you about the party tonight?' asked Adelaide excitedly.

Penny nodded.

'And, you know about Alessia?'

'Alessia?' Penny asked with a flick of her free hand.

'DJ Allora,' Adelaide tried.

'Oh, of course!' said Penny.

'Well, obviously I have nothing to wear tonight,' said Adelaide, rolling her eyes dramatically. 'Mind if we go shopping?'

AS the three women walked into the powder-puff interior of the boutique, Penny let out a low whistle. 'I think I have nothing to wear also,' she said.

They all laughed as the sales assistant emerged from the back of house. 'Hello again. Drowned luggage, right?' she said

'Well remembered,' said Adelaide.

'We all have nothing to wear to Electric Blue tonight,' said Xena on behalf of the group.

'What a problem!' exclaimed the sales assistant.

As Adelaide and Penny waited for Xena to emerge from the dressing room, Penny leant in conspiratorially. 'So is my brother still following you around like a fool?' she whispered.

Adelaide turned her head sharply, a look of bewilderment creasing her brow.

'Come on! It was so obvious, wasn't it? I practically had to shoo him away from you when we were kids,' she said, laughing.

'He was never... I mean, he didn't. I was just an annoying kid to him.'

Xena flung the dressing room door open before striking a dramatic pose, her back leaning against the doorframe. She wore a tailored, man-style suit, in wide black and white stripe, with a lace bralette beneath. Penny whooped her approval and Adelaide applauded while her thoughts whirred. She scanned her memory for any evidence that what Penny said was true but came up blank.

'This is it,' Xena said to the sales assistant, smoothing the fabric of the jacket adoringly.

Once she had disappeared to change, Adelaide turned to Penny.

'You're not really serious though, are you? Alec would never have had a crush on me,' she said, trying to sound casual.

'Crush!' she scoffed. 'He was in love. You should have seen him after you went home to Australia. It was the most pitiful thing I've ever seen.'

Xena emerged and Penny jumped up to take her turn in the dressing room.

Adelaide stared, unseeing, at the closed door, the sound of Xena chatting with the sales assistant unable to penetrate her runaway thoughts.

Adelaide got up to pace around the store, running her hand absentmindedly over the fabrics. She had been so accustomed to the belief that her interest in Alec was unrequited that this new information shocked her. Feelings of injustice and loss washed over her. The embers of her attraction to Alec, ignited two decades prior, had glowed steadily throughout her life and now here she was on the brink of singledom, learning that she may have had a chance, but was too late.

'You should totally try this.'

Xena was beside her, indicating a dress that Adelaide hadn't noticed she was gripping the hem of. Adelaide extracted it from the rack, feeling its weight on the hanger. It was a capped-sleeve shift dress, covered entirely in sequins in varying metallic tones. It moved like liquid, reflecting the light in celestial flashes. She turned it around to reveal a deep scooped back.

'I don't think so,' said Adelaide, shaking her head. 'I'm too old for this, Xena. You should try it,' she said, trying to hand the dress over.

'I've made my choice,' said Xena, holding up her hands, 'and you are not too old,' she scolded.

Penny wandered over wearing a black leather pencil skirt and a cream guipure lace halter top. She put her hands in the air proclaiming, 'I have found it.'

'Adele is going to try this on,' said Xena, taking the hanger from Adelaide's hands and walking towards the change rooms.

'*Nai, nai, nai*,' said Penny, nodding as she pushed Adelaide to follow Xena.

'Okay, okay. I'll try it. But I'm not buying it.'

She marched into the dressing room where Xena had hung the dress and closed the door.

Adelaide wiggled out of her clothes, letting them drop to the floor. 'You can't even wear a bra with this dress,' she shouted over the door.

'So don't,' said Xena.

Adelaide muttered to herself as she removed her bra. The silk lining felt cool on her skin as she slipped the dress over her head. She regarded herself in the mirror, turning this way and that, the sequins emitting a faint maraca sound as she moved. She had to admit, it looked good on her.

She cracked open the door to reveal just her smiling eyes.

'Come on! Show us! Come out!'

Adelaide flung open the door and wiggled her shoulders causing the dress to play its soft music. Raucous applause and whooping filled the small shop and Adelaide laughed. 'Enablers!' she yelled over the din before retreating to change.

AS the Kombi meandered back towards Ilios Choros, Adelaide stared out the window, Penny and Xena's chatter on the outskirts of her awareness.

She still reeled from Penny's revelation about Alec. How would she be able to look at him tonight, without her heart shattering?

Pulling into the carpark, Adelaide snapped back into reality. She hadn't realised that her mind had wandered off so thoroughly. *Try harder to act natural*, she told herself, not wanting to alert the others to her inner turmoil. 'Okay, ladies, what's the plan?' she asked brightly.

'Perhaps some *mezedes* before we party?' Penny suggested.

'Sure,' said Xena shrugging. 'I don't want to go home anyway. I can get ready at Alessia's villa and meet you in the restaurant.'

'Adele, do you want to get ready with me at Alec's place?' Penny asked.

'Um, no. I'll give you time to settle in and catch up, we can all meet at the restaurant later.'

Somehow the idea of doing her hair and makeup in Alec's presence was unbearably intimate. The women gathered up their belongings and made their way inside the grounds of the resort.

'So how is Joe? He must be a saint to look after the children while you take a break,' said Penny.

Xena let out a squawk which she tried to suppress by clapping a hand to her mouth. Adelaide felt her neck flush scarlet.

'What did I say?' Penny asked, dumbfounded.

Like a band aid, Adelaide thought. 'Joe has left me for someone else,' she said.

Penny's face turned to stone.

'There's no need for the face. I'm coming to realise that it's actually for the best. I have a sneaking suspicion that I'm too good for Joe,' she said, her posture straightening.

Xena clapped Adelaide on the back. '*Bravo!*' she said.

Penny's face went from grave to impressed in a matter of seconds. 'There goes my fantasy of Australian men.'

THE sky was awash with pink when Adelaide emerged from her room a few hours later, the sun low on the horizon. The heat of the day had given way to a balmy sea breeze that caressed her naked back. The sound of her beaded dress kept time as she strolled along the path towards the restaurant. When she arrived, Xena and Penny were seated at a small table, three narrow glasses of cloudy white liquid sitting in the centre.

'Ouzo? Really?' Adelaide asked, sitting down.

'When in Greece,' said Penny cheerily, picking up a glass and handing it to Adelaide who raised it and exclaimed, '*Yammas!*' before taking a small sip. She marvelled at how the icy liquid elicited such a warm feeling, her hand instinctively rising to her neck.

'Did you have a chance to see Alec?' Adelaide asked Penny, trying to sound casual.

'Barely,' she said, replacing her glass, 'he has a million things to do tonight.'

'I saw him,' said Xena.

'At Alessia's,' said Adelaide, quietly.

'He came by to wish her good luck, not that she needs it,' said Xena, turning a menu over in her hands. She threw it down on the table. 'I don't care what we eat, you two decide.'

'I'm easy,' Adelaide agreed.

'Okay, so it's me?' said Penny, picking up the menu and scanning it.

She raised a hand to catch the waiter's attention, rattled off some instructions in Greek and clasped her hands in front of her. 'So, tell me everything,' she said, addressing Adelaide.

When Adelaide finished recalling the recent events of her life it was Xena who piped up. 'You tell it differently,' she said.

'Differently?'

'It was sad before. You were kind of pitiful. Now, I don't know, you have courage. How do you say it? You have more balls.'

'And,' said Xena, addressing Penny, 'now she has a project to distract her.'

Adelaide smiled on as Xena gave Penny a comical account of her idea for Alessia and Giovanna to commission embroidery work from her family. 'Beats the hell out of selling the occasional *trapezomántilo* to tourists,' she concluded.

AFTER dinner, the friends made their way towards the thumping beat reverberating from the main pool. Penny hooked an arm around each of the two women and proclaimed, 'Tonight is ours!'

Adelaide and Xena laughed, their mood as light as meringue. Tonight, the real world could wait.

Arriving poolside, Adelaide scanned the area for Alec and Alessia but came up short, her eyes falling instead on the gleaming faces of Cora and Dave. Her wave was reciprocated tenfold by the excited Mancunians.

'Friends of yours?' Penny asked.

'Yes, they're the ones I climbed a mountain with,' said Adelaide and then launched into the, now hilarious, story of survival.

'O *thee mou*,' Penny exclaimed when confronted with the sight of Adelaide's badly bruised hip.

Xena nodded with raised eyebrows. 'I'll go get drinks,' she said and strode off without asking what they wanted.

'I just can't believe you're here,' Penny said, taking Adelaide's hand and giving it a squeeze.

'I didn't realise I needed this holiday as much as I did,' Adelaide confessed.

A nearby lounge had just been vacated, so Penny abruptly dropped Adelaide's hand and strode over to claim it. She stretched her arms out wide and patted the seat for Adelaide to sit beside her.

Adelaide looked over at the DJ. He played a monotonous thumping track that reminded her of when the towels bunched to one side of the washing machine during the spin cycle. She lowered her gaze to smile into her lap.

When she looked up, Alec stood in front of her, his smile shining its glorious light upon her. She felt elation and heartbreak in equal, devastating measure. In lieu of the voice which had momentarily left her, she offered up a genuine smile.

Xena arrived with a tray carrying a large jug of something effervescent and placed it down on the low table where they sat. 'Should I get another glass?' she asked Alec.

'I'd love it, but no,' he said. He turned his attention to Penny. 'You look very pleased to be back with your girl,' he said, indicating Adelaide with a slight tip of his head.

'Not as pleased as you,' she countered, crossing her arms.

Adelaide thought he was blushing but no, surely it was the patina of whirling lights emanating from the DJ booth, tinting them all in fuchsia hues.

Adelaide felt like the oxygen was being slowly sapped away from the atmosphere. She stood, ready to make an excuse about seeking out Cora and Dave. Her dress shimmered and sparkled as she moved. Alec stepped forward and took her hand to help her up.

'Yowza,' he said, echoing her reaction to the hot springs.

She had been close to tears but instead she laughed, a lilting sing-song sound, and she was once again at ease. 'Well,' she said, feigning confidence, 'I thought I'd better lift my game to keep up with you.'

Adelaide could practically hear Penny's eyes rolling in their sockets. 'Here we go again,' she said.

'I have some friends to say hi to,' said Adelaide, letting go of Alec's hand.

'Of course, I have a few things to take care of and then I'll come back to join you all,' he said, addressing the group.

Adelaide turned and walked towards Cora and Dave, who were right in the thick of the dance floor. She wiggled her way in past limbs being thrown about. Her "sorrys" and "excuse mes" mute in the clamour, she broke through to her friends and they embraced her. Adelaide couldn't make out anything Cora and Dave said but her wide smile and enthusiastic head nods seemed to suffice in place of comprehension. She danced with them for a while, letting herself be lightly jostled to the beat by the crowd. Despite her best efforts, she found it difficult to be swept up in the party atmosphere. Her brief encounter with Alec had left her heartsick and, she was loath to admit, jealous of Alessia. She mimed to Cora and Dave that she was going to get a drink and rode the wave of revellers back to her friends.

Adelaide took her place on the lounge. Xena leant in and Adelaide planted a kiss on her mop of thick hair. Xena's eyes smiled. 'I've done some research on how to become a real business, you know?' she said sheepishly.

'You have? Oh, I'm so pleased to hear it! I was a little worried that you might not be too keen on the idea of working with Giovanna. I was worried I had been too pushy.'

'No,' said Xena matter-of-factly and handed Adelaide a drink that sparkled like her dress.

Adelaide sipped the floral-tasting liquid and willed her mind to stop chasing its tail over Alec. What was it about heartbreak that accompanied her like a shadow lately?

Xena consulted her chunky gold watch and proclaimed, 'Alessia's set starts soon.'

She downed the remainder of her drink in one gulp, as if it were she about to take the stage and needed the courage.

Adelaide's eyes scanned the party, taking in the scene. A cluster of young women was huddled together, one holding a selfie stick at arm's length. They each angled their faces, widening their eyes and pouting their lips into unnatural shapes. Some feigned laughter, their mouths open, but not too open, heads thrown back in a pantomime of enjoyment. Once captured, they each dropped their poses and their smiles vanished as they huddled around the image, scrutinising. From behind them, Alec and Alessia emerged. She was a sight to behold in all white, her full lips made even more striking by a saturated, raisin-coloured lipstick. It was the type of colour that Adelaide had stared at while visiting makeup counters, wondering about the type of woman who could possibly pull it off. She found her answer in Alessia. Alec leant in to kiss her and Alessia offered her cheek to him, presumably not wanting to disturb her perfect pout. She climbed the stairs to the platform and, even though the current DJ continued to play, the audience applauded and whooped. Dave and Cora looked positively effervescent. The beat slowed into a mellow funk and the DJ leant into the mic to announce, in a cockney lilt. 'And now, it is my absolute pleasure to introduce one of the hottest acts in the world right now. Let's make her feel welcome. DJ ALLORA!'

The crowd erupted and Adelaide was surprised that her heartbeat quickened. She clapped so hard her hands stung, and she felt a sudden rush of pride that she was intimately acquainted with this woman who was such a source of enjoyment for so many. Alec made his way over to stand between her and Xena. Adelaide could feel his towering presence next to her but dared not look at him. The mellow beat thumped on as Alessia took up her headphones and positioned them around her neck. She dipped an ear to listen from one side as she cued the next record. The atmosphere was bursting and the crowd leant forward expectantly. Alessia looked up towards Alec, her eyes sombre. She gave a brief questioning nod, and then an almost imperceptible smile at the response this must have garnered.

Adelaide's stomach felt hollow for reasons she didn't understand. Alessia parted her dark lips to speak, leaning into the microphone.

'*Allora*, I have something of an announcement to make here tonight…' she said, barely able to contain her smile.

Smartphones flickered to life in the crowd like candles at a vigil.

'I've decided that what I need is a change of pace. It's time for me to take things… slower,' she said, slowing down the beat to match her drip of words. 'This will be my last show for… maybe ever because, the thing about it is, I'm in love and I'm going to take some time to enjoy it.'

Gasps, whistles and applause punctuated the subdued backbeat. Alessia's eyes sparkled.

'Baby, I know you're shy,' she said, her eyes locked on Alec, 'but I want everyone here to know that you're mine.'

White hot noise erupted in Adelaide's eardrums and her windpipe constricted. Everyone at the party seemed to hold their breath but it was only Adelaide who could not breathe. She placed a hand up to her heart and tried desperately to swallow the lump in her throat. Time stood still.

'XENA KARAKOSTA!' Alessia bellowed into the microphone, 'I love you and I want the whole world to know it.'

She flicked a switch, releasing a vicious track that all but drowned out the elated screams of her audience.

Adelaide looked past Alec to Xena, whose typically stern face had opened like a flower bathed in sunshine.

Adelaide felt as though she were in a dream, floating high above, looking down at her own stunned face, her motionless body standing next to Alec who was, in turn, smiling broadly at Xena. Xena. *Alessia is in love with Xena.* Adelaide repeated this phrase to herself over and over as if it would cease to be true if she stopped. *Alessia is in love with Xena.* Adelaide opened her mouth to say something to Alec but before the words could form in her mouth, the sound engineer waved him over and he made his apologies to her and strode away. Adelaide looked at Xena who was trying in vain to contain her smile.

'So another one bites the dust,' said Penny, with feigned scepticism as she drew Xena in for a one-armed hug. Xena turned her attention to Adelaide, her smile disappearing. 'You are shocked,' she said.

How could Adelaide explain her surprise without sounding like a fool?

How could she tell Xena that she had seen something that was never there, and then built an entire narrative on the foundation of that hallucination? How could she tell her that every molecule of her body felt like it was erupting with possibility, and relief, and blinding hope, and that the feeling was so intensely pleasurable it was almost painful?

'Oh, Xena, I had no idea but I'm so happy for you. For you both,' she said and embraced her friend.

'She wants to stay here, you know, in Ikaria. We're going to get a place together. My father may never talk to me again but... that's his choice I guess.'

She gave a resigned shrug that did nothing to conceal the depth of her heartbreak.

Adelaide's eyes darted towards a woman approaching and Xena turned to see what had caught her attention. The woman unleashed an outpouring of what seemed like well wishes in Greek, and Adelaide stepped slightly away from them, allowing their moment together.

'So...' Alec's deep voice cut through her thoughts, 'are we ready for dancing?'

His eyes sparkled mischievously, awaiting her response.

'I've never been more ready for this dance,' she said to him, her eyes so intense he flinched.

18

AS Alessia deftly wove together old-school funk tracks and set them adrift on a ceaseless sea of contemporary beats, Adelaide and Alec fell into rhythm with the crowd. The dance floor had traversed the tipping point where a group of people transforms into a sanctuary of anonymity and privacy. Adelaide drew nearer to Alec, slowing her movements and allowing herself to be guided by the feelings bursting within her. Emboldened by circumstance and the effervescent cocktail, she dared to reach a hand up to stroke his face, cupping his cheekbone before running her hand down his soft beard, her thumb gently parting his bottom lip from his top. Before he had time to react, she lifted onto her toes and took his bottom lip between hers, gently sucking it before coaxing him into a kiss. His mouth was warm and accepting and tasted of spearmint and aniseed. She felt a wave of surprise, and relief, and pleasure, pulse through his body, mirroring her own. Setting herself back down onto her feet, she opened her eyes and looked up at him. He smiled at her and there was something breathless in it. 'What took you so long?' he mouthed before leaning down to continue their tryst, hidden in the throng.

She pushed away gently, and his eyes searched as she clasped his giant hand in hers and turned away from him. He ran the open palm of his free hand down the length of her exposed back and she felt an electric charge shudder through her.

From the corner of her eye, Adelaide noticed the good-natured laugh that Penny let out as they walked away from the party. As they wove their way along the now deserted paths, they stared at each other in wonder, unable to hide their elation.

Alec's bungalow glowed like a beacon in the distance, its doors and windows open, gauzy curtains undulating in the night breeze. They climbed the stairs in a dream, Alessia's music providing a distant, primal beat. The light inside the welcoming space was subdued and golden, bathing them in amber. Alec looked at her with longing, a flash of sadness rippling over his features before he could censor it. He brushed a strand of hair away from her face and asked, 'Are you sure this isn't too soon?'

'Well, I've wanted this since the nineties,' she said grinning broadly. 'I hardly think it classifies as rushing in.'

He laughed, his eyes dancing with pleasure.

He gathered her up in his arms to kiss her, lifting her slightly off the ground in the process, then buried his face in the fragrant softness of her neck. His large hands caressed her exposed back, the slight roughness of them making her skin tingle. She wanted that feeling over her entire body. Pushing away from him, Adelaide relaxed her posture, rounding her normally square shoulders. Her heavy dress slid down her body in one swift motion, hitting the floor with the soft *cha* of a brushed cymbal. Alec's green eyes blinked with the rapidity of a camera shutter, and he appeared to be momentarily stunned. He ran his hands up and down her arms, kissing and gently biting her neck and shoulders. He scooped her up—her shoes clunking on the floorboards as they dropped—and carried her the short distance to the sofa where he placed her down, kicked off his shoes and knelt before her.

'You are even more beautiful than I imagined,' he said, his eyes devouring her all-but-naked form.

He looked at her with such adoration that Adelaide felt herself become more beautiful under his gaze. Running his hands down her ribs, he traced each small bone as if taking stock of them, then across her stomach and down the length of her.

She leant forward to unbutton his shirt, revealing the swirl of chest hair she had longed to touch. 'I wanted to do this so badly the other day at the hot springs,' she muttered into his neck.

He pulled back to seek out her eyes. 'Why didn't you?'

Adelaide grimaced. 'I thought you were with Alessia,' she admitted.

'You what?' he said, laughing heartily. 'So that wonderful imagination of yours can sometimes work against you too?'

He returned to her mouth before gently pushing her body backwards into a nest of cushions. Running his hands down her reclined neck, he traced her sternum until both hands swept outward, encompassing her breasts in Rorschach symmetry. His dark-lashed eyes sought hers for confirmation of her pleasure before daring to take her nipples in his mouth in turn. He moaned quietly, as if tasting something delicious, and Adelaide emitted a light and glinting laugh in response to the completeness of her delight. Raking her fingers through his lush hair, she willed herself not to wake if this was a dream.

Adelaide felt a warm flush pulse from the centre of her body and breathed against her desire to rush. Alec repositioned himself slightly and tugged at the miniscule cobweb of black lace that had, until now, kept her from complete nudity. She ran her hands over his chest before tracing the silky pathway leading to his belt buckle, which she loosened. Her hand sought beyond the confines of his trousers but she was stopped short by a forceful hand halting hers. 'Let me taste you,' he murmured, and she let out an involuntary groan which straddled the space between pleasure and torture.

His mouth meandered down the length of her bare torso, his hands washing over and under her in a half-time rhythm of her hammering heart. Finally, his hands and mouth came together, and Adelaide felt herself unfurl in endless waves, like a *mise en abyme* recursive image. The heat of his mouth gave way to icy cold as he gently exhaled close to her wetness. Adelaide felt as though she was being commanded—an instrument expertly played. She raised her head, staring down in disbelief. Alec's intense eyes met her gaze briefly before he was capsized by his enjoyment once more.

She had wanted to wait. Had a romantic notion of them climaxing together in one exquisitely elegant arc. She had been doing her best to resist succumbing to the unstoppable surge he created in her, but this only served to intensify what was ultimately too tempestuous to stifle. She cried out in an ascending tone that sounded more musical than guttural. Pressing her cheek into one of the many cushions that surrounded her, chin raised at an almost unnatural angle, she emitted her chorus until all was silent.

When her body went limp, she felt his breath on her, felt him tracing her with a finger that barely even met her flesh, but even that was too much. She thrust her hands downward, grasping his strong wrist, demanding that he stop moving, stop breathing, until she could rejoin the earth-bound. She realised she had been holding her breath until now, writhing subtly from the aftershock of her pleasure, her mouth frozen open in a silent scream. Her awareness returned in increments and she dared to open her eyes. Alec looked up at her in wonder. The sight of him was too much for Adelaide to languish before so she reached down, pushed the shirt off his shoulders and ran her fingers hungrily over his smooth, golden skin. He paused to remove the garment, then ran his large hands down her thighs, pushing her knees outward. He leant over her, alternately taking her nipples in his mouth as if trying to decide which he preferred. Adelaide squeezed his torso between her thighs, her yearning made new.

'I need you,' she said huskily, her lips brushing against his earlobe. She felt his face move into a smile. He stood, his belt buckle clanging as he undid his trousers and let them fall to the floor. Adelaide sprang to her knees, pulled him towards her by the waistband of his boxers and smiled up at him before pushing them down to his ankles. He stood before her, proudly displaying his arousal and she let out a half-laugh.

'Is there anything about you that isn't perfect?' she asked.

He smiled broadly and leant down but she stopped him, taking him in her mouth.

'Adele,' is all he could say, 'Adele, Adele, Adele.'

She contracted her lips, feeling how hard he was, enjoying how impossibly silky he felt on her tongue. He stroked her cheek, her jaw, her nape with adoring fingers and her hands explored everything within reach, as if recording every detail for future recollection.

His body moved in unison with hers and then suddenly jolted.

'Wait,' he implored her and, as much as she wanted to continue, she did not. 'Wait,' he said it again, but this time to himself. 'I'm sure I have something, somewhere… but where?'

He kissed her deeply before disappearing into the depths of the house and she traced the journey his mouth had taken, savouring the way her body still tingled.

He returned, the rustle of a plastic wrapper crackling beneath his fingertips. Once he was satisfied that everything was in place, he kissed her gently on the mouth, taking the time to cup her face and whisper, 'This is more than I could have…' He searched for the words in vain before settling on the phrase, 'This is everything to me.'

She pulled him down to sit on the sofa and straddled him, holding her hips high enough so that the object of his desire was just out of reach. She leant forward, gently rotating her hips, using him to pleasure herself.

'Who are you?' he said into her neck and braille bloomed down the length of her body. He traced it with his fingers, seemingly awed by her responsiveness to him.

She lowered herself onto him at a glacial pace and he leant his head back, letting out a soft, low groan before straightening to meet her gaze. Her hair hung down around them like a veil, concealing their slow, deep kisses as she bobbed. She felt him position his hand where their two bodies met so that with each rhythmic movement, she brushed his thumb. She smiled into his kiss, her eyes opening, dancing, acknowledging his expertise. He covered each breast with hand and mouth, his fingers mirroring the twirling of his tongue, whipping her into a frenzy. *This time*, she told herself, *I will resist.*

Adelaide felt her eyes rolling as she made her body dance to Alec's beat, and she threw her head backwards, feeling her hair caress the top of her shoulders like fingertips. She was in a place where she had ceased to form coherent thought, and so forgot the pact she had made with herself to stave off her second climax. In a distant universe, she could hear Alec's low, pleasured breathing, could smell the woody cologne that radiated from his warmed skin, could feel the soft hairs that fringed his wet lips.

'Oh, Alec,' was all she could manage before she ceased to exist altogether.

'Adele,' he whispered.

He moved his hands underneath her and, taking care to avoid her bruised hip, hoisted her upward so he could set their final rhythm. Their breathless moans mingled, making her pleasure indistinguishable from his, and then all was still save for the drumming of their hearts. Alec rested his head back momentarily before looking up into Adelaide's glowing face. He licked a single bead of sweat that pooled in her collar bone and muttered something inaudible in Greek. They smiled at each other, kissed each other, but dared not separate, instead reclining into the cushions which surrounded them. Adelaide rested her cheek on Alec's chest, inhaling the clean scent of him as he muttered confessions into the top of her head. They traded stories of their twenty years of longing for one other, each taking turns to feign disbelief and accuse exaggeration, all the while laughing as they reminisced.

'Do you know what would make this night perfect?' she finally said, eyes sparkling.

'It's not perfect?'

'I mean, almost,' she said cryptically, her eyes glinting in the half-light.

Picking up her mischievous tone, Alec played along. 'In any case, I would hate to leave a woman with unfulfilled desires,' he said.

'Food,' she said decisively. 'We need food.'

He laughed, a deep delighted sound that dispelled the intimacy of the space and returned it to something homier.

'That might be the second-best idea you've had all night,' he said before striding off into the bedroom and returning, still shirtless, in loose fitting linen trousers.

Adelaide retrieved Alec's shirt from the floor and slipped into it, feeling like the lead in a romantic comedy and not disliking the sensation. She followed him into the kitchen where he opened some retsina, which he poured into thick tumblers before fossicking around in his refrigerator for ingredients.

She watched as he deftly peeled and diced two potatoes with a paring knife and set them to fry with crushed garlic in olive oil. They crisped and sputtered in the smouldering pan, which he removed from the heat before breaking in two eggs and scrambling them with a fork. Next, he crumbled in feta and stirred it through roughly, completing the dish with a sprinkling of oregano. He retrieved two forks and napkins which, she noted with an approving smile, were cloth, and sat down beside her. They devoured the meal almost as hungrily as they had devoured each other and then made their way to Alec's bed to begin their entire dance again.

19

ADELAIDE had enjoyed a precious few hours of sleep, limbs entwined with Alec's, when she was prematurely roused by the melodic drip of her Skype tone sounding from the next room. It was still dark out, the horizon showing only the vague promise of daybreak. Alec grunted and rolled away with the ease of someone who is childless. Adelaide felt a rising terror that propelled her out of bed, to scramble around in the lamplight of the lounge room for her cast-off belongings. She had just located her phone, glowing like a beacon from the confines of her clutch bag, when it fell silent. It was just after 5:00 a.m. which, she quickly calculated, put Melbourne at just gone 12:00 p.m. Her phone sounded again, startling her. It was Joe. She looked down at her nakedness and panicked.

'Jesus,' she spat into the darkness, quickly rejecting the call and writing a message instead. "Give me five, I'll call you back."

She dressed hurriedly, careful not to wake the still-sleeping Alec, and scurried out the door, holding her mules. Adelaide noted that Penny wasn't back yet and prayed that she didn't run into her friends on their way home. Once outside, she popped on her shoes and tried to adjust her demeanour to match the partygoers she encountered. Inside, her heart threatened to thump free of her ribs with the unbearable thought that something had happened to her children. *Please let them be okay*, she willed. *Please let them be okay.*

Once inside her hotel room, she shucked her dress and pulled on her bathrobe. Then, unaware that she was holding her breath, she Skyped Joe. His unshaven face came into view looking grave and a full decade older.

'Are the twins alright?' she asked, desperately.

'The twins?' he asked. 'Yeah, shit, sorry. They're fine. They're just at Mum's.'

Adelaide's relief quickly turned to anger. 'Fuck, Joe,' she said, placing her free hand up to her brow.

'Sorry, sorry,' he said, shaking his head. 'So, how's it going over there?' he asked, in a tone she didn't recognise.

'How's it going? What is this about? Why are you calling me at the crack of dawn? I was… asleep,' she faltered.

'Yeah, sorry,' he said. 'I didn't think. I guess, I just wanted to… I just miss you, is all.'

Adelaide reeled back in repulsion. 'You miss me? You're divorcing me. Aren't they kind of opposing ideas?' she spat, unable to keep the sarcasm out of her voice.

'Yeah, I mean, about that…'

Adelaide's eyes turned into saucers.

'Maybe we were a bit, you know, hasty in that respect.'

Adelaide scrunched her face as if smelling something rancid.

'Look Adelaide, I know I stuffed up and I'm going to have to live with that forever, but I love you and we're a family, and I just think that what we have is worth saving,' he blurted.

Adelaide squinted, trying to sift through his avalanche of words. Back and forth she sifted until just three words remained.

'You *love* me?'

The question hung in the air, unanswered and Joe's pitiful expression suddenly infuriated her.

'So, what? You've changed your mind about Kimmy and you're trying to run back over the bridge you just set fire to?'

Adelaide's laugh was full of a venom she hadn't realised she possessed.

'It's not just about us,' he said desperately, 'there are the kids to think of.'

'I'm not the one who forgot that, Joe!'

He hung his head, looking ashamed and Adelaide felt a pang of regret for having been so cruel.

'Look, Joe, this is a lot to take in,' she said, softer.

His eyes darted up hopefully.

'I just need a minute to process what all this means, okay?'

'Of course,' he said hurriedly, 'take your time.'

'I have to go,' she said and hung up as he opened his mouth to respond.

Adelaide sat for a moment still holding her phone, her brain a boulder between her ears. She texted Alec, "Sorry I had to run off, I thought something terrible had happened with the children, but it was a false alarm."

She turned her phone to silent and crawled under her covers seeking the respite of sleep.

ADELAIDE blinked, trying to focus on her surrounds. Where was she? The cube of her hotel room came into focus and for a moment she thought that her night with Alec had been a dream. She retrieved her phone from the entwinement of her sheets and squinted at the screen. It was midday. Two names appeared on her screen and the effect of seeing them together made her stomach flip. The worlds of Joe Spiteri and Alec Leventis had never collided, until this moment. Adelaide stared at the screen, unblinking. *Which should I read first?* she wondered, as if the answer mattered. She considered the question and finally decided that she would read them chronologically. The first text had come in from Joe not long after they Skyped. It read, "You have the right to be angry, but I meant what I said. I love you and I'm sorry. Your the best thing that ever happened to me and I've been a complete idiot."

Adelaide cringed at his spelling mistake and checked the text from Alec.

"When I woke alone, I thought I had been dreaming. It turns out all my years of dreaming were nothing compared to the reality of you. Good to hear there was no emergency at home."

LYING on the beach with her face covered by her giant sun hat, Adelaide's eyes traced the weave of the sisal braid, illuminated by the afternoon sunshine. An anvil had taken up residence in the pit of her stomach and she couldn't shake a feeling of intense dread. The last two wishes that Adelaide had sent out into the universe had come true and she could not be more miserable about it. Hadn't she come on this foolhardy trip with the express purpose of making her husband repent? Instead of fixating on that, she had… she couldn't exactly say "gotten over it" but her mind had shifted. She had basked in the warm glow of Alec's attention, even when she believed it to be platonic, and it had given her a glimpse of what was possible, maybe even what she deserved. If she were unattached, there would be no debate. She would pack up her life and leave Australia to be with Alec. But she was getting ahead of herself. There was nothing to indicate that last night with Alec would amount to anything more than a holiday romance. Perhaps it was something they each needed to get out of their system. A twenty-year-old itch that needed to be scratched. But the point was, Adelaide wasn't unattached, she had her children to consider. From the moment they were born every one of her decisions was made with their wellbeing at the forefront. Even this trip, this seemingly impetuous trip, was intended to make their father see sense. And now here he was telling her that he no longer wished to leave. If she decided not to reunite with Joe, Adelaide herself would be the home wrecker. The weight in her stomach grew.

The corn-yellow glow inside her hat was momentarily extinguished.

'Adele, is that you?'

Xena eclipsed the sun and stared down at her, eyes peaking above her aviators.

Adelaide lifted herself into a sitting position and made room for Xena to sit beside her.

'You and Alec ghosted us last night,' she said, in a tone of mock confusion.

Adelaide blushed and did a terrible job of suppressing a grin. 'How was the rest of the night?' she asked.

'It was special for me, for Alessia, but I worry about her slowing down. I'm not sure she knows how.'

Xena pulled a squashed pack of cigarettes out of her back pocket. 'You mind?' she asked, tapping out a cigarette.

Adelaide shook her head and waited for her friend to go on.

'She has other ventures of course, but the lifestyle she's been used to…' Xena trailed off, lighting her cigarette and inspecting its glowing ember.

'You know, my love, worrying is just a sign that you care.'

Xena considered this and gave a slight nod. She bumped Adelaide's shoulder with her own and offered her a wry smile. 'So, tell me. How is *your* heart this morning?'

Adelaide smiled as bravely as she could, but the tears that had threatened to burst since her Skype call with Joe could not be staved off any longer.

'*Gamoto*,' Xena swore, wrapping an arm around Adelaide and drawing her in.

Adelaide sobbed into her friend's neck as she recounted the entire story, leaving out the slightly embarrassing detail of how she had convinced herself that Alec and Alessia were an item. She described the terror she felt when she thought something had happened to her children, and the sickening shame that she was on the other side of the world, entangled in passion instead of with them. She spoke of how visible she felt in Alec's presence, and how invisible she felt in Joe's.

'I'm not naïve enough to think that Alec is in love with me, but that doesn't change the fact that my time here has changed me,' said Adelaide, straightening. 'But anything other than going back home to Joe just feels selfish.'

Xena took a long drag on her cigarette, turned her head and exhaled a thick cloud of smoke. 'You can't live your life by prioritising the happiness of your family over your own,' said Xena.

'What have you told your father?' Adelaide asked.

'Nothing about Alessia yet. I've kept it hidden away, so he doesn't ruin it with his small-minded views. What we have is beautiful. He will make it ugly.'

'Surely he will see reason though? You're his daughter, for God's sake,' Adelaide said.

'Yes, but my father's love is conditional,' she said, extinguishing the cigarette in the sand before carefully replacing it in her crumpled pack.

Xena sprang to her feet and extended a hand to Adelaide, pulling her up in one effortless motion. The women walked back along the beach towards the resort.

'I don't suppose you want to go over my notes for your business model now, do you?' Adelaide ventured, half expecting to be rebuffed.

'Sure,' Xena said, shrugging. 'At least those problems can be solved.'

BACK at Alessia's villa, Adelaide set up a template which Xena could populate once she had conducted timed embroidery samples for each of Giovanna's designs. The preloaded formulas would then calculate the various financials required for a sustainable commercial operation, as well as estimate the turnaround time for production.

'So, you said you have looked into business registration?' said Adelaide.

'Sure. My mother reminded me that I have a second cousin working in the Chamber of Commerce. He will help.'

'Xena, that's amazing!' said Adelaide, pleased to see her hare-brained scheme coming to life.

Xena shrugged.

Adelaide's text tone announced the arrival of a message from Alec.

"Crazy day today, sorry I haven't come by. Dinner at my place with Penny? I'm cooking."

Adelaide's anguish grew wings and flew away, and she couldn't help breaking into a wide smile. Xena, witnessing the full unfurling of her demeanour, merely raised an eyebrow.

Alessia strolled in from the sundeck and retrieved a bottle of water from the fridge.

'I should go,' said Adelaide, rising. 'You'll start work on the samples tomorrow?'

Xena nodded.

20

ALEC'S bungalow glowed like a beacon as Adelaide approached, and she experienced a rush of adrenalin at the memory of last night. The two of them had practically scrambled to get here, stumbling up the path, giddy with anticipation.

Adelaide rapped on the front door, her heartbeat echoing the sound. Penny answered the door, her face sallow. '*Ya*,' she said and turned to replace herself on the sofa.

Adelaide had a flashback of straddling Alec on that sofa, his wet mouth encircling her breast, and shook her head rapidly to dispel it. 'Big night?' she asked.

'I'm too old for this shit,' Penny groaned.

Adelaide laughed but the sound was sympathetic. She breathed in deeply. The rich scent of roasting meat, garlic and lemon wafted in from the kitchen, making her mouth water. 'It smells amazing in here,' she said to Penny, who groaned her disagreement.

As Adelaide approached the kitchen, she heard Greek music and Alec's sporadic, off-pitch vocal accompaniment. She paused in the doorway, silently observing him as he chopped cucumbers for a salad, a blue and white chequered tea towel slung over one shoulder. He went to retrieve something from the fridge, then turned and saw her for the first time. They stood at opposite sides of the kitchen, smiling at each other until the open fridge beeped impatiently, breaking the spell.

'I didn't hear you arrive.'

'My knocking can hardly compete with your singing,' she said.

He grinned. 'Not much can compete with my singing. Would you like a beer?'

Penny let out a pained groan from the sofa and Adelaide and Alec exchanged laughing eyes.

'She could do with a shandy,' said Adelaide knowingly.

'Shandy?' said Alec.

Adelaide smiled. 'Do you have any lemonade?'

'In the fridge.'

'Okay, I'm on drinks.'

She skirted around Alec and felt an overwhelming urge to wrap her arms around his waist where he stood cutting tomatoes. Instead, she retrieved the beer and lemonade from the fridge and pulled down three tall glasses from the shelf beside it.

'Want ice in your beer?' she asked, as if it were a test.

He raised an eyebrow. 'Ice? In beer?'

'If you haven't tried it, you haven't lived,' she said airily.

'Well, in that case.'

Adelaide filled the glasses with ice and poured in the amber liquid, taking care to only half fill Penny's glass before topping it up with lemonade. 'Shandy!' she said brightly, holding up the glass and walking into the lounge room. She offered it to Penny who looked at it with trepidation. 'Strictly medicinal,' she reassured.

Penny sipped cautiously, her face displaying a look of begrudging acceptance.

Adelaide rejoined Alec in the kitchen, sidling up beside him and placing a glass by his chopping board. He wiped his hands on the tea towel, took up his glass and offered a, '*Yammas*!'

They clinked glasses and took a sip, an exaggerated look of appreciation crossing his face. 'Ice in beer,' he said. 'My life is complete.'

He leant down and kissed her as if it were the most natural thing in the world.

By the time they were seated at the dining table, Penny was feeling a little better. She told them about Alessia's set, the way she manipulated the crowd into a frenzy. Adelaide thought of how Alec had done the same for her but forced her mind back into the conversation.

'Half the people on the dance floor jumped into the pool at the end! I was about to myself when I realised my new leather skirt might not survive a swim.'

Adelaide and Alec marvelled at the recount but neither of them uttered a word about wishing they'd been there.

Alec cleared away the dishes as the women continued talking. Penny told Adelaide about the wacky things patients had said in the operating room as they were coming out of anaesthesia.

'He was tripping, looking at his hand, which is actually very common, but then he turns to me with this look of horror and asks, "why are there five penises here?" Then he starts screaming, "They've given me the wrong operation!"' Penny laughed at her own well-worn story as Adelaide gasped and gulped with laughter.

Alec returned and set a dish down on the table. 'Penis hand, right?' he asked, obviously familiar with his sister's repertoire.

Adelaide turned to the dish Alec had set down. 'You did *not* make dessert!'

'I didn't? Then where did this *rizogalo* come from?' he asked, looking around the room with an exaggerated flair.

'Who are you?' she asked, boldly echoing his question to her the night before.

A lingering smirk passed between them and Penny, sensing the energy of the room shift, pushed her chair back from the table. 'I need sleep,' she said, simply.

'Are you sure you don't want a little dessert?' Alec asked after her retreating figure.

She raised a hand in the air. '*Kalinikta!*' she said.

Alec walked over to an art deco drinks trolley in the corner of the room and selected a tall bottle containing a honey-coloured liquid. He poured two small glasses and placed one in front of Adelaide. '*Metaxa*,' he said. Noticing her confused expression, he elaborated, 'It's brandy.'

She took a tentative sip and, as she swallowed, felt her throat blazing before settling into a pleasant warmth. Alec dished out two modest helpings of the steaming rice pudding.

'Like it?' he asked.

'I like it's effect,' said Adelaide, feeling as though she were being illuminated from within, though how much could be attributed to Alec and how much to the brandy was unclear to her.

Alec took the seat closest to her, taking a sip of his own drink, his eyes never leaving hers. Adelaide's heart rejuvenated and broke apart on a maddening, endless loop. *How much should I tell him?*

She opened her mouth to speak but before she could utter a word his mouth was on hers, the warm taste of raisins mirroring the taste on her own tongue.

'Alec,' she tried again.

'You must taste this,' he said, his gaze as warm as the brandy.

He took a small scoop of the creamy pudding onto his spoon and raised it up to her lips. Adelaide felt a rush of sheepishness at the gesture but opted to accept the morsel rather than wound Alec's pride with a rebuff. The subtle flavours of vanilla bean and lemon rind rose from behind a velvet ripple of cream, punctuated with tender grains of rice. She reflexively closed her eyes as the spoon touched her lips. She opened them to behold the full penetration of his gaze. *I am here*, she thought, *and here, I am yours.*

He ran his thumb down the corner of her mouth, catching stray cream and slowly licked it, his eyes smiling. Adelaide wondered if he could hear her heart beating. She took his hand and placed it over her silk blouse, between her breasts. Feeling the drumbeat, he looked at her in astonishment. A single tear sprang rebelliously from the corner of her eye, disobeying her command to stay put.

'Adele?'

'I'm sorry, it's just that...'

How could she convey to him all that she felt? The bittersweetness of it all? How every beautiful moment they shared was shadowed by a ticking clock calling her home.

'I'm leaving in a few days and my heart... I know I'm not supposed to... but I just feel...' she faltered.

He placed his hand on her forearm, halting her. 'There is no "supposed to",' he said, simply. 'Whatever you are feeling is the right thing. Since I met you, a part of my heart has belonged to you. I could ask you to stay here with me, but I know you cannot. Your children come first and that is one of the things I love most about you, your selflessness.'

She lowered her head, feeling helpless.

He went on, 'But Adele, we may not be fortunate enough to have forever, but we do have now.'

She gave a sad smile and nodded.

'And…' he said, his cheeky grin reappearing, 'this *rizogalo* is not going to eat itself.'

She sniffed away her tears and returned his look. Then, furrowing her brow she leant in and pledged, 'I will not let you down.'

'*Ella*,' he said, standing and gathering their bowls, 'we can listen to some music.'

Adelaide picked up their glasses and followed Alec into the lounge room, noticing for the first time he did not own a television. She set the glasses down on the low coffee table and followed Alec to the large bookshelf. He opened a cupboard to reveal records and a player. She ran a hand appreciatively over the books that filled every possible space, crammed in at odd angles.

'Oh. My. Goodness!' she exclaimed laying eyes on a small, framed photograph. She pulled it down, dislodging it from a stack of art books.

The image was faded and yellowed but the three young faces were unmistakable. Adelaide stood at the centre, her gaze intense. To her left Penny was captured mid eye-roll, clearly the product of some jibe of Alec's. He could be seen laughing at his own hilarity to Adelaide's right.

'Look at my hair, it's so long,' she said, fingering her own hair absentmindedly.

Alec dropped the needle on a record and stood to look at the image over her shoulder, he was so close she could feel him smiling. She turned to him.

'I can't believe you have this, I don't even remember having it taken. I need to take a photo of this,' she said, pulling out her phone. She turned the photo this way and that, until she was satisfied with the result in the low light, then snapped.

'Maybe we need an updated one too?' he said, sounding a little bashful.

'Definitely,' she said.

She sidled in close to him and he pressed his cheek to hers. She could feel the slight tickle of his facial hair as his face opened into a bright smile. Holding her phone at arm's length, she smiled in response to his face on her screen. Once the photo was taken, the smiles remained. They sat on the rug, close to the speakers, enjoying the sound of Spanish guitar music. The low volume, designed to respect Penny's sleep, inadvertently added a layer of intimacy to the already cosy surrounds. There they sat, devouring the rice pudding, making conversation which evolved from light-hearted to the deepest confessions of the soul, as effortlessly as the ferry Adelaide arrived on had cut through the waves.

When the last track on the last record gave way to the soft purr of the player's infinite revolution, Alec asked if Adelaide would stay the night. The two of them were slumped on the floor, in a nest of cushions, just one slow blink away from sleep. Adelaide wondered if she had in fact dozed off because the sound of Alec's voice, low though it was, startled her.

'Mmmm,' she murmured.

He helped her to her feet, and they walked to his bedroom, holding hands like children.

21

ALEC'S room came alive under the glow of the morning sun, the flimsy white curtains powerless against the dazzling light. Adelaide's limbs explored the bed, searching for Alec, but they found nothing. She lay there a moment, her eyes running over his various possessions. This was the first time she had been in Alec's bedroom in the daylight. She smiled, noticing an open book on his nightstand and imagined him lying in bed reading before sleep swept him away to his dreams. *His dreams of me*, she recalled, still in awe of this strange new reality. She heard the shower being turned on in the adjoining ensuite, slipped out from under the sheets and eased the bathroom door open.

'Room for one more?' she asked.

Alec turned and the sight of him wet and naked sent a warm pulse through her. His long eyelashes, slick with water, stuck together in mascara-like points.

'I'm going to be late for work, aren't I?' he asked, smiling as she stepped in beside him.

ALEC had indeed needed to make a hasty departure for work, which Adelaide tried her best not to laugh at. Now she sat drinking coffee in his kitchen and wondering if Penny would emerge. Her phone vibrated next to her, announcing a text from Celeste.

"Hi lovely, hope the trip was awesome! I know you're probably super jet-lagged but any chance you could swap some shifts with me?"

Adelaide replied to say she was still away, was sorry she couldn't help and would see her in a few days. By the time Adelaide finished her coffee, Penny still hadn't woken, so she gathered her belongings and set off in the direction of her room. Melancholy descended as she imagined the moment she would have to leave but, recalling Alec's sentiments, she quickened her pace and tried to outrun it. Cora and Dave would be heading off today. She made for the restaurant, hoping to catch them at breakfast.

Adelaide walked through the pergola of magenta bougainvillea and into the restaurant. Time and familiarity had done nothing to dampen the effect that this view had on her. She sighed, thinking of the bleak Melbourne winter and bleak Melbourne life she would return to.

'There's our girl!' Dave called out.

'We thought we'd miss you,' said Cora, pulling out a chair at their table.

'We looked for you the other night, wasn't DJ Allora banging?' Dave asked, eyes sparkling at the memory.

'She was amazing,' Adelaide replied, not having the heart to tell them that she'd missed the entire set.

'And her announcement!' said Cora, eyes wide. 'The internet is buzzing about it.'

'Yeah?' said Adelaide.

Cora and Dave nodded enthusiastically.

'Well, I'm glad I caught you anyway. It was really great hanging out. Well, most of the time,' she said, rubbing her hip with a grimace.

They all chuckled.

'Well, give us your email. If we're ever down under we can all climb the Sydney Harbour Bridge together!' said Dave, handing over his phone.

ADELAIDE was still waving at the Aston Martin as it shrank into the horizon when she heard Xena's familiar voice.

'*Kalimera.*'

'*Kalimera.* Heading home?' Adelaide asked.

Xena nodded, lighting a cigarette. 'What are you doing today?'

'Actually, I have no idea,' said Adelaide.

'Want to come and help us time the embroidery work?' said Xena, smirking.

'You know what? Yes, I do,' said Adelaide.

It was a better prospect than being alone with her thoughts.

They walked across the carpark and paused next to Xena's quad bike while she finished her cigarette.

'Alessia is looking at a house for us this morning. I think it's too big but she says she wants to put in a recording studio so she can continue producing for other artists,' said Xena.

'Gosh, what an amazing place to come and record music,' said Adelaide.

Xena shrugged and stamped out her cigarette, clearly unable to appreciate the astounding beauty of where she lived.

Xena strapped her belongings onto the back of the bike and climbed on. Adelaide followed and soon they left the coastline behind. Adelaide threw her head back, enjoying the sensation of the warm wind ruffling her hair. The trees became thicker as they climbed, creating a canopy that filtered the bright morning sunshine, making the road look like the glittering surface of a lake.

Xena pulled into the town square and parked the bike alongside a cluster of Vespas and other quads. Adelaide looked over discreetly at the same gathering of men she had noticed during her first visit to Xena's home. Every pair of eyes were focused on them and Adelaide could have sworn she heard muttering. Xena had already climbed off the bike and was striding towards the church, her jaw tilted at a jaunty angle, her eyes locked straight ahead. Adelaide clambered off the bike and hurried after her friend, falling into step beside her as they disappeared from the group's view.

'Poú eísai, Mamá?' Xena yelled into the house.

Xena's mother called out from the kitchen and Xena headed in. Adelaide, unsure of whether she should follow, stayed standing in the lounge room feeling superfluous and awkward. The women's whispered exchange was so quiet that Adelaide wasn't sure she could have made out any of the words, even if they had been spoken in English. She wondered if she should leave but, having no way to get back to Ilios Choros, was forced to stay. Eventually, Xena's mother emerged to greet Adelaide, her face arranged into a welcoming smile. Xena trailed behind wearing a scowl.

Seated at the kitchen table, the women scrutinised Giovanna's working drawings before Xena marked out the designs onto small pieces of linen. They chatted and drank aromatic mountain tea, all the while stitching and timing their work. Adelaide, having nothing else to contribute, entered the times and order quantities into their spreadsheet and made sure no one's teacup was empty. She estimated how long the entire order would take to complete and compared it to Giovanna's launch date.

'I'm just not sure you can get an order this size completed in time,' said Adelaide, evaluating the numbers, 'even if you have your *theia* working with you.'

A crease formed between Adelaide's eyebrows. Had she inadvertently lured everyone into something unrealistic?

Xena turned to her mother and said something in rapid Greek, to which she replied nodding.

'We have more women, we could practically ask anyone in this town. Everyone has this skill,' said Xena with an air of nonchalance.

'Well, okay then,' Adelaide said, relaxing. She looked over her spreadsheet and thought about how easy it would be to manage all these variables in an App. She chewed absentmindedly on her nail, watching Xena's deft hands manipulate the needle like a conductor's baton.

The front door clicked open and Adelaide felt the two women tense.

The dark sinewy man who stalked into the kitchen was barely taller than Adelaide, yet he seemed to fill the small space and push out all the oxygen. He spat out a string of Greek words, as if they were bitter in his mouth. Xena's mother rose, trying to swat him away, her fearful eyes occasionally darting towards Adelaide, who lowered her gaze so that her face was practically parallel with the table. She felt as though she was intruding and should leave, but the only way out of the small kitchen was past Xena's irate father so she remained sitting, holding her breath and trying to make herself small. Xena sat, her eyes locked on an invisible point in front of her. Her father leant down to yell directly into her ear, spittle spraying from his mouth. He straightened, noticing Adelaide for the first time, and thrust out a hand towards her as he continued to bark at Xena. Adelaide looked up at him wide-eyed and paralysed, until Xena stood to yell at him with the same ferocity he had unleashed upon her. Finally, she picked up the small stack of embroidery samples and shook them in his face. Xena's father leant down to place his palms on the table and glare at Adelaide. She gulped involuntarily.

'You. You are the one filling their heads with stupid ideas. Do these look like businesswomen to you?' he growled in a thick accent, cocking his head towards his wife and daughter.

He snatched the fabric swatches from Xena and threw them down on the table in disgust, a couple of them landing in Adelaide's lap.

Rage surged from the pit of Adelaide's stomach. 'Yes, as a matter of fact, they do,' she said, her face steely.

He scoffed and Xena's mother, sensing that his energy was waning, successfully shooed him out of the kitchen. She turned, her eyes brimming with tears and tried to placate Xena's anger with a quick succession of low murmured phrases. Xena turned her back.

'He is old fashioned,' said Eleni, addressing Adelaide in a desperate tone. 'He feels that Xena has disrespected him. Even in this small town, the internet, everyone knows about Xena and this… musician.'

'Her name is Alessia, and he can go to hell,' said Xena, packing the laptop and fabric samples into her backpack.

She disappeared into the depths of the house and returned with another bag, stuffed with clothes.

'He just needs time, he will come around,' said Eleni, desperately.

Adelaide was unclear if Eleni was suggesting that Xena's father would come around to his daughter's sexuality or the notion that his wife was becoming an entrepreneur, but now wasn't the time to clarify.

Eleni placed a timid hand on her daughter's shoulder but was instantly rebuffed. A thin veil of torment descended upon her weary face. Adelaide cast her eyes downward to inspect her sandals.

'He's a pig,' Xena spat, storming out of the kitchen.

Adelaide gave Eleni's arm an encouraging squeeze before jogging to catch up with Xena.

ADELAIDE felt foolish pressed in close to Xena on the back of the quad bike. She could sense Xena seething, and it felt wrong. Adelaide was torn between compromising her personal safety and infringing on her friend's privacy, which resulted in her holding on to Xena in pulses that coincided with tight bends and acceleration. Adelaide thought about what Xena's father had said, about her filling their heads with ideas. There was only one way to change small minds like his and that was to succeed despite their disapproval. Adelaide decided that he would eat his words and she hoped they tasted as bitter going in as they had sounded coming out. Xena pulled the bike over to the side of the road and killed the engine. She turned and

Adelaide could see that her face was tear-streaked and blotchy.

'I'm sorry,' she said, so quietly that Adelaide almost missed it.

'You have literally nothing to be sorry about,' said Adelaide.

'He's just such a…'

'He sure is,' Adelaide agreed.

Xena smiled.

'The way I see it, my darling, you have two options.'

Xena looked at Adelaide with curious eyes.

'You can either move in with the woman you love and start a successful business, or…'

'Or?' said Xena, beginning to laugh a little.

'Or you'll have to come and live with me in Australia.'

Xena sniffed and laughed. 'Plan B, huh?'

'Plan B.'

Xena wiped her eyes with the back of her hand and nodded thoughtfully. 'And you?' she asked, furtively.

'Me?'

'What's your Plan B?'

Adelaide thought for a moment, feeling a knot form in the back of her throat.

Xena went on. 'You're busy teaching me and my mother how to be independent but you're planning to return home to Joe. To what? Pretend that nothing has happened? To pretend that you're happy?'

Adelaide felt a sudden flare of animosity towards Xena, toward her simplistic, ideological judgment of her.

As if reading her thoughts, Xena went on. 'Look, I'm not judging you. I can't pretend to understand how having children complicates things. But shouldn't we make the choices that are right, not the ones that are easy?'

'There are no easy options that I can see,' said Adelaide shortly. 'We should head back.'

ONCE back at Ilios Choros, Adelaide said a cool goodbye to Xena. As her feet crunched across the gravel, she could feel Xena's eyes on her until she walked through the gate and out of view. Adelaide wondered if perhaps she had painted Joe in a harsher light than he deserved. Apart from the recent betrayal, Joe had been an adequate husband and he loved his children more than anything. Perhaps this whole mess was the wake-up call they needed to build a stronger and happier partnership? They could go to couple's counselling like Rosemary and Adam. Those two had been through the wringer and it looked like they were coming out the other side more committed than ever. It was like the pain of their experience had stripped everything bare, clearing the way to create something more authentic. The sale of Grasp Digital would be finalised soon, so she and Joe would have the resources to dedicate to the rehabilitation of their marriage. Xena was young and idealistic, she had no idea of the complexities Adelaide faced.

Adelaide was so lost in thought that she all but walked past Penny who was coming back from the beach, a striped towel slung over her tanned shoulder.

'Hey!' said Penny, gesticulating wildly.

'Oh my God. Hi! I'm so sorry, I was a million miles away.'

'That's a long way,' said Penny with a quizzical look.

'Where are you headed?' Adelaide asked.

'I was going to go back to Alec's and text you. He's working tonight. Do you want to hang out? I go back to Athens tomorrow.'

'That sounds perfect. Do you want me to come now or meet you later?'

'I just need a shower. Give me an hour?'

AS Adelaide stepped into her hotel room, she was gripped by a surreal sense of displacement. It seemed so long since she had been here, or was it another person in another life? Her sequined dress lay in a glittering heap on the floor where she'd discarded it before taking Joe's Skype call. Adelaide thought of returning home and was engulfed by dread. Was her life as neat as a puzzle? Waiting for her, the missing piece, to slot back in? Or was she so altered that the entire picture would have to change to accommodate the person she had become? She kicked off her sandals and crawled onto the bed to rest her weary head.

A text sounded from her back pocket, and she lay there a while, unmoving, trying to predict who it could be from. Her phone, sensing her procrastination, was silent. She was so invested in her pointless game that the second alert of the text startled her, and she felt embarrassed, even though she was alone. She retrieved her phone and read, "Our bed feels so empty without you. Can't wait for you to come home."

Adelaide stared at her phone, unsure how to respond. This was the first time Joe had ever sent her a text like this. A text that wasn't operational. A text that told her he was thinking only of her. She tried desperately to stifle the pettiness that welled up in her and was shouting, *Your bed was pretty warm while Kim was in it, Joe!* She lay there a while, tears spilling from her clamped eyes, indulging her heartbreak. Leaving the text unanswered, she decided that the best course of action was a hot shower and a change of clothes.

22

ALEC'S front door opened to reveal Penny sporting the same pink, freshly scrubbed face and wet hair that Adelaide wore herself. She made way for Adelaide to enter, and they walked through the lounge room into the kitchen.

'Wine?' Penny asked.

Adelaide nodded. She had an overwhelming desire to get drunk. Very drunk.

Penny grabbed a bottle of white wine from the fridge and gestured to the cupboard. 'Glasses are in there. Let's sit outside,' said Penny, disappearing out the back door.

Adelaide followed with two glasses and stepped out of the kitchen into the lush private space, taking a seat on a weather-beaten lounge chair. Penny poured the wine.

'That was one hell of a party,' said Penny. 'It was totally worth the hangover.'

Adelaide laughed.

'I miss the old days. I could party and work and party and work and all I felt was...'

'Young,' said Adelaide, finishing the thought.

'Exactly,' said Penny, laughing and extending her arm so they could clink glasses. 'I can't believe you and my brother!' she said, sticking out her tongue and scrunching up her nose in jest.

'And I can't believe that we've both had a crush on each other this whole time,' said Adelaide.

'I thought you had better taste,' said Penny, her eyes dancing with mischief.

'It's actually impossible for me to imagine a more perfect man,' said Adelaide, before she could filter herself.

'Well, maybe you two can work something out. Love is all you need, right? Or are the Beatles totally full of shit after all?'

'If only that was an option,' Adelaide murmured.

'So, what? You shake hands and say goodbye and go back to being pen pals?'

'Maybe. Although after all of this I'm not sure how Joe will feel about my choice in pen pals.'

'Joe?' said Penny, snapping her head to look at Adelaide.

'He wants to get back together, says he made a huge mistake.'

Penny clenched her jaw and looked into her wine glass. 'Have you told Alec?' she asked.

'No, but… what difference will it make? The outcome is the same for him. I still leave in a few days.'

Penny bit her bottom lip and gave a restrained shake of her head. 'He would never have…' She sighed gruffly. 'He would never have… *pursued* you if you were married. If you were *staying* married.'

Her voice was even and measured, the kind of tone designed to conceal profound irritation.

Adelaide felt a cold sweat bloom over her skin. She was suddenly acutely aware that Penny was Alec's sister first and foremost, and her friend only secondary to that. She had confessed too much and now the whole situation threatened to spiral out of her control.

'Was this whole thing just to make your husband jealous?' asked Penny.

'Well, I mean… No. Kind of,' Adelaide stammered.

'I see.'

'No, you've got it wrong. I mean, when I came here, I *had* hoped that Joe would miss me and come to his senses. But then, this thing with Alec. I had no idea he was even interested in me in that way. God, I don't know anymore. The whole world is completely upside down,' said Adelaide, hopelessly.

A long and deafening silence followed in which even the breeze seemed to hold its breath. Finally, Penny spoke, 'The whole world isn't upside down, Adele, only you.'

Adelaide wasn't sure why this retort stung so badly, but she felt as though the verbal punch was physical. She sat in silence a moment, clutching her wine glass so hard that her fingertips turned white. She felt foolish and wanted to retreat.

Beside her, Penny visibly seethed.

Adelaide wished her body would turn to sand and blow away.

'You must have a lot of packing to do,' said Adelaide, her words like glue in her mouth.

'Yes, I do,' said Penny, drawing her knees into her chest and cradling them with her free hand.

Adelaide set down her wine glass and rose. 'Thanks for the wine. It really was nice to see you. I'm sorry I…'

Penny turned her head slightly away from Adelaide, which had the curious effect of muting her mid-sentence.

Adelaide sighed and skulked away into the night, thankful that she was leaving the day after Penny and wouldn't have to endure an entire ferry ride with her tomorrow.

If Adelaide had felt the urge to get drunk at the beginning of the evening, then she was hell-bent on it now. She racked her brain trying to remember if Xena had mentioned whether she'd be working at Tazo tonight. The prospect of remaining sober was infinitely more terrifying than the risk of running into Xena, so Adelaide decided to scope out the bar in the hopes that someone else was working.

Adelaide rounded the now familiar corner and hid behind the taxidermy zebra, scanning the small space for Xena. She was peering between its ears, feeling completely ridiculous, when a group of tanned boys approached from behind, startling her so thoroughly she jumped. They shot her odd looks and one of them muttered something under his breath to the others, sending a muffled ripple of laughter through the group. Adelaide dropped her head and exhaled loudly before straightening and walking in behind them. She took a seat at the bar, noting with no small measure of relief that the bartender was a squat young man with a penchant for facial manscaping and Xena was nowhere in sight.

A short time later, a cluster of shot glasses and disfigured lemon wedges lay before Adelaide, her left hand crusted with salt. It had been more than a decade since she had drunk tequila and she'd forgotten how it burned her throat like a liquid insult. Tonight, the unpleasantness of it seemed poetic to her, as though this was actually what she deserved. Adelaide felt her head loll and could hear herself enunciating words in an attempt to conceal her extreme intoxication. As she ordered another, she realised that she was beginning to sound like she was from England and laughed before saying, 'Oh helloooooooo,' to herself in a caricatured impersonation of Queen Elizabeth. She laughed stupidly, before rearranging her face into a shape she hoped resembled that of a serious person.

'Well, what's all this?'

Adelaide turned to see two Alecs smiling down at her, but neither of them would stand still. She closed one eye and tilted her head up. 'Uh oh,' she said.

'You look like a pirate,' he said, amused.

'Well in that case… Arrrgghhhh.'

'It might be time for you to go home,' said Alec.

She nodded solemnly, turning her mouth into an arc. 'Home to Joe,' she muttered.

Adelaide felt so tired, she closed her eyes, lost her balance and head-butted Alec in the chest. He caught her and helped her into a standing position. 'I'll walk you back to your room.'

'Everybody is mad at me,' she said, dragging her feet beside him. 'It's because I'm the worst and you're the best. But of course, I love you. I always love you. But it doesn't matter what I love. No, no, no. It never matters what I love.'

They arrived at her door and Alec rummaged in her bag, located her key and unlocked the door. Adelaide squinted up at the pink neon sign which implored her once more to "Trouble the Darkness".

'What does that even mean?' she yelled in vain.

23

ADELAIDE woke in stages. Her brain was first but, due to the unholy throbbing in her temples, it did not alert her eyes, which remained closed. Her mouth was so dry that when she attempted to moisten it there was an audible *click*, like a boot treading through mud. She wanted to groan but even that felt like an effort too great to muster. She remained still, hoping that sleep would reclaim her but in the spirit of the way things were going, she remained wide-awake. A wedge of light spliced through the ajar bathroom door, dimly illuminating the space. She sat up slowly and shuffled to the bathroom where she drank cold water directly from the faucet.

An hour later, Adelaide had managed to down paracetamol and shower. She sat on the edge of her bed trying to remember how she had gotten home. She had a vague sense that she had seen Alec, but it could easily have been a dream. She rummaged around in the rumpled sheets for her phone. The text from Joe remained unanswered so she replied, "Can't wait to come home," which was partially true now that all her friends were furious with her. Maybe she should just hide in her room until it was time to leave tomorrow? Adelaide felt sick to her core and had a nagging suspicion that it was more than the hangover at work. She had acted unkindly towards Xena, who was clearly just trying to help. Adelaide had been petulant and felt ashamed. She could not leave without trying to make amends. She texted Xena apologising for her behaviour and received a reply instantly. "Don't be silly, no need for apologies. BTW—we got the house!!" Xena's text did more to sooth her pounding head than the pills she had just taken. Feeling buoyed, she ventured to text Penny and apologise to her also but, although the message displayed a read receipt, she received no reply.

After making plans to meet Xena that afternoon, Adelaide chewed pensively on her thumbnail, desperately trying to recall how she got home last night. She tried to conjure the memory of it only to have the images crumble and turn to dust in her mind. Fatigued by her efforts, every tiny movement sent jolts of nausea through her. She lay back on the bed and stared up at the ceiling, the timber knots in the ancient crossbeams morphing into sinister faces. She drifted into a fitful sleep and dreamed of dancing devils and a blazing fire. A shrill scream rang out as the flames flickered higher consuming the beasts, and Adelaide woke with a start to hear her text tone. "I think you may have drunk all the tequila at Tazo last night. How are you feeling?" It was from Alec.

DESPITE her sunglasses, Adelaide squinted in the bright afternoon sunshine as she exited her room. She felt like an astronaut taking her first steps on an alien planet. Every breath, every step, laborious. She picked her way along the path towards Alessia's villa, making impossible resolutions regarding alcoholic abstinence. She longed to return home to her children, to their insatiable need for attention, which would cocoon her from her own self-absorbed neuroticism. She missed them, she missed who she was when she was with them. Stoic, dependable, selfless, loving. Not the self-sabotaging train wreck of a person who was currently debating whether or not to throw up in an agave bush. She stood regarding the plant, whose glossy green leaves glistened with a vitality that Adelaide could never hope to match. She thought back over her text exchange with Alec. She had tried to sound self-deprecating and even flippant, to deflect from the shame she felt over her extreme inebriation the night before. She wondered what Penny had told him by now. The anticipation of their impending dinner date niggled at the frayed edges of her mind.

When Adelaide arrived at Alessia's villa, she and Xena were just about to pop a bottle of champagne.

'To celebrate our new house and Xena's new business,' Alessia explained, smiling broadly.

Alessia offered Adelaide the first glass but the sight of it made her stomach turn. She declined but offered up her sincerest congratulations.

'Giovanna has accepted the quote and the timeline. We will start the order and when we are ready to invoice, our business registration should be finalised,' said Xena.

'It's just so wonderful,' said Adelaide.

Coming here had been the right decision. If she remained in her hotel room, as every cell in her body had instructed, she would be drowning in a pool of self-pity right now.

'And the house?'

'It's vacant so we move in immediately. Maybe next time you visit Ikaria you can stay with us. The house is big enough,' said Xena, flashing a look at Alessia who nodded sarcastically in response.

Adelaide smiled and nodded but inwardly she knew she would probably never come back. Would she ever even see these people again?

'I have some work to do,' said Alessia, before retreating to the bedroom.

'Let's go outside,' said Xena, picking up her glass and cigarettes off the kitchen counter.

They sat beside each other on the polished cement bench-seat overlooking the fire pit. Xena flicked a cigarette from the soft crumpled pack and studied it. 'I'm sorry about yesterday, I know I offended you,' she began, cautiously.

'No, I'm sorry. I acted like a brat. I have no idea what the hell I'm meant to do, you know? Nobody plans for this shit when they get married and have children,' said Adelaide.

The two sat in silence ignoring the majestic vista.

'I can't just cut him loose—Joe I mean—I have to at least try to move past this. If there's even a ten percent chance that I can avoid telling my kids that their parents are splitting, then I'm going to take it.'

'And Alec?' Xena asked, still fingering the unlit cigarette.

'I've held Alec in my heart for twenty years…' Adelaide began, but her constricted throat prevented her from going on. She dropped her head and Xena placed an arm around her. Adelaide slumped against her friend and scrunched her eyes tight. 'I have to tell him tonight,' she whispered.

24

ADELAIDE scanned the crowd of diners looking for Alec's face. Her whole body felt at odds with her environment, like a transplanted organ slowly being rejected. Adelaide wasn't sure where her hangover ended and her dread began, but they were in league to destroy her. She looked around at the sun-kissed faces of the restaurant's patrons and fought hard not to despise them. A toothy American threw her head back emitting a raucous laugh in response to, what one could only assume was, the greatest joke ever told. Adelaide made a move to step forward and almost collided with a waiter labouring under a burden of dinner plates. Predicting the outcome of her trajectory she redirected her foot backwards and teetered slightly before being steadied by a large and reassuring presence. Alec had appeared at her side, placing a hand at her elbow. She looked up at him and felt as though she were melting over and over into oblivion like a surrealist painting. She attempted a weak smile but wasn't sure if she landed it. He smiled at her, and she thought she saw a flicker of melancholy in it. *Let him be mad at me*, she silently begged.

'Shall we?' he asked.

Adelaide managed to nod.

He pulled out a chair for her and she could barely stand herself under the glare of his innate kindness. She sat.

'Shots?' he asked, picking up the menu.

All but his eyes were concealed, and she could see his smile at their corners.

She groaned and covered her face with one hand. 'Never again as long as I live.'

He laughed. 'So, were you celebrating or commiserating last night?' he asked.

Adelaide felt her eyes burning. *How many tears can one person cry?* She smiled sadly, trying to communicate all that she felt for him with a single look. How her heart would break itself on a ceaseless loop every day for the rest of her life, every time she thought of him. How her heart wasn't her own, how it belonged to her children. How she would not only miss him, but herself in response to him.

He reached out and placed a hand on her arm. 'It's okay, I understand,' he said, softly.

'I'm not just going home tomorrow. I'm going home... I'm going home to Joe.'

'I know,' he said.

They sat in silence a while. A silence that Adelaide could feel herself drowning in. She must have been looking at him expectantly because when he spoke, he tried to explain. 'I would be lying if I said I wasn't disappointed that you are returning to Joe. I could beg you to stay. I could tell you that I can make you happy, but I would be deluding us both.'

Adelaide leaned in to hear Alec's quiet words in the din of the crowded restaurant.

'The fact that I love you, have always loved you somewhere in my heart, shouldn't matter. I am not going to compete for you, Adele. I am not going to add to your obvious turmoil, by demanding you choose me.'

Adelaide realised that her wish for Alec to turn on her was completely in vain. She was not surprised to discover that his light shone brighter, through darkness.

Her face must have been contorted to stifle an outpouring of emotion because Alec's face suddenly inclined towards her, slipping out of the seriousness he had worn just a moment ago and said, 'So... we are two old friends having dinner together, one last time.'

She let out an involuntary sputter that was somewhere between laughter and tears.

ADELAIDE was astonished to find that after the excruciating anticipation of her confession, the remainder of the evening passed pleasantly. She chose to skirt around the subject of her impending reunion with Joe, side stepping it like the gargantuan elephant it was. Instead, she focused on how excited she was to see the twins. Adelaide idly worried that she was being one of those exasperating parents who gush about their children, believing them to be more remarkable than other children, but she hardly cared. She was so close to holding their wriggly bodies and peppering them with kisses, that she could barely contain her excitement. Alec talked about his upcoming plans for the resort and how much press attention Alessia's bombshell had garnered.

'We are completely booked out for the rest of the year, even through winter. And we're looking at hosting a whole calendar of parties next summer. Alessia has so many connections, and with her planning to start producing music here...' he trailed off, noticing Adelaide staring dreamily at him. 'What?' he asked, cocking his head self-consciously.

Adelaide, who hadn't realised she was staring, blushed. 'No, nothing. I mean, it's great, I'm so interested, that is… It's really interesting to hear you talk.'

She inwardly winced at the sound of her own voice but pushed through.

'It's going to be quite the hive of activity over at Alessia and Xena's place. Xena is poised to become a textile mogul,' said Adelaide.

'Thanks to you and your crazy ideas!' said Alec, smiling broadly.

Adelaide smiled into her water glass and took a sip. There was a comfortable pause in conversation and they each took in their bustling surroundings. The vast inky blackness of the ocean gave the effect that they were suspended in an orb of glittering light, adrift in the night sky.

'So, you would like me to drive you to the port tomorrow?' Alec asked finally.

Adelaide felt the lump rise in her throat again and was unsure how to answer. She wanted to reach for his hand, feel it envelope hers but she knew she shouldn't. She thought about sitting in close proximity to him for the entire journey, how she would be able to feel him breathing next to her.

'Oh, that's not necessary. Xena actually offered to take me, so…'

He nodded, offering a rueful smile. He looked around the wreckage of their dinner plates and asked, 'Dessert?'

Adelaide shook her head realising that they would soon part ways, probably forever.

'I will walk you back to your room,' he said.

'No,' she said, too quickly.

She reached out to cover his hand with hers and the warmth of his skin tugged on a thread that threatened to unravel her. She tried again. 'No… I just don't think I can bear…'

He placed his free hand over hers, silencing her, then lifted it to his lips. He closed his eyes and Adelaide noticed that his dark lashes were slick with tears. She reached her free hand across the table to touch his face before standing. His eyes remained closed, his face cast down. She walked away, her world imploding.

25

THE Kombi screeched to an abrupt halt, disrupting a group of competing seagulls locked in a disagreement over the rightful ownership of a discarded souvlaki. Adelaide took in the port and felt reflective. She turned to Xena, searching for words that would express how much her friendship meant. Adelaide had been set adrift in a cruel and unforgiving sea and Xena had appeared like an unexpected lifeline.

'Xena…' Adelaide began, her eyes welling.

'I know, me too,' said Xena quickly and drew her in for a rough hug.

Adelaide laughed, she would miss this gruff young woman who concealed so much warmth.

They climbed out of the van and Adelaide gathered her belongings.

'Try to hold onto your bag this time, eh?' said Xena.

Adelaide laughed. 'Goodbye, Xena.'

'*Yassas,* Adele.'

ADELAIDE had Skyped her family before checking out of Ilios Choros that morning. Their excited faces jostled for space on her phone's screen and she laughed at their exuberance about her return. Adelaide had left under the pretence of preparing herself for a divorce, but now she was on the cusp of returning to a life that would remain unchanged. It was like experiencing a deeply disturbing dream and then waking to discover that everything is as it should be, only you can't shake the last wisps of disconcertion. On the surface, Adelaide was getting everything she hoped for. Her husband had repented, and her family would remain intact. Why then did she feel more like a prison inmate on death row? To make matters worse, her brain was repeatedly recasting perfect strangers as Alec. First, he was checking tickets at the pier. Then, he was a refreshment vendor, lazily mixing frappes. Now, he was a honeymooner taking endless photos of his new wife, her hair whipping around her face in the wind. Adelaide closed her eyes, allowing the man with the camera to change back to who he really was. Adelaide's body was leaden. She resisted the urge to hurl herself off the side of the boat and into a watery slumber.

Having dozed off, Adelaide was roused by a booming bilingual announcement that they had arrived at Mykonos. She jolted awake, and then, realising where she was, felt a rush of adrenalin at the idea that she could disembark here and return to Alec. *If this was a movie, I would*, and then, *If this was a movie I wouldn't be a mother of two, nearing middle age.*

TRAPPED in a ceaseless waking dream, Adelaide seemed to journey upon every mode of transportation ever invented. She was now about to board a plane for the final leg of her journey home. Her phone battery had died, leaving her disconnected and anxious. She shuffled onto the plane with her fellow passengers and took her seat in a bank of three with a woman no more than twenty. She chattered excitedly in the first few hours of their flight, eventually petering out to what, at first, was an uncomfortable silence by sheer contrast. Adelaide couldn't help but be reminded of her younger self, owing more to the practically hypnotic state of reflection she was now in, rather than any tangible parallels. She looked at the young woman and wondered at the ebbs and flows that were inevitably stretched out before her. How would she navigate them? Would she prevail? How many times would her heart be broken by the time she was Adelaide's age?

With an unoccupied seat between them, the women ended up in a disconnected yin and yang configuration, so close together and yet never touching. Adelaide drifted in and out of sleep, each short cycle yielding yet another bizarre dream that lingered for a moment before dissolving. She woke again, unable to get comfortable on her injured hip, and received a piercing eyeful of bright dawn sunshine from the window shade being opened in the row ahead. She squinted around the cabin at her fellow passengers in their crooked positions, their open mouths glistening with drool at the edges. Bodies straightened, and plastic groaned all around, as more window shades were pushed upward, revealing the sunbathed clouds below. Adelaide opened her own shade and peered downward at the verdant countryside. The rolling, tree-covered hills looked no more authentic than the felt-covered landscapes meticulously crafted by model train enthusiasts. She had vowed to stop dipping into her memories of Alec once she arrived home. She owed it to her family to be present with them, not only in body, but in mind too. Now she gently closed her eyes trying to conjure how he looked, how he felt, how he smelled, how her body unfurled and beckoned in response to him. Already, she feared the images had lost their sharpness and that soon they would fade completely.

'Tea or coffee this morning, ladies?'

A glossy-haired air hostess appeared holding up a stainless-steel jug. Adelaide stared at her for a moment. Clearly the pot she held only contained one of the beverages, but which one? Adelaide's seatmate muttered something inaudible before repositioning herself to continue snoozing. The air hostess looked at Adelaide expectantly, a false eyelash beginning to peel away from one heavily made-up eye.

'Tea or coffee?' she tried again.

'Tea. No, coffee! No, tea. I want tea.'

'Tea will be a sec,' she said, indicating another crew member making his way down the aisle. Adelaide felt as though she had failed some kind of test.

DESPITE Adelaide's protestations, Joe had insisted that he would pick her up from the airport. She navigated her way through customs, deciding that having "Nothing to Declare" would be her position towards Joe. She made her way past the stern looking officers. *Why do people in uniform make me feel so guilty?* The double doors opened to reveal a railing over which bored-looking people leant limply, awaiting family and friends that one could only assume they didn't like very much. She scanned the faces, aware that she was holding up the flow of passengers who spilled through the doors. Seeing no one familiar, she veered left and made her way along the line, feeling as though she was a contestant on a reality TV show about to walk into some unknown prank.

'Adelaide!'

Her own name sounded odd to her and she flinched. She was so accustomed to being Adele. She turned to see Joe, holding a comically large bunch of flowers, flanked by the twins. He leant down to them and pointed as they looked around frantically for her. Darcy spotted her first and took flight. Estée followed a beat behind. Adelaide crouched down in anticipation, bracing herself for impact. They knocked into her at full speed and she absorbed the impact expertly. She breathed them in, the sweet clean smell of them. She couldn't stop kissing their doughy cheeks and nuzzling into their necks.

'My babies, I missed you,' she said, her eyes filling with tears.

Joe ambled over and looked down at them. Adelaide's bones turned to rubber, and she closed her eyes. She hid her face in Estée's soft waves, wishing she could float away on them. Darcy wriggled free and launched into the middle of a story about a dead possum found at Nanna's house. Adelaide mustered her courage and stood, meeting Joe's eyes. He held the flowers out to her—a giant bunch of pink-centred, white lilies. Adelaide had always found their perfume oppressively strong. So much so, they once gave her a blood nose. She forced a smile and accepted them.

'Hello, Joe,' she said, in a voice that was not her own.

He leant in tentatively to kiss her under the watchful gaze of two sets of eyes. She offered her cheek, despite his trajectory aiming at her lips. They each understood their misjudgment a moment too late and fumbled. Adelaide emitted a strange, forced laugh, before Joe successfully deposited a hasty peck on her cheek. If he was crestfallen, he didn't show it. He took charge of her luggage trolley and led them towards the exit, Adelaide feeling like the runner-up in a beauty pageant, under the burden of the pungent blooms.

THE morning sky was draped overhead like an over-laundered bed sheet. She thought of the black velvet Ikarian sky that would be dotted with twinkling stars now but blinked the image away, knowing that her mind would soon meander down the leafy path to Alec's door if she allowed it. As Joe drove them home, she shared simplified fragments of her trip, skewing the stories to highlight topics that the twins would find most interesting. Finally, they pulled into their driveway. Adelaide felt as though she was arriving on a movie set.

The feeling continued as she walked through the front door and surveyed her surroundings. She was struck with the disconcerting notion that the scale was wrong, but she wasn't sure if she was too large for the space, or too small. She breathed in deeply and the familiar, yet strange smell of home triggered a memory, but she wasn't sure of what. Her life, she supposed. She knew she was suffering from jetlag and that her perception of reality was coloured by it so she resolved to push through the bulk of the day and force her body clock to reset. She was determined to realign herself with her family.

Joe threw the car keys down onto the hall table, their clatter making her start. 'We've really missed you, the place just hasn't been the same without you,' he said, walking past her to the kitchen.

The breakfast dishes lay discarded across the bench, following a trail of toast crumbs, like Hansel and Gretel. The dishwasher door hung open revealing clean dishes that longed to be unpacked. Adelaide peered beyond to the dining table, which was littered with laundry and art supplies, to the sofa which was missing some cushions and strewn with last night's pyjamas. Adelaide felt weary.

'Mummy, we're hungry,' said Estée, appearing at her side. Adelaide smiled down at her and nodded.

Adelaide supposed it was a good thing that the house was in such disarray. Setting things right would keep her mind from wandering. She plugged in her dead phone and rolled up her sleeves.

ADELAIDE was lost in a maze of domestic duties. Each time she believed she was coming to the end, she would stumble upon yet another task, and another, and another, leading her in deeper. She and Joe hadn't had a moment alone to talk since she arrived home and Adelaide had the strange sensation that she had dreamt the whole scenario in which he was leaving her.

She padded downstairs after putting the twins to bed, her eyes feeling like they were being scooped out of their sockets, and sought out Joe. The television flickered with a generic action sequence, the volume turned down low, the rumble of Joe's snoring providing an alternate soundtrack. The scent of lilies wafted through the air, filling her nostrils with a sense of foreboding. She rubbed her hip absentmindedly, its sickly yellow tinge her only tangible evidence that she had not imagined the entire journey. She looked over at her phone, still plugged into the charger by the fridge. *Perhaps*, she thought like an addict trying to kick their habit, *I could just take a quick look at the photo of me and Alec.* She stood for a moment, thinking, listening to the tidal melody of the dishwasher's hum. Just a quick look and then she'd take herself up to sprawl across her bed, leaving Joe on the sofa.

She picked up her phone and unplugged it. The screen glowed bright in the low light, alerting her that two voicemails had been left while her phone was dead. She swiped and put the phone to her ear.

She heard a harried voice. It took her a beat to realise it was Celeste. But what was she saying? She punched the keypad to play the message again from the beginning.

'Adelaide, it's me. I just can't believe it. I mean, how can this have happened? I only took the day off because I had a stupid assignment due. She said she'd be fine without me. Oh my God. Oh my God. Call me when you get this.'

Adelaide was sure she was missing some key piece of information that had only escaped her because she was so very tired. What was Celeste on about? A disconcerting feeling burrowed into her sternum but Adelaide refused to acknowledge it in the hope that it would go away. Celeste had always been a bit on the flighty side, and this was just a classic example of her overreacting to some insignificant occurrence. She swallowed hard as a second voicemail began to play.

'Adelaide, this is Roger,' began a quavering, elderly voice, 'I'm calling to tell you...'

His voice broke and for a few seconds all that could be heard was laboured breathing, until he tried again. 'I'm calling to tell you that Ivy has had a fall. She isn't... She didn't make it, dear. She's gone.'

There was a string of unidentifiable sounds that could have been throat clearing or nose blowing or a combination of the two.

'We'll be holding a service the day after tomorrow. Celeste has all the details. She said you'd be back today. I'm sorry to leave a message like this, I was hoping to talk to you. You meant the world to her.'

There were more muffled sounds and then nothing.

Adelaide placed a steadying hand on the kitchen bench. Her mouth hung open slightly and her lips were dry.

She must be misunderstanding something. Ivy—more a mother than an employer—couldn't be dead. She scrunched her eyes tight and shook her head as if to clear it. She would listen to the voicemails again and this time pay better attention. Ivy would think this whole situation was a hoot, once Adelaide relayed it to her over espressos at work tomorrow.

26

SITTING in Rosemary's kitchen, Adelaide nursed a cup of tea as she watched the children playing in the backyard. Their noses were pink from cold, their dexterity severely impinged under the burden of their mittens.

'Better that than losing a finger to frostbite,' Rosemary joked, when Charlie protested their application.

Adelaide had imagined the moment she would share everything about her trip with Rosemary, but the revelation of Ivy's passing had eclipsed all else. Despite the lateness of the hour, Adelaide had phoned Celeste immediately after replaying her voicemails the night before. Her workmate answered in a slow drawling voice which, coupled with the unmistakable bar room din, told Adelaide that sorrows were being drowned. Despite Celeste's inebriation, Adelaide was able to gather that Ivy was descending the stairs at Retrograde, holding the excessively large ledger, and her heel got caught in the hem of the kaftan she was wearing. When she didn't arrive home on time, and didn't answer her phone, Roger drove to Retrograde and found her.

'He said she was unconscious but still breathing. She died on the way to hospital with Roger holding her hand,' said Celeste, her voice breaking on the last word.

It had been as if Celeste was speaking a different language and Adelaide's brain struggled to translate what she was saying, word by excruciating word. All at once, the meaning became clear and Adelaide felt all the energy of the universe contract into the size of a pinhead with the sharp, painful clarity of comprehension. She stood there, holding the phone up to her ear, her mouth moving slightly but emitting no sound.

She just couldn't reconcile the fact that Ivy had been afraid of her demise at the hand of Alzheimer's but instead fell to her death while descending the stairs she had been clomping down for the last twenty-seven years, holding a book she had forgotten they no longer used.

'It's all my fault,' Celeste said in halting, pitiful gulps. 'I should have been there.'

'Should have been there,' Adelaide repeated, entranced, before ending the call without saying goodbye.

She had covered her face with her hands and cried under the illumination of the range hood in the otherwise darkened house. The woman who had been like family to her was gone, and Adelaide couldn't even remember the last thing she had said to her.

'IT just goes to show,' said Rosemary, breaking through Adelaide's thoughts, 'it can all be over at any time. There's something so self-centred that happens in the aftermath of a loved-one's passing. I mean, everyone left behind just goes all introspective, taking stock of their own lives. It kind of disrupts the bubble, you know? Forces you to stop and acknowledge your own mortality.'

Adelaide nodded, disappointed to realise that her internal musings revealed her to be a cliché. Since learning of Ivy's passing, one question plagued her. *Is this really my best life?*

THE morning of Ivy's funeral was a rain-streaked Impressionist painting and Adelaide drove to the cemetery with her windscreen wipers on the highest speed. Having arrived early, she sat in her car a moment, steeling herself. The sound of the rain reverberated around her car like jeering and Adelaide was weary at the prospect of fighting her way through the rain to the burial plot. She rummaged around the back seat for her umbrella, somewhat restricted by her outfit. Roger had requested that mourners wear bright colours to honour Ivy's vibrancy. This was to be a celebration of her life not the mourning of her passing, he insisted. Adelaide thought it would be fitting to wear the very outfit she wore the day she met Ivy. After the children were asleep, she ventured out to the garage to rummage through her boxes of stored clothing. The collection represented the pieces that she couldn't bear to part with despite Joe's incessant teasing that prevented her from wearing them. Now she wore a 1960s A-line coat with Peter Pan collar and matching shift dress constructed from a heavy turquoise and gold-lamé brocade. The fabric was stiff and unyielding and the lamé fibres scoured her skin around the armholes. She was unable to locate the gold-buckled pilgrim pumps she used to wear with this outfit but suspected that her feet, like her waist, had gone up a size since having the twins. Having located the umbrella behind the driver's seat, and lost a few layers of skin to the abrasive personality of her shift dress, Adelaide placed her hand on the door handle and took a deep breath. Joe's stinging reaction to her attire, 'What are you going as?' still rang in her ears, making her question her choice.

It was at that moment that the rain chose to ease and come to a stop. Adelaide's eyes filled with tears, and she laughed. *Oh Ivy*, she thought, even though she was neither religious nor superstitious. All around her, car doors opened and brightly-dressed people emerged, emitting a flurry of delighted exclamations and spontaneous sing-song bursts of laughter, in response to the weather's about-face. *What unusual sounds to be greeted with at a cemetery, and just exactly what Ivy would have wanted.* She joined the parade of people snaking their way along the pathway into the grounds, their uncharacteristically cheerful garb confirming that they were all headed to the same plot. The clouds dispersed to reveal patches of blue while rainwater flowed away from the slick bitumen path, making the gutters sparkle in the sun. There was an irreverence about the unorthodox procession that Adelaide knew Ivy would have enjoyed immensely. Perhaps Roger was right, maybe they could celebrate rather than mourn. In the distance, Adelaide saw an elderly man step out from under a white marquee and extend his right arm in a beckoning wave.

Roger wore a royal-blue velvet jacket with shiny brass buttons, his silver hair covered by a fuchsia-coloured felt fedora which, along with the silk kerchief tied around his neck, Adelaide knew to be Ivy's. She smiled in his direction even though he was motioning to the group at large. To Roger's left, a hard-faced woman reprimanded her two sons for giggling as their father sat slouched, engrossed in his phone. Except for the boys' white runners, the family was entirely dressed in black.

Adelaide looked at the casket and tried not to imagine Ivy's shrivelled body within. It was gloriously hand painted with wide-eyed faces and crude animals, in rich autumnal tones—presumably the work of one of Ivy's friends. Adelaide scanned the crowd, trying to guess who the artist was and settled on a broad-faced, doughy woman whose own gigantic eyes resembled those depicted. She wore a roughly-tied velvet turban and huge disc earrings that whacked her in the cheeks with every turn of her head.

'Adelaide,' said Roger, walking towards her.

'Oh, Roger. I'm so...' she trailed off before deciding on a more positive angle. 'Ivy would have loved this,' she said, sweeping a hand across the scene. 'I'm just sorry she's not here to see it.'

'Oh, she's seeing it alright. She just badgered someone upstairs to turn off the rain,' he said, his watery eyes darting skyward as he laughed. 'Always telling everyone what to do,' he added, shaking his head.

A slim man, in a beautifully tailored mustard suit, stood off to the side and he caught Roger's eye.

'I'll leave you to greet your guests,' said Adelaide, giving his gnarled hands an encouraging squeeze before stepping away. Her heels sank into the sodden lawn, and she suspected her gait resembled that of a flamingo. Adelaide smoothed her outfit and surveyed the crowd. A small knot of attractive women, around Ivy's age, enjoyed a private reunion within the larger gathering. Adelaide wondered if they were friends from Ivy's days as an in-house model for George's Department store.

When Adelaide had begun working at Retrograde, she was astounded by the many lives Ivy had led. She was like a Russian nesting doll concealing layer after layer of interesting personas. Adelaide admired how Ivy managed to live all these lives, in addition to being a mother. Adelaide always felt as though her existence had diminished her mother's life, which is why she made sure the twins knew they were appreciated and valued in hers. She would often look at Darcy and Estée's bright, innocent faces and wonder how any parent could feel disappointed at their child's existence. Adelaide lived her entire life knowing she was a mistake.

Adelaide felt a small hand on her shoulder and turned to see Celeste wearing a forced smile. She leant in heavily to accept an embrace and Adelaide felt the younger woman's body relax into hers. She pulled away and looked down at herself, tracing her outfit with a double handed sweep. 'This is the best I could do,' she said, indicating her slate-coloured dress. 'My whole wardrobe is black, I'm from Melbourne for God's sake!'

'You look perfect,' said Adelaide, as her eye was caught by the arrival of two gentlemen wearing felt hats, trimmed with excessive plumes of feathers. The first man was abnormally tall and lanky, with a bushy set of mutton chops. The second man was rosy and rotund, the buttons on his paisley waistcoat visibly straining under the expansive girth of his midsection. Walking side by side, the odd pair resembled the number ten, which made Adelaide smile. *Where did all these exotic birds come from?* she wondered, falling in love with Ivy all over again for having been at the centre of such a menagerie.

'LET us gather now to farewell our dear friend,' a booming voice cut through the polite volume of chatter. All eyes turned toward a stout, middle-aged man, wearing a dark purple cape, who resembled a community theatre actor, playing Count Dracula. People shuffled under the marquee, allowing older guests to be seated on the white folding chairs placed at the front. Adelaide ushered Celeste into the gathering, all the while fingering the small packet of tissues in her coat pocket. Once the murmuring died down, The Count began.

'We are here today to farewell our dear friend Ivy,' he bellowed. 'Ivy is survived by her darling husband Roger, daughter Amy, son-in-law Kevin and grandsons, Rhys and Liam. But those who loved her were many and varied, and it is so touching to see all your beautiful faces here today as we celebrate the life of a truly extraordinary woman.'

He paused for effect, surveying the crowd.

'Now, Roger thought it might be fitting to see if anyone had any stories they'd like to share about Ivy. Please, only the family-friendly ones,' he said, chuckling preemptively at his own joke as others followed suit. 'Of course, our dear Roger will begin.'

Subdued sounds of encouragement rippled through the crowd as Roger rose laboriously to his feet and made his way to the front. He stood, silently regarding the guests for a moment. His eyes glistened with the promise of tears. Closing his eyes, he breathed in deeply. 'I've only loved one woman in my life, but folks, what a woman I chose!'

Cheers and loud clapping rose in a raucous wave, disturbing two spotted doves foraging in the grass nearby. Roger grinned through his square, black-framed spectacles, transforming him momentarily into a boy.

'The first time I saw Ivy, I was working as a lift operator in Georges.

I'd only just started working there a few months prior so it must have been 1963. She was riding the lift to the fourth floor, to interview for a job as a telephone operator. Well, I took one look at her and told her she should go straight to the open call-out they were having for house models that day. She thought I was flattering her, of course, but she took my advice anyway. House models earned four times what phone girls did back then, so when she got the job, she promised to treat me to lunch with her first paycheque. And well, we've been eating lunch together ever since.'

Everyone applauded as Roger removed his spectacles to dab his eyes with his handkerchief. He took his place next to his daughter, who offered him a tight-lipped smile.

Without prompting, a woman with raven-coloured hair and ruby lips, dressed entirely in clashing leopard prints, raised her hand and shouted, 'I've got one!'

'Please, regale us,' The Count boomed, his hand outstretched theatrically.

'I'm afraid it might be a shocking revelation,' she began salaciously, 'but our Ivy was once the mastermind of an ingenious racketeering operation.'

Good natured giggles and gasps rang out, encouraging The Leopardess to go on.

'Ivy and I were working at the magazine at the time. I was on reception, and she oversaw the print ads, and Ivy got to asking all the advertisers if they would send in samples of their accessories. Bags, and purses, and scarves were arriving by the box full. She'd give a few of them over for the fashion shoots and the rest she would take to Camberwell Market and sell.'

Laughter rippled through the gathering, some people doubled over or clutched their sides. The Leopardess, encouraged by the reaction her story elicited, added, 'I can still see her sitting on her little fold out stool in a sea of designer handbags. She paid for her first shop that way! You know, the little knick-knack store she had in Ivanhoe?'

Adelaide saw Roger's daughter give him a sharp look, in response to his own wheezing and thigh slapping, which he remained unaware of. At length, the raucousness died down and The Count once again addressed those gathered.

'Who will share next?' he asked, face still glowing from his own participation in the uproar.

Adelaide felt a rush of adrenaline pulse through her body and realised her hand was raised. 'Me,' she said, meekly. 'Me,' she tried again, more firmly.

'The floor is yours, my dear,' said The Count.

Adelaide picked her way to the front. She looked over at Roger who gave her an encouraging nod while, next to him, his daughter studied her ringed fingers. Adelaide was struck with the alarming realisation that she had no idea what to say. The collective seemed to be holding their breath, eyes unblinking, expectantly urging her to begin and ease their empathetic feelings of awkwardness.

'I'm Adelaide,' she began, in a quavering voice, 'I work with Ivy... worked with Ivy.'

A hearse passed by silently and Adelaide's eyes followed it. One of Ivy's grandsons sniggered, and she snapped her attention back to the group, startled to realise they were still waiting.

'Does anyone remember Ivy's old Sandman?' she asked the group at large.

Adelaide could see a few nods and smiles at the memory of the beat-up panel van that was once the makeshift mascot of Retrograde.

'When I first started working for Ivy, we would go driving around suburbs that were having hard rubbish collections. "Cruising for street treats" she used to call it,' said Adelaide, laughing.

Murmurs of recollection and appreciation rippled through the gathering.

'Well, it kind of became a tradition for us. We'd pack a lunch and get coffees and just drive around, talking. All while keeping an eye on the kerb for "treats". She had an eagle-eye too. She could home in on a teak sideboard like a sniper. And then out we'd jump and load it into the back. Ivy was strong too. The first time she hoisted up a leather armchair on her own, I just stood there gawking like an idiot until she told me to "Quit staring and open up the back!"'

Adelaide laughed at the recollection.

'Back then, our expeditions were fruitful. Not so many people appreciated mid-century modern decor. And then, it must have been about five years in, we'd been out so many times without finding so much as a lamp. So, I said to her, "Should we really keep going? Isn't it kind of a waste of time?" And she says to me, "But, darling, our best conversations happen when we're in the Sandman." I'd never really had anyone find me interesting before, let alone someone as...'

Adelaide's eyes filled with tears. She had intended her story to be humorous but now every face was offering her sympathetic smiles and sad nods. She looked at her shoes.

'Well...' said The Count, coming to her rescue, 'we have certainly all felt the warm glow of Ivy's attention at some point or other. Thank you, Adelaide, for sharing your beautiful memory with us.'

BACK at Roger's house, Adelaide stood holding a sandwich she wasn't eating and a glass of chardonnay she most definitely was drinking. She smiled weakly as strangers offered her kind smiles and words of condolence. She seemed to be over the worst of her jetlag, so she supposed the pain in her head, which felt like a too-tight bicycle helmet, was due to the unnatural amount of crying she had done since learning of Ivy's passing. In the small hours of the morning, she lay in her darkened room alone, thinking of how she had squandered her last days with Ivy in a cloud of self-absorption. She resented Joe, not only for putting her through all this upheaval for nothing but also for how his selfishness had robbed her of time with Ivy. What was more, Joe had made no attempt to talk to her about anything that had transpired, instead adopting a maddening "business as usual" strategy. Worse still, he would be flying to California this week to visit the headquarters of the company acquiring Grasp Digital. Adelaide looked down at the sandwich she held. The creamy chicken filling was beginning to ooze out of the sides owing to the warmth of her hands. She deposited it on a discarded plate piled with crusts and strawberry tops and tried not to think about whether Kim was still working at Grasp. Surely Joe couldn't have ended their relationship and continued to see her every day at work? She chewed absentmindedly on a ragged cuticle, wishing she had sipped her wine instead of gulped it. Adelaide had no idea how to talk to Joe and the more time that passed, the more impossible it felt to even broach the subject of how to mend their marriage. How would she ever be able to look at him again without anger welling up inside her, threatening to spill out and ignite everything in its wake? Perhaps while he was away, she would find a marriage counsellor they could go to. All they needed was a kind of emotional Sherpa to help them scale this mountain of infidelity and shattered trust. He ended his affair and returned to her, she reminded herself for the millionth time. That had to count for something.

'How are you holding up, my dear?' asked Roger, appearing at her side.

'Forget about me, how are you?'

'Oh, well, me. I keep turning to tell Ivy something and then realise she's not next to me. But she spent our entire life telling me that she would go first. She was always right, that woman,' he said, shaking his head.

Adelaide smiled sadly and nodded.

'Amy! Amy dear, come over and meet our friend Adelaide.'

Amy looked over at her father and opened her mouth to say something. Her eyes shot towards her two sons who were scuffling in the curtains on the other side of the room. She sighed heavily and ambled over to join them.

'Adelaide, this is my daughter, Amy,' said Roger, placing his translucent hand on her black sleeve.

Adelaide extended her hand and received a flaccid handshake.

'It's so lovely to finally meet you, Amy,' said Adelaide. 'Although I wish it could have been under happier circumstances. You've come down from Brisbane?'

'Yes, we're heading home the day after tomorrow.'

'Oh, that reminds me,' said Roger, turning to Adelaide. 'I was wondering, dear, if you would join us for the reading of Ivy's will tomorrow.'

Amy's eyes darted from Adelaide to her father, her mouth fell open, giving her the appearance of a fish.

'The will?' Adelaide asked, taken aback.

'Yes, tomorrow morning. At our solicitors in Toorak. It'll just be immediate family, but Ivy considered you to *be* family.'

He put extra emphasis on the "be" adding a weight to the sentiment that Adelaide could hardly bear. She blinked slowly and nodded, fearing that any verbal response would come out choked.

A dull thud broke through the reverent murmur of mingled

conversation, and everyone turned towards Amy's sons. Rys held Liam in a headlock, and they were frozen in their positions, looking over at their mother, wearing the same fish-mouthed expression she was. Amy emitted a guttural sound of exasperation and stormed over to reprimand them, without saying goodbye.

WHEN Adelaide returned home, Joe's suitcase was at the foot of the stairs, in preparation for his early departure the next morning. The weight of all they should have said to one another threatened to crush her. She kicked off her shoes, which were beginning to give her blisters, leant down to pick them up and heard a sickening rip as the brittle, aged fabric of her coat split down the centre back seam. *I'm falling apart*, she thought in serene detachment. Deciding she couldn't cope with the confinement of her attire any longer, she undressed and climbed the stairs in her underwear, holding her bundled garments to her chest. She wished desperately that she could talk with Alec. To be on the receiving end of his kind attention. She considered emailing him, reasoning that they had agreed to resume their friendship, but she knew it was too soon. Thankfully, she had managed to make amends with Penny since her return. Or at least she thought she had. It was so difficult to interpret tone via email but surely receiving a reply, even a short one, was progress?

Adelaide pulled on the first clothes that came to hand and heard the front door click open.

'Mumma!' Darcy's high-pitched voice rang out.

Adelaide appeared at the top of the stairs to see Joe struggling to remove coats and shoes from the wriggly, non-compliant bodies of their children.

Estée looked at her solemnly. 'Are you okay, Mummy, from saying goodbye to Ivy?'

Adelaide padded down the stairs and sat at the foot. Estée wiggled her way between her knees, while Darcy sat beside her. They looked up at her with their bottom lips dropped in a mime of sympathy, awaiting her response.

'I feel really sad actually, you guys. Today was hard,' she confessed.

Estée nodded wisely.

'Poor Mumma,' said Darcy.

'After people are dead, you don't see them anymore, but they are always in our hearts,' said Estée, parroting the explanation Adelaide had given to them.

'That's right, baby,' said Adelaide, feeling a wave of pride at her children's concern for her.

'What's for dinner tonight?' asked Joe.

Adelaide looked at him in disbelief.

'Yeah, I mean. Let's get something delivered tonight, shall we?' he said.

27

LYING awake in bed, Adelaide heard the stairs creak under Joe's heavy footsteps as he crept down to depart for his business trip. After putting the children to bed last night, she had resolved to push through her fear and talk to Joe about what on earth they were going to do with the mess of their marriage. There was only one thing more terrifying than talking to him and that was continuing to say nothing. But when she returned to the living room, she found it abandoned. Now she slid out of bed and made her way through the silent house to the kitchen. There he stood in the darkened room, his face illuminated by his phone.

'Morning,' she said, making him jump.

'Jeez,' he said, 'you scared me.'

'Sorry,' she mumbled.

Just get it over with, she thought.

'So, I was thinking I'd line up a marriage counsellor for when you get back.'

He shifted his gaze from his phone to her. He wore the exact expression he gave to the twins, when they asked for something they knew they were not allowed to have.

'Is that really necessary?' he asked, looking back down at his phone.

'Well, yeah. I mean, you could hardly call us functional right now.'

'We just need time for everything to settle,' he said.

'I disagree. I don't know about you, but I can't just ignore what happened. Clearly, we need to do some work. We need to rebuild what was broken.'

'Look Adelaide, I said I'm sorry. It won't happen again. I get it now, I appreciate you, okay? Maybe I didn't before but when Kim couldn't cut it even for a week, I suddenly realised…'

'I'm sorry, what did you just say?'

Joe's eyes darted towards her as if frantically scanning what he had just said for flaws.

'She left *you*?' asked Adelaide, incredulous. 'Oh my God, Joe!'

'Bloody hell, Adelaide, do we have to get into semantics? She left me but… she was just never going to measure up to you, okay? I would have realised that eventually.'

'You mean she was never going to put up with your shit like I do!' she spat.

Joe's phone rang in his hand and they looked at it in unison.

'Yes? Oh, right. I'll be right out,' said Joe tersely, before ending the call. 'My car's here, I have to go.'

Adelaide shook her head, trying to understand the world from this grotesque vantage point.

'Look, organise a counsellor if you want to, okay. Whatever.'

He made a move to kiss her but halted when she visibly recoiled. He sighed impatiently, pocketed his phone and left the room. Adelaide heard him manoeuvre his suitcase over the threshold and shut the front door.

Adelaide climbed back up the stairs and peered into the twins' room. The glow of the nightlight revealed their smooth, slack faces, their little chests moving up and down with each peaceful breath. She thought about what Alec had said that first night they had dinner together. *You can teach them how to overcome adversity with grace and courage. You can show them that they can be their own heroes. How to create their own happiness.*

Adelaide crawled back into bed and fell into a deep sleep. She dreamed of Xena sitting in her lounge room, the sheer white curtains billowing around her. A blind faceless creature stalked in and sniffed at Adelaide threateningly. Paralysed, she looked into its unseeing eyes as the monster gouged out her insides. Streams of red string, braid, ribbon and thread poured out of her as she screamed, and just as quickly as the monster arrived, it was gone. She looked over at Xena, horrified, clutching at her stomach but her friend just looked at her serenely and said, 'Don't worry, Adele, it can all be stitched back together.'

'Mummy!'

'Mumma!'

The twins bounded in and threw themselves onto her bed. Adelaide, disoriented from her nightmare, squinted at them and sat up, her hands seeking out her stomach. Golden morning light poured through the open door. What time was it? She craned to see her bedside clock, but the twins bounced up and down, flapping the covers around her like a parachute. She wrestled Darcy down onto her pillow and managed to register the time— 8:14 a.m. Her little human alarm clocks had overslept.

'We're late!' exclaimed Adelaide, trying to extricate herself from the octopus in her bed.

AFTER dropping the twins off at kindergarten, Adelaide clawed her way through the post-peak hour traffic, her shoulder muscles bunched tight. It was as if her children were allergic to the notion of departing the house quickly. She was fairly confident she would only be a few minutes late, but she texted Roger to let him know anyway. He replied with an accidental selfie of the top of his ear, which helped Adelaide uncoil from her self-induced stress.

When Adelaide arrived at the address Roger had given, she thought she must have made an error. She walked through a glass door and was confronted by a long corridor with a water feature running down the left side. Her heels clicked along the polished concrete pathway that appeared to be floating in mid-air. The space was adorned with so many paintings and sculptures that Adelaide was convinced she had inadvertently found herself in a contemporary art gallery. But as she reached the end, the hallway veered to reveal an expansive waiting area. A sweeping desk, impressive enough to belong to St Peter at the gates of heaven, sat at the far end. The name "Baxter, Baxter and Pritchard & Associates" was emblazoned across the front in gleaming copper letters. Atop it sat a perfectly cut square of earth with red tulips growing from it. Behind the desk sat a small, taut-faced woman, whose black bob was so thoroughly hair-sprayed into place it resembled a motorcycle helmet. She looked up, removed her headset from one ear and smiled.

'Welcome to Baxter, Baxter and Pritchard. Are you expected?'

'Well, yes, I suppose so. I'm Adelaide Jones. I'm here for the reading of Ivy Volcek's will,' said Adelaide.

The receptionist removed the headset and slid her chair out from under the desk with a flourish.

'They're waiting for you in the boardroom,' she said, clip clopping toward a set of ceiling-high double doors. She rapped briskly and stepped in to announce Adelaide's arrival.

Adelaide entered the long, sleek room to find all eyes on her.

'I'm sorry I'm late,' she muttered to no one in particular.

Roger stepped forward to greet her. 'Not at all, dear. You remember my daughter Amy, and this is her husband Kevin and our solicitor Bernard Baxter.'

Amy and Kevin each gave a tepid acknowledgment but remained seated while the silver-haired solicitor rose.

'Lovely to meet you, Mr Baxter,' said Adelaide, extending her hand.

'Please, call me Bernard.'

Once they were all seated, Bernard spoke. 'I would like to commence by stating that this is a completely informal meeting, arranged at Roger's request. There is really no legal requirement to read the will of a deceased person. In fact, in most cases, letters would simply be sent to the beneficiaries. But Roger has advised me that a gathering of family is what Ivy envisaged, which is what brings us all here today.'

'I think she watched one too many movies,' said Roger, chuckling.

Bernard smiled and continued, 'As you may expect, the bulk of Ivy's estate will go directly to Roger but there are a few items which Ivy chose to bequeath others. After her Alzheimer's diagnosis recently, she came to see me and together we drafted this letter,' he said, producing a single typed page.

Adelaide let her mind wander to the conversation she'd had that morning with Joe. Like the nightmare that followed, fragments of it kept floating up to the surface of her thoughts. He had not returned to her, and somehow the knowledge of that hurt more than the infidelity itself.

Tired from her sleepless night, she was having trouble focusing on the solicitor's words and, although she had been invited, she felt like the odd person out.

She tuned back into Bernard reading out a passage written by Ivy to Amy who was now dabbing at the corners of her eyes with a tissue.

'...some of my fondest memories are of us sitting side by side on that piano stool as I taught you how to play. When you play, I hope you will hear our music and the melody of my love for you.'

Amy leant into Kevin and sighed. Adelaide knew that Ivy's relationship with her daughter wasn't always an easy one. Ivy confessed to Adelaide that she believed Amy was ashamed of her, and from quite a young age. 'Why can't you wear a tracksuit to pick me up from school, like the other mums?' she once asked, after Ivy arrived wearing a black and white leather skirt suit. Ivy, deeply offended had retorted, 'I'll wear one when I'm dead.'

Bernard now listed various items of jewellery Ivy had left to Amy. *Perhaps Ivy has left me a brooch or something I once admired*, thought Adelaide idly but the jewellery portion seemed to have come to an end because Bernard was now talking about a yacht that Adelaide thought Ivy sold years ago. Ivy had left it to Kevin who was surreptitiously looking at his phone under the board table. Amy poked him in the ribs just as Bernard read, 'for Kevin. Take the boys out on the water and leave the phones at home.'

Adelaide couldn't help smirking at Kevin's bemused expression as Amy leant in to repeat what he had missed.

'And finally, to my dear friend, Adelaide Jones, I leave my business, Retrograde.'

Adelaide's gaze snapped from Kevin to Bernard, and she blinked several times before looking over at Roger who nodded and smiled at her.

'...including all inventory, contracts and the building title,' continued Bernard.

All eyes fell on Adelaide, and she muttered, 'I thought I was here to get a brooch or something.'

Adelaide surged with adrenaline and wasn't sure if the sensation was pleasant or not. She sat, unmoving, through the remainder of the reading. When everyone rose, Adelaide did the same, but she was acting in imitation of them, not of her own volition.

BACK home, Adelaide sat in her car, parked in the driveway. Something occurred to her on the drive home and she feared that if she moved the feeling would dissolve. She sat there chanting it over and over like a mantra, willing the feeling to gain strength, willing herself to turn it into action. If she had indeed just been gifted a business, a livelihood, a life, then she could leave Joe. *Leave Joe, leave Joe, leave Joe.*

ADELAIDE plunged her fingers into the rubbery dough, luxuriating in the tactility of it. She added more oil and let her mind wander to the afternoon Alec had massaged warm oil tenderly into her skin. Since the reading of the will, and having her epiphany, a profound feeling of calm and happiness descended upon Adelaide. She felt a bright energy pulsing through her body, the same feeling she experienced when she had finally come to the end of her studies.

At the time, she had been making plans for what she saw as the commencement of her real life. By day, she made lists and wrote emails, applied for jobs and made contacts. And by night, just before she fell asleep, she would lay awake imagining where life's journey would take her. It had been the first time in her young life that she didn't know what the future held. And the mystery of it, coupled with the naive surety that whatever it was would be wonderful, was exhilarating.

Adelaide couldn't say for sure what it was about inheriting Retrograde that made everything click into place, but she supposed it had to do with having something that was hers. Although she hadn't meant it to happen, she had become defined by her roles as wife and mother and saw her job as more of a hobby than a career. Now she would have something to focus on, something to challenge her, somewhere to channel her energy other than her marriage and children. She rolled the dough into a sphere and thought of how excited the twins would be when she told them they'd be making pizza tonight. Adelaide knew there would be difficult times ahead if she was going to build a new life for herself and her children. But she decided that, just for tonight, she would put all thoughts of that on hold and enjoy this feeling of clarity. For the first time in a long time, she was completely in control of her own destiny and emancipated from her mental entanglement.

28

RETROGRADE had been closed since the accident but now Adelaide put her key into the lock and turned. She paused with her hand on the door, took a deep breath and pushed. The space within was cold and quiet, and Adelaide was struck with the musty smell of old timber and leather. She hadn't realised it until now, but to her that smell was Ivy. A gust of emotion swept through her body and tears blurred her vision. Adelaide walked around running a hand over the surfaces, as if seeing everything for the first time. She hadn't been here since before she went to Greece but, of course, she hadn't known she was going to Greece then. She thought of her mother and felt a pang of guilt. She hadn't spoken to her since the harried phone call she made from the airport. Not quite believing it herself, she had tried her best to explain that she wouldn't be coming to stay with her in Mornington because she was about to board a flight to Athens. Her mother laughed and farewelled her by saying, 'Enjoy your mid-life crisis.' Adelaide had tried not to be offended, reminding herself that her mother always had what you would call a dry sense of humour. Saharan, in fact.

Coming to the foot of the staircase, Adelaide stared upwards, trying not to imagine the moment Ivy tripped. The strange thing was, Adelaide had to keep reminding herself that Ivy was gone. Everything around her was so familiar, so unchanged, that she expected Ivy to emerge at any moment. 'Good morning, darling,' she'd say, 'Coffee?' But there would be no more coffees with Ivy, no more telling her everything about her life, basking in her attention, soliciting her wisdom. Adelaide placed a hand on the banister. She would need to go up at some point, there was work to be done and Celeste would arrive soon. The sound of her boots echoed as she clomped up the stairs. She sat down at Ivy's large desk, the leather chair creaking under her weight. On the desk sat an empty espresso cup with a scarlet lipstick imprint on its rim. *Ivy's last kiss.* Adelaide succumbed to a tsunami of tears.

ADELAIDE didn't hear Celeste come in, so when she appeared by her side and placed a hand on her heaving back, she screamed. The reaction was so comically exaggerated that the two women erupted into raucous fits of laughter. It took several failed attempts to compose themselves but when they finally did, their formally waxy pallor was replaced by a rosy-cheeked vitality.

'What the hell was that?' asked Celeste, getting her breath back.

'You scared the shit out of me!' said Adelaide.

'It wasn't like you weren't expecting me,' Celeste retorted.

Adelaide wiped under her eyes with a tissue, grimacing at the mascara streaks left behind.

'Coffee?' asked Celeste, walking towards the kitchenette.

'Coffee,' agreed Adelaide and followed.

'Well, it turns out Ivy included me in her will,' said Adelaide, as Celeste spooned coffee into the pot.

'Um, yeah,' said Celeste, unsurprised.

'She left me this place. All of it. Even the building.'

'Hello. Excuse me. What?'

'Yeah, I know. Pretty wild huh? So, I was wondering if… That is… I'm really going to need you,' said Adelaide, feeling like a total imposter in her new role as "boss".

'You got me, babe,' said Celeste, simply.

Adelaide reached out and pulled Celeste into a hug.

'Come on,' said Celeste, giving Adelaide a playful shove, 'come and see what I put together for the West Gate sets.'

CELESTE'S pride in her work was obvious as she swiped through her pitch for the TV mini-series. She had taken great care, even including such miniscule touches as ashtrays and drink decanters. When she went through everything, she looked at Adelaide expectantly, a rare and endearing flush of self-consciousness visible beneath her usually brash exterior.

'Celeste, it's perfect. It's somehow better than perfect. I'm speechless.'

Celeste's face erupted into a childlike smile, before being dialled back into a measured interpretation of mild pleasure. 'Okay, awesome. I'm glad. I'll send the proposal off to Televisual today.'

Adelaide nodded.

'So, in other news, it turns out I'm leaving Joe,' said Adelaide, saying the words out loud for the first time.

'Wow. I was going to ask you about that. So what? He wants you back and you're like, "Hell no!"'

'Yeah, pretty much.'

'Yes!' cried Celeste, shoving Adelaide's shoulder.

'Actually,' said Adelaide, feeling inspired, 'I've been trying to figure out the best way to tell him. He's in California this week so I wanted to get everything ready so that all our bullshit doesn't happen in front of Darcy and Estée.'

'Think he's gonna flip out?'

'Maybe. He can be kind of a child when he doesn't get his own way.'

'Crazy. What are you thinking? Ambush him at the airport?'

Adelaide had a vision of hiding in a shrub, wearing camo gear and running out to tackle Joe to the ground and smirked. 'Actually, that could work. I was also thinking that I'd set him up with somewhere to stay, move all his stuff there. I have to show him that I'm not just playing games, making empty threats.'

'Wouldn't he just go stay with the home-wrecker?'

'She broke up with him!'

'Ha!' exclaimed Celeste before the pair erupted into laughter once more. It was such a relief to laugh at the situation that had twisted and tugged at her ceaselessly since Joe first uttered his fateful confession in their kitchen, less than a month ago. Adelaide had assumed the most challenging times lay ahead, but she was beginning to suspect that she had already emerged from the darkness and was now seeking out the light.

'You're gonna need a village, girl,' said Celeste, wisely.

Adelaide thought of her mother and nodded her agreement.

LISTENING to the ringtone, Adelaide was nervous. She wished she had been in contact with her mother sooner, rather than waiting until she needed something from her. She felt an overwhelming impulse to end the call and try to manage everything on her own but, in truth, she needed the support.

'Well, if it isn't the jet-setting daughter!'

'Hi, Mum.'

'Nice to hear you're alive and well,' said Sia.

'Yeah, sorry I didn't call, Mum. Things have been a bit full-on since I got back. Ivy passed away actually and I kind of forgot about everything else.'

'Oh, sweetheart. I'm so sorry to hear that,' said Sia, her voice losing its edge.

'But that's not why I'm calling. I've decided that Joe and I aren't going to be able to work things out and I...' Adelaide's words caught in her throat.

'Do you need me to come?'

Adelaide was stunned by the swiftness of her mother's offer. Sia was always so quick with her jibes that Adelaide found it difficult to discern any semblance of a caring side in her.

'Yes please, Mum,' said Adelaide, her voice childlike.

'Right. If I leave now, I might be able to beat the traffic. I'll just throw some things in a bag. I'll see you soon.'

Sensing that her mother was about to end the call Adelaide said, 'Mum?'

'Yes, sweetheart?'

'Thank you. I mean, really. Thank you.'

'Of course, see you soon.'

A light mist of rain fell so Adelaide remained in her car, parked outside the kindergarten gate. Fog crept up the car windows and she absentmindedly drew squiggles through it with her index finger. She heard knocking and turned to see Rosemary's beaming face framed by the hood of her polka dot raincoat. She opened the door and leapt into the passenger seat before enveloping Adelaide in a soggy embrace.

'Oops, sorry!' said Rosemary, noticing the mottled water marks she left on Adelaide's white shirt.

'Oh who cares. It'll dry,' said Adelaide, waving away Rosemary's apology. 'Rosie, I'm leaving him. I'm leaving Joe.'

Rosemary's mouth fell open and she was momentarily silent. 'You sound very sure about that,' she said, squaring her gaze at Adelaide.

'I am. He has never loved me. Never respected me. Underestimates me,' she said, counting each point off on a finger. 'And he only came back to me because Kimmy dearest dumped him!'

'She did not!'

'She did too,' said Adelaide, replacing her hands in her lap. 'Plus, Ivy left me the business in her will.'

'You inherited it?' said Rosemary too loudly.

Adelaide nodded.

'So, what's the plan? What can I do?'

'My mum's coming up from Mornington now. If she's around to help with the kids, then I can move Joe's stuff out before he comes back from California.'

Adelaide looked down at the hem of her shirt and tugged at a loose thread. 'If I've got everything in place, hopefully he'll see that I'm serious and won't try to manipulate me into changing my mind.'

Rosemary nodded.

'It's so strange, Rosie. It's like I'm finally able to see him for the first time, instead of seeing what I want him to be. I was so desperate for him to love me that I pretended he did. And now that I have seen things as they really are...'

'You can't unsee it,' said Rosemary.

'Exactly. I just hope we can work together. For the kids, you know.'

'The kids!' exclaimed Rosemary, noticing other parents leaving the kindergarten with their children.

'WHY is Si Si coming to stay?' asked Estée, as Adelaide removed her gumboot, taking care not to spill any of the sand within.

'She misses you. She hasn't seen you since...' Adelaide stood and scratched her head, trying to remember.

'I think it was feaster,' said Darcy, his eyebrows a calligraphy curl of concentration.

'That's right. It was Greek Easter,' said Adelaide, smirking.

She leant down to kiss his mop of hair that was so long it curled around his ears and nape. He had informed her, in no uncertain terms, that he wouldn't need a haircut since he had decided to grow it long enough to tie into a ponytail like Charlie's.

'Will we dye red eggs when Si Si gets here?' Estée asked.

'No, my darling. That's only for Easter but I'm sure Si Si would like to do some other fun activities with you while she's here. Maybe we could ask her to make some *galaktoboureko* for a treat?'

'Which one is that?' asked Darcy, all eyebrows again.

'It's the custard pie. Remember the one where you paint the pastry with butter and then put the custard "to bed" in it?'

'Oh, yeah! That one is my most favourite,' said Darcy, nodding his curly head vigorously.

'Yummy,' agreed Estée.

To Adelaide's surprise, she looked forward to her mother arriving. Her immediate response to Adelaide's call for help was so unexpected and so heartening that a nostalgic calm settled upon her. As if on cue, there was a knock on the door and the twins shrieked. Darcy tried desperately to reach the latch on the door, while Estée jumped up and down calling, 'Si Si, is that you?'

Adelaide opened the door.

The twins flew at their grandmother's legs as she tried to simultaneously hug them and shuffle her way into the house.

'Now that's what I call a welcome,' she said, dropping her weekender bag in the hall.

'Hi, Mum,' said Adelaide. 'I'm so pleased you're here.'

Adelaide's mother looked at her intently as if scanning her demeanour for cracks. She nodded to herself, having decided something, and pulled Adelaide into a hug.

THAT evening, Adelaide sat on the sofa drinking a glass of wine. After bathing the twins and getting them into their pyjamas, she had brought them back downstairs to say goodnight to her mother and found her sitting in a spotless kitchen, wearing her trademark inscrutable smile.

'Can Si Si put us to bed tonight, Mummy?' Estée asked as Darcy implored her with his doe-eyes.

Adelaide looked over at her mother who nodded and rose.

'I'm going to tell you a story I used to tell your mummy when she was little,' she said, leading them up the stairs. 'It's the story of how I came to Australia on a boat when I was a little girl.'

'A boat!' exclaimed Darcy, already enthralled.

Adelaide listened to their chatter trail off as they ascended the stairs and felt uneasy in the face of having nothing to do. She was so used to riding the ceaseless conveyor belt of responsibilities that motherhood demanded, she immediately felt cast adrift whenever she was relieved of duty. If Joe had partial custody of the children, she would find herself alone far more than she was used to, perhaps far more than she was comfortable with. She thought of Retrograde and how thankful she was that Ivy had bestowed this lifeline upon her. Had she somehow known?

ADELAIDE heard the stairs creak and saw her mother's small figure darken the doorway to the kitchen. She picked up her wine glass and made her way back into the kitchen.

'Wine?' asked Adelaide.

'Why not? It's not like I have to drive home,' said Sia, amiably.

Adelaide retrieved a glass from the cupboard and poured a generous measure from the open bottle on the bench. She handed it to her mother and clinked her glass.

'It's so nice to have you here, Mum,' said Adelaide, climbing onto one of the stools.

Sia mirrored the gesture and smiled. 'It's nice to be here. Especially without... especially seeing as it's just the four of us,' she said.

Adelaide laughed. It was no secret that Sia and Joe weren't, what you would call, fond of one another. Anytime they were all together, Adelaide felt like she was on buffer duty between them. She had always assumed the rift occurred because her mother was being disagreeable, but she was beginning to question that theory.

'It is nice, isn't it,' agreed Adelaide. She sipped her wine and appraised her mother with a focused gaze. 'You never liked him, did you?' she asked, emboldened by the wine.

'Well... he's just...' Sia trailed off and sipped her wine. 'He just has a very, shall we say, elevated sense of self,' she finished.

Adelaide laughed at her mother's unexpected candour.

'He just always acted so entitled. And I'm sorry, sweetheart, but you just followed him around like a little lost puppy, kissing the ground he walked on. I just couldn't bear to be around it.'

Adelaide groaned and buried her face in her hand. 'Oh God, I did, didn't I? What's wrong with me?' she said, her eyes peering through spread fingers. 'You know he cheated on me?' said Adelaide, enjoying the feeling of camaraderie.

'What a prick hole!' said Sia, trying out swearing for the first time and failing.

Adelaide clutched the kitchen bench and laughed. 'He really is a prick hole, isn't he?' she said, trying to suppress the last vestiges of her giggles.

29

AS weak daylight illuminated the bedroom, Adelaide enjoyed the warmth of her bed and the clarity of her mind. Last night was another, in what seemed like a long line of blissfully uneventful nights, where her children were concerned. Adelaide couldn't explain it, but Darcy seemed to have turned a corner and was no longer waking at night. As with so many experiences in her parenting journey, Adelaide was surprised at how fleeting each stage was. Just when you thought you were being driven to the brink of your capabilities, a particularly difficult stage would give way to reveal something new, something more manageable. Each time this happened, she felt a mixture of relief and mourning because even the conclusion of challenging times represented yet another marker in the relentless passage of time. Her babies were growing up and one day they would leave altogether. She blinked away the thought and reached for her phone. An email had come through from Xena with the subject heading "First batch complete". Adelaide opened it to reveal a photo of Xena posing dramatically, draped with beautifully embroidered fabric. Adelaide flushed with pride in her friend. She typed a quick reply of congratulations and almost instantly received an email in return. "You're awake? Do you want to Skype?"

"Just woke up, give me five".

'YASSAS,' Xena crooned excitedly, her face momentarily flickering into a Cubist painting.

'You finished an order? That's amazing!'

'I know, we have worked day and night.'

'Xena, that's fantastic, well done.'

'So, how are you? How are things at home?'

Adelaide raised her eyebrows. 'Eventful.'

'Tell me.'

'I've finally decided to leave Joe.'

'*Bravo*! What made you decide?'

For the next few minutes, Adelaide explained to Xena about Ivy's passing, the revelation that Joe had been dumped, and her inheritance of Retrograde.

'You mean you will stay in this job?' Xena asked.

'Well, yes but the business is mine now. I can really put my mind to growing it.'

'But… furniture? It is not your passion.'

Adelaide was stung. 'Well, maybe I will make it into my passion,' she retorted.

'Okay,' said Xena, elongating the word.

'Look, Xena, I think the kids are awake. I should go,' Adelaide lied.

'Okay, so… Good luck with Joe. Let me know how it goes, *endaxi*?'

'Sure,' said Adelaide and ended the call.

Adelaide sat on her bed sulking. So what if she wasn't passionate about the work? All that would change now that it was her name on the door. And besides, the notion of finding every single part of your life inspiring and fulfilling was such a symptom of privilege that it made her sick. Didn't the true key to happiness lie in finding joy in the mundane? Not for the first time, she felt deflated by Xena's abrasive assessment. She thought longingly of how positive she had felt when she woke this morning, until Xena had ruined it. Sighing heavily, she tried to refocus her thoughts. There was work to do.

AFTER the rest of the household woke, Adelaide retrieved old filing boxes from the garage and snuck them upstairs. The twins were making pancakes with her mother, their sing-song voices drifting upstairs as they worked. She could hear Sia's measured, patient instructions as she guided them through the process.

'That's it, Darcy, now poke your thumbs into the crack and pull the shell apart,' she said. 'Estée, you mix the eggs in. Slowly though, we don't want our batter to escape, or we'll have nothing for breakfast.'

Adelaide's heart swelled and she fought the urge to go downstairs and watch them working together. Instead, she pulled out armloads of Joe's shirts, slipped them off their hangers and folded them carefully. Rosemary would arrive soon and together they would take all of Joe's belongings to a serviced apartment close to his office, while her mother took all three children to the park.

'Pancakes are ready, Mummy,' Estée called from the foot of the stairs.

'Save me some, baby, I'll be down in a minute,' she called back, getting started on Joe's trousers.

How quickly a life could be packed into a few boxes. Adelaide looked over at the newly vacated side of the walk-in wardrobe and wondered what on earth she would fill the emptiness with. Hearing a meek knock on the front door, followed by a more purposeful rap, she made for the stairs just in time to see her mother opening the door for Rosemary and Charlie.

'Morning, Rosie. Hello, Charlie,' said Sia, stepping aside to welcome them inside.

'Hi, Sia, you're looking well,' said Rosemary, kissing her on the cheek.

Rosemary looked up at Adelaide, descending the stairs towards her.

'There's my warrior princess,' she said, grinning impishly.

Gratitude washed over Adelaide at how effortlessly the women in her life had rallied around her in support. *Even posthumously*, she thought.

DOWN to their sweaty shirtsleeves, Adelaide and Rosemary trudged up and down the stairs conveying boxes of Joe's belongings to Rosemary's car. Although he wasn't arriving home until the day after tomorrow, Adelaide wanted everything completed today.

'You're so organised, you even factor in time for the calm before the storm,' Rosemary joked.

When the final box was loaded, they drove the short distance to the serviced apartment and collected the key.

'This is nice,' said Rosemary, walking in. 'Some of these places can be like... where hope goes to die, you know?' She looked back at Adelaide who stood perfectly still in the doorway, her expression grave. 'Are you okay, my love?'

Adelaide, rooted to the spot, nodded unconvincingly.

'Come in, let's close the door and talk.'

Rosemary closed the door and led her to the small sofa, gently pulling her to sit down.

'What you thinking there?' Rosemary prompted.

'I just don't want him to think that I don't care, you know? I don't want him to hate me for this.'

'I know,' said Rosemary, 'but you said it yourself. He has never really loved you. So this will ultimately be good for him too. Maybe the whole point of you and Joe was to create those two miracle babies of yours? And now it's time for you both to move on.'

Adelaide furrowed her brow and nodded, turning the idea over in her mind. A picture of Alec drifted into view, but she blinked it away. She had resolved not to contact him, even after deciding she was leaving Joe. The last thing she needed was to be confused about her motivations for ending her marriage.

'What you're doing is brave. I mean, so many people just stay in their rut, composting, because they don't have the guts to make a change.'

Adelaide forced a weak smile and leant to rest her head on Rosemary's shoulder. Her friend's soft curls tickled her nose as she breathed in her sweet scent. They sat there a while before Rosemary kissed the top of Adelaide's head and nudged her away. 'Shall we?'

Adelaide nodded and rose.

30

THE next morning would have been perfectly ordinary, if it didn't precede such a momentous event in Adelaide's life. Colours were vivid, details more poignant and the air itself buzzed with a nervous and volatile energy, making everything simultaneously beautiful and terrifying. She'd had barely any communication with Joe since he left and the few texts that had been exchanged were strictly operational. He didn't ask her about the contents of her heart following their exchange in the kitchen before his departure, so she didn't divulge them. It was as though every feeling was dividing and multiplying at an unfathomable pace within her. She looked at the innocent, carefree faces of her children as they played with her mother and felt sick with the guilt of what she planned. On more than one occasion, her hugs lingered a little too long and they wriggled free impatiently to resume their play. By lunchtime, her expression was so mournful that her mother all but shooed her out of the house.

'You need to go out and get some air, clear that head of yours,' said Sia, her eyes stern.

Adelaide blinked rapidly, shocked that her interior existence was so thoroughly on display.

'Sure, yes, right,' she stammered, grabbing her keys and kissing the twins goodbye.

She sat in her car for a few minutes, considering her options. She wondered if she should go and help out at Retrograde but decided she would be more distracting than helpful to Celeste in her current frame of mind. Instead, she started the engine and made for the shops.

The bright expanse of the supermarket made Adelaide feel conspicuous and strange. Everyone seemed to be staring straight into her thoughts. She grabbed for the least noxious shopping basket and wandered the isles in search of Joe's favourite foods and a comprehensive selection of basic staples with which to furnish the apartment's kitchenette. Coffee pods, ice cream, potato chips, bread and toast spreads, and a selection of frozen ready meals for one, the symbolism of which made her cry, sandwiched by the freezer door. It was only when a mother quickly shepherded her children away from her that Adelaide came to her senses and moved on, her eyes darting around furtively. Craving a glass of wine, even though it had barely gone noon, Adelaide made for the liquor department. She gazed around at the overwhelming selection, wondering what kind of sedative Joe might appreciate. *Whiskey for if he's devastated and beer for if he's not*, she decided, grabbing his favourite brands.

WHEN Adelaide let herself into the serviced apartment, she noticed for the first time how cold and uninhabited it felt. Its too-clean sterility started with the vague smell of bleach and extended to the polyester sheen of the carpet, upholstery and bedding. She set about unpacking the groceries, hoping their very presence would provide a layer of hominess. She lined up jars and packets in a cupboard, taking care to display their labels frontward, then removed them all to try out an alternate layout. She removed the stickers from the apples, before placing them in a salad bowl in the middle of the kitchen table. *Sorry Joe, I can't stay married to you but here's an apple*, she mocked herself.

WHEN Adelaide arrived home, her mother was seating the children for dinner.

'Si Si taught us how to make *pastitsio*,' reported Estée proudly.

'First you put the pasta tubes, then you put the meat sauce, then you put more pasta tubes and then you put the "betcha smell" sauce and then you sprinkle all the cheese on top,' said Darcy, miming the steps with his chubby hands.

'Béchamel,' corrected Sia, smiling.

'It looks delicious,' said Adelaide. She drew her mother into a one-armed hug, marvelling at how neatly she fit in the crook of her armpit. *Will my own children tuck me into theirs one day?*

'And we made a big one so we can freeze some for another day when we don't feel like cooking,' said Estée, parroting Sia.

'Ready to eat?' Sia asked, looking up at her.

'Yes, just give me a minute to wash up.'

Adelaide climbed the stairs, looking at the family photos which lined the wall. Would they have to go, once she and Joe divorced? Surely he didn't need to be erased from all memory like an alien encounter in a sci-fi film? She turned away from their smiling faces and tried in vain to silence the internal voice telling her she was selfish.

When Adelaide returned downstairs a few minutes later, she slipped into her seat and gazed at the faces of her children as they devoured their meal.

'She's doing it again, Si Si,' said Estée.

'Me? Doing what?' asked Adelaide

'You keep staring, Mumma,' said Darcy.

Adelaide blushed. She looked at her mother and received a conceding tilt of the head. Adelaide looked down at her plate and laughed. 'I'm sorry, you're right. You know what it is though?'

'What?'

'I just love you so much and it makes me go all...'

Adelaide made a heart shape with her hands, rested her chin on top and batted her eyelashes rapidly, making the twins giggle.

'Again!' shouted Darcy.

'SO, you'll take Joe's car to the airport tomorrow morning?' Sia asked, once the twins were tucked in bed.

Adelaide nodded. 'I'll get an Uber back from the apartment I guess.'

'How are you feeling about it?'

Adelaide glanced inside herself like an explorer charged with the identification of an entire ecosystem of hitherto undiscovered species. Where should she begin? 'I'm feeling like it's the right thing and I'm feeling like it's the hard thing. It would be so easy to stay. To pretend I hadn't seen what I've seen. To pretend I'm an actor playing a part.'

'That doesn't sound easy,' countered Sia.

Adelaide exhaled. 'I think I'll try for an early night,' she said, rising from her stool and walking to pour a glass of water.

'It breaks my heart, you know?'

'What does?' said Adelaide.

In the half-light of the kitchen, Sia's face looked smooth and wistful.

'I just wonder if I did something wrong,' Sia began. 'It's just that… for you to end up in the same situation as me. Married to the wrong man, I mean. Are you repeating my history? Did I set a bad example for you?'

Sia's often brash demeanour had completely dissolved, revealing a touching vulnerability that Adelaide wasn't sure she had seen before, perhaps never even suspected was there. She looked like she was on the verge of tears. Adelaide skirted the bench to where her mother sat and lowered herself onto the stool next to her. She clasped her mother's small hands and met her gaze.

'Maybe from you I learned to be brave? Learned that I deserve more?'

Relief washed over Sia's face and Adelaide felt her breathe again.

'I always wished I was more. I could have made something of myself, you know? I was smart but there weren't any opportunities. Not like you girls have now and especially not for migrants. All they thought we were fit for was housework and babies.'

Adelaide felt her old shame return and said, 'Look, I know you regretted having me, but I always appreciated everything you did for me.'

'Regretted having you?' said Sia, incredulous. 'Sweetheart, you're my greatest achievement.'

31

LYING in the dark, Adelaide felt like she was straddling the border between two realities, like those cheesy tourist pictures taken at the equator. She thought of Alec, bathed in sunshine on the other side of the world. Thought of how she herself had bathed in the sunshine of his attention. She recalled his kisses, how hungry they had been. How she had felt beautiful and interesting and worthy by pure virtue of his belief that she was all those things. In Joe's presence she always felt like an inconvenience, never really wanted but rather, tolerated. She accused him once, early on in their marriage, of giving her "go away kisses" instead of "come here kisses".

Newly pregnant at the time, she had woken from an impromptu post-work nap. Lying in bed, she waited for the familiar wave of morning sickness to descend upon her, but there was no trace of the queasiness that had plagued her day and night for the past month. In fact, she felt an elemental sense of wellbeing. Every cell in her body seemed to hum with vitality and life. She sat up, taking care to roll onto her side before pushing up, as the obstetrician had instructed. Although her stomach displayed only a slight protrusion, she was determined to follow all the advice she was given. Perched on the end of the bed, she placed a hand underneath her blouse and rubbed her belly, marvelling at its new density. She stood, resisting the urge to be pulled into the waddle, which her altered centre of gravity commanded, and made her way to the full-length mirror. Although strangers may not guess at her condition, to Adelaide's eyes the changes to her body were profound. Her breasts, once modest, had swelled to a volume that captured her awareness with every movement. Her shirt buttons pulled and every bra she wore produced a bountiful cleavage. The word "buxom" sprang to mind several times a day and the novelty of it made her feel as though she enjoyed a private joke. What was more, her once unremarkable bottom had transformed into a firm shelf of flesh that followed her around wherever she went. She could actually feel it moving around back there. Creating a bouncy rhythm with each step. She had never felt so present in her body. Never felt so powerful. While everyone else went about their day, here she was doing everything she usually would, all while creating two new human lives. *How on earth had women ever been perceived as the weaker sex*, she wondered, *when we are the provenance of life itself?*

Engulfed by an unexpected wave of primal desire, Adelaide cocked her ear, listening for Joe, and was rewarded with the distant rumble of the television. Padding downstairs, she found him sitting on the sofa, scrolling through his phone.

'Sorry, I must have dozed off. Who knew making babies was so exhausting,' she said, sitting down.

She leaned into him, seeking his mouth.

With his eyes still on his phone, he turned his face slightly towards her to deflect her with his lips.

Inwardly wounded but undeterred thanks to the smouldering undercurrent of her hormones, she placed a hand on his chest and tried again. When she received the same nudging away, she said in a light-hearted tone, 'Sometimes you give me "go away kisses," instead of "come here kisses".'

Lowering his phone and turning to her with an exasperated exhalation, he asked, 'For Christ's sake, Adelaide. What is it that you want from me?'

Adelaide felt heat spring up her collar but managed to produce what she hoped sounded like a nonchalant laugh. She gave him a gentle shove to complete the act and stood.

'Dinner should be about ready. It smells good, right?' she said, walking towards the kitchen and swallowing her hurt.

Adelaide scrunched her eyes tight against the memory and begged for sleep to take her, but it was not to be. Instead, she kept watch over the night. She lay on her side, her unblinking eyes waiting for the digital clock to tick over from 4:59 to 5:00, signifying her triumph over the night and her long-awaited emergence into the day. *Click.* She sprang up, thankful that the marathon she had run through her own thoughts was over, even if she wasn't sure that she'd won. By the time the twins appeared, she was in her third outfit change and drinking her second coffee. Today was the day. The wait had been so torturous, so thoroughly excruciating that she was almost looking forward to it. Or perhaps, more accurately, she was looking forward to it being over.

'Good morning, sleepy heads,' she greeted her children, drawing them in to kiss their rumpled, sleep-softened faces.

Sia followed behind, woken by their ruckus.

'Morning, sweetheart,' she said, offering a smile that seemed to be laced with sadness, or was it sympathy?

'Morning, Mum. Will you be okay to do kindergarten drop off today?'

'Yes, I'm sure I'll manage. Can you put the address into Goo-Goo maps for me?' she asked, her almost non-existent accent comically noticeable on the word "Google".

'Of course,' said Adelaide, concealing her smile inside her coffee cup.

It was so delightful having her mother stay. They had settled into a symbiotic rhythm that had alleviated a loneliness that Adelaide hadn't realised she felt until it was gone. During her night-time musings, Adelaide was struck by a thought. It must have been at least twelve months since Sia had retired from the homewares store she worked at on the coast. Adelaide knew that her mother's dwindling number of friends were fleeing the southern chill in favour of more tropical climates up north. Feeling encouraged by the newfound ease of their relationship, Adelaide ventured, 'So Mum, have you ever thought about moving back to the city? It would be lovely to have you around closer to us.'

Although Sia was turned away, pouring herself a cup of coffee, something in her posture told Adelaide that her mother was smiling. She turned around slowly, wearing the last glimmer of it on her face. 'Well,' she said, 'that might be something to consider.'

'I should get going,' said Adelaide, draining her cup and standing.

Sia's smile evaporated and she sighed. 'Yes, the traffic.'

32

THE interior of Joe's car smelled like the man himself and, as Adelaide climbed in, she immediately felt nervous, as if he were present and scrutinising her. She had only driven the car once since he bought it the year before and the powerful vehicle intimidated her. It had been his gift to himself when the negotiations for the sale of Grasp Digital began. He came home with the idea of buying a sports car and, although Adelaide expressed her hesitation in parting with such a huge sum of money before the deal was finalised, he drove the yellow Porsche into their driveway the very next day. She had tried to conceal her hurt feelings by acting impressed and excited by the machine, when in truth it made her feel small and insignificant every time she laid eyes on it. She adjusted the seat and mirrors and checked, and double-checked, that she was clear to reverse out of the garage. Adelaide was at least ten minutes down the road when her hands began to ache, and she realised her knuckles were white from gripping the wheel too hard. *Relax*, she silently implored herself, *relax, relax, relax.*

Adelaide had allowed time for bad traffic. The last thing she wanted was for Joe to hop into a taxi because she couldn't head him off at the airport in time. This morning, however, the roads seemed to clear before her. Lights turned green and motorists were uncharacteristically good-natured. She pulled into the airport's short-term car park and cringed at the thought of the car ride they would soon take to the serviced apartment. The stocked shelves she had prepared for Joe's stay seemed foolish now and she wished that she could erase all that she had done yesterday. For some reason, the notion that she had taken great pains to merchandise the pantry items into a visually appealing display, made her hate herself. Maybe she was as ridiculous as Joe thought. The smell of aeroplane fuel and duty-free perfume greeted her as she walked into the terminal, fooling her brain into releasing endorphins in response to a holiday she wasn't taking. She stood motionless, wondering how she would kill the spare time she had, as the airport buzzed around her. Her legs felt weak, pre-empting her suggestion that she roam around the shops browsing. She needed to sit, to gather her thoughts, to ready her mettle. Inspiration struck when she saw a dozen paunchy thirty-somethings, wearing matching custom-made bucks party t-shirts and novelty sombreros, walk into a tacky looking, faux mahogany-panelled bar. *The airport*, she thought with relief, *is the only place in the world where it's cocktail hour, at any hour.* Adelaide slunk into the dimly lit space and muttered her order to the bartender.

'Bloody Mary please, extra spicy.'

'Already on holidays, aye?'

The bartender wore a black waistcoat, the sleeves of his white shirt rolled up at the cuffs. His thinning hair was combed over his spherical head which gleamed greasily under the green-glass pendant lights. He looked like a caricature of what a barman was meant to look like. Adelaide wondered if she should spill her secrets to him, but instead she swapped her credit card for the palm tree of a cocktail and sipped. The Tabasco burned her mouth, reminding her of the way her lips had felt after an entire night of devouring Alec's bearded mouth. Pleasure pulsed through her body in response to the unexpected memory. Pocketing her card, she was startled by a jaw-rattling chorus of approving whooping from the bucks' party. She forced a smile, offered them an air cheers and slunk off to the farthest corner of the bar. Adelaide's thoughts lost focus as the vodka danced a tango with her fatigue and she resisted the urge to rest her head in her hands. She blinked hard and shook her head, wondering if perhaps a shot of espresso would have been the more responsible choice. She looked over at the bucks' party. Some of the men had tucked the front hem of their t-shirts in at the neckband and were adopting feminine affectations. Adelaide gaped at them, transfixed by the gelatinous rippling of their hairy bellies. Coming to her senses, she consulted her phone for the time. 'Shit,' she spat, realising that Joe had disembarked ten minutes ago. She slid from her seat and hurried from the bar as one of the bucks yelled 'Run Forrest, run!' to a chorus of laughter.

Approaching the arrivals gate at a trot, Adelaide frantically searched the faces of the passengers for Joe's. When she was satisfied that she hadn't missed him, she leant forward, hands on hips, trying to catch her breath. *I really need to start exercising*, she thought, panting.

'Adelaide?'

His voice came from behind her, and she turned, her face red and hairline damp from her exertions.

'What are you doing here?' he hissed, eyes darting around.

This was the moment. She had a dozen prepared openers but before she could remember any configuration of them, his face recoiled in sickened recognition.

'You're checking up on me? What? You thought I was off fucking around instead of working?'

He leant in close to her ear and she could feel his hot breath emphasising every righteous word. She was confused and unprepared in the face of his anger. When she planned this out in her mind, it was she who saw him first, walked over and calmly explained that they needed to talk. Then, they would drive to the apartment where she would explain that he had been right, they were better off apart. Remembering this, she tried to bring the situation back on track, but he grabbed her wrist hard, demanding she respond to his accusation.

'Nnnn, no,' she stammered, 'Nothing like that.'

'What? What then?'

'I just...'

She tried to focus, tried to look inside herself and find any shred of the gumption she had been cultivating for days. Taking a deep, purposeful breath she looked him in the eye with such steely determination that he dropped her wrist, as if it were something scorching.

'I am here because we need to talk, alone. You were right, we are not in love, and we need to move on.'

He blinked rapidly, trying to process her words in the correct order. Finally, he refocused on her and narrowed his gaze.

'Yeah, I see,' he said cryptically, nodding his head in a way that made him resemble a chicken scratching for grubs in the dirt. 'You're just trying to get back at me. Give me a taste of my own medicine? Okay sure. Well done. Look, Adelaide, I said I'd go to your stupid couple's counselling or whatever,' he said, dropping the handle of his suitcase and making air quotes with his fingers either side of his face.

Adelaide had never realised how ridiculous he was until now. He was a spoilt child, and she was the one who had spoiled him.

'Joe, it's not that, really. I'm not playing games with you. I'm here to tell you that you were right. I mean, maybe you went about it in the wrong way by having an affair but, essentially…' she trailed off.

He squinted at her suspiciously. 'Have you been drinking?'

She rolled her eyes but didn't answer.

'Look, I drove your car here to pick you up and take you to…'

She faltered for a second, during which time his eyebrows shot up in a smarmy, impatience. 'Ttttt, to?' he said.

'To a serviced apartment where you can stay until we sort out a plan,' she blurted, before adding, 'together'.

He emitted a scornful scoff but followed her when she made a move towards the exit.

Adelaide climbed into the passenger side of the Porsche and waited. The engine purred to life, but they didn't move. She looked over at Joe who wore an expression of extreme annoyance.

'Oh,' she said with a start, realising he didn't know where they were going.

She pulled out her phone and her heart sank as it dropped to the ground. Joe sighed angrily as she muttered an apology from underneath her seat. She retrieved it, practically dislocating her shoulder in the process, punched the address in and let the unperturbed voice of the navigation lady calm her.

When they pulled into the apartments' carpark, Joe shook his head, his chin jutted out, giving him an exaggerated under bite.

'Packing me off to the land of divorced dads, I see.'

Adelaide said nothing as he killed the engine and got out of the car.

She pulled out the key and walked towards the door, predicting that if she offered to carry any of his bags, he would lose it.

Once inside, she seated herself at the kitchen table, deciding at the last minute that the small sofa was too intimate for the situation. What she needed now was a nice expanse of lacquered pine between them. Her eyes flicked guiltily toward the pantry door and she hoped that when Joe discovered the contents later, he might assume it all came with the apartment. Joe discarded his belongings at the door and sat opposite her. He reached for an apple and took a bite out of it, his menacing eyes never leaving hers.

'So I guess what I wanted to say to you is, in a way, thank you. I didn't realise it at the time but when you said you were leaving… well, it was like… well, first I freaked out, but then, what you said was right. We thought that just because we said we would love each other, that we could.'

He crunched the apple, regarding her with disdain. 'I thought you said you did love me?' he challenged, as if trying to catch her in a lie.

'Joe, I did love you, but I guess it's a bit wearing loving someone who doesn't love you back. Maybe your indifference towards me extinguished it, okay?'

She heard her voice becoming terse and resolved to centre herself. She was determined to present a focused, perhaps even detached, aura of calm. She knew for a fact that spoilt children could turn nasty in an instant.

He set down the ravaged apple core on the table and Adelaide resisted the urge to clear it away. He leant onto his elbows, hunching his shoulders. He looked like an ogre.

'Yeah, well, I may not love you, but I love our children and if you think that I'm going to let you have them while I get to be king dick for one weekend a month, you've got another think coming.'

He was using the tone of voice normally reserved for talking about sports with men he had just met, and was trying to impress.

'Nobody is trying to take your children away, Joe.'

'I'm not going to be like my dirtbag dad, okay?'

'I know, you would never be.'

'I want them half the time,' he said, his words quick as a whip.

'Half the time? How could you possibly look after them half the time? You don't know the first thing…'

'There it is!' he shouted, throwing his hands out towards her as if highlighting her outrageous behaviour to an invisible audience. 'I know plenty!' he spat. 'I looked after them alright when you were off on the other side of the world doing God knows what with God knows who!'

'Well, you couldn't even manage it without passing off Kim as a goddamn babysitter. And the house looked like a bomb had hit!'

Her voice sounded shrill, and she scolded herself for losing her cool. He sat back in his chair, looking as if he'd won.

She closed her eyes in a long blink, trying to compose herself.

'Look, Joe, I'm sorry. I'm sure with a little help, a housekeeper, a nanny, you'll be more than able to have the children some of the time.'

'Half of the time,' he corrected, the raising of his eyebrows emphasising the word "half".

'Have you told them?' he asked.

'Told who, what?'

'The twins! I mean, you've shipped me off here. Maybe you've already told them and changed the locks as well.'

'Of course I haven't told them. I thought we could do that together, present a united front, minimise their trauma, you know,' said Adelaide, regurgitating phrasing from her insomniatic Googling.

'Mother of the year,' he huffed, looking down his nose.

'Look, I should go,' she said, not wanting to push her luck. 'I brought your stuff here the other day so you should have everything you need. I got the apartment for a week, after that you can decide what to do.'

'You're too kind,' he said, sarcastically.

AS Adelaide stood at the kerb watching the little icon of the Uber round the corner on the map, her phone rang in her hand, making her jump. She fumbled to answer it.

'Hello? Adelaide Jones speaking.'

The Uber pulled up and Adelaide, indicating the phone to her ear, mouthed the word "sorry" to the driver as she climbed into the back seat.

'Hi, Adelaide, it's Bernard Baxter here, from Baxter, Baxter and Pritchard.'

'Oh, hello, Mr Baxter, how are you?' said Adelaide, wondering idly if his firm handled family law.

'Ms Jones, I have something of a sensitive issue to discuss with you. Is now a good time?'

Adelaide placed her hand over the mouthpiece and whispered to the driver, 'Could you turn the music down please?'

'Yes, now is fine,' she replied.

'It's concerning Ivy's bequeathment of her business to you.'

'Yes?' prompted Adelaide, feeling mildly annoyed by the solicitor's sluggish preamble.

'It's just that…'

Adelaide wanted to shout into the phone 'spit it out man!'

'It's being contested.'

'Contested?'

Adelaide stared out the window at the houses rushing by, her reflection atop them creating a double exposure.

'By Mrs Dwyer,' he went on.

'Who the hell is Mrs Dwyer?' asked Adelaide, feeling like she was being led into a punchline.

'Mrs Amy Dwyer, Ivy Volcek's daughter.'

Adelaide met her eyes in the reflection and her mouth fell open.

'Amy is contesting Ivy's will,' Adelaide paraphrased for her own clarification.

'Mrs Dwyer is claiming that her mother was not of sound mind when she made the amendment which included you in her will,' he went on.

'Because of the Alzheimer's,' said Adelaide.

'Exactly.'

'But Mr Baxter, Ivy *was* of sound mind, wasn't she?' Adelaide asked, turning her head away from the driver, whose eavesdropping was obvious.

'I believe she was and so does Roger. If it goes to court, I'm sure we will have no trouble gaining the testimony of Ivy's neurologist to support this.'

'Court,' repeated Adelaide.

An invisible force pushed down on Adelaide's shoulders and her head ached. She closed her eyes and massaged her temple with her free hand.

'Roger is hoping he will be able to reason with his daughter. If this can all be sorted out amongst you, then it won't have to go to court at all,' he said.

'Yes, I'm sure we can sort it out,' said Adelaide, unconvinced.

'I'll be in touch with further details,' said Bernard, signing off.

Adelaide looked at her phone in disbelief. She felt as though she was stuck in a dream, where the people kept shapeshifting. If inheriting Retrograde had jolted her into leaving Joe, what did it mean if it were taken away from her? There was nothing else for it—she hung her head and cried.

'Are you okay, lady?' the driver asked, stopping in front of her house.

'Yes, I'm sorry, thank you,' Adelaide blurted.

She opened the door and made to get out but was pulled back by her seatbelt. Mortified, she unclipped and successfully fled the car, muttering another, 'Thank you, sorry,' before closing the door.

Stumbling in through the front door, Adelaide was met by her mother heading upstairs with a basket full of freshly laundered clothes. The sight of this simple act of kindness, that so thoroughly displayed a depth of love and care for her, made Adelaide all but liquefied in the face of it. She sat at the bottom of the stairs and buried her face in her hands. Sia set down the basket and sat beside her, wrapping Adelaide in her arms as she sobbed. Adelaide could not explain the barrage of feelings that overwhelmed her. She sat on the step, small and fragile as her mother muttered soothing phrases into the back of her head about how the hardest days were behind her.

33

ROSEMARY pushed the door open to Adelaide's bedroom. 'Hey there,' she said, into the darkness.

'Hi, Rosie,' said Adelaide in a small voice from the bed. Thanks for picking up the kids.'

'Mind if I open the curtains?'

'Sure, of course.' Adelaide sat up.

Muted winter daylight struggled to illuminate the farthest corners of the bedroom. Rosemary sat beside Adelaide, put an arm around her and kissed her on the head. 'How'd it go?'

Adelaide rested her head on Rosemary's shoulder. 'It went.'

'Yep, that sounds about right,' said Rosemary, nodding.

They sat in silence, huddled together, watching a few solitary leaves and bristly seed-balls on the skeletal plane tree outside bob in the biting wind.

'Ivy's daughter is contesting the will,' said Adelaide, breaking the silence.

'Annie?'

'Amy, yep.'

'What the hell for?' asked Rosemary, squaring her body to face Adelaide.

'She's saying that Ivy wasn't of sound mind, because of the Alzheimer's.'

'But that's not true, is it?' said Rosemary.

Adelaide shook her head.'

'So, you fight it,' said Rosemary, defiantly.

'The last thing Ivy would have wanted is fighting,' said Adelaide, in a voice that belied her battered spirit.

'Well, she started it,' said Rosemary, sounding like the children.

Adelaide smiled, accentuating the exhaustion she wore on her face.

'You know the first thing my mother asked me?' said Adelaide after a while 'She asked me if I even want Retrograde.'

'What did you say?' asked Rosemary.

'I said I didn't know.'

AT the dinner table, Adelaide sat between Sia and Rosemary. She felt like they were holding her up on either side, like a drunk being escorted out of a bar by concerned friends. She poked her fork at the tender chunks of pork on her plate until they were cold and covered in a thick film of congealed fat.

'Mumma, when is Daddy coming home from Mamerica?' asked Darcy, as Sia cleared away the dinner plates.

'He's not in America, silly. He's gone to Califormina,' Estée corrected, haughtily.

Threads of guilt and regret encircled Adelaide's heart and tightened, but she tried her best to arrange her face into something bright. 'Tomorrow afternoon. And you're both right. He went to California which is in America.'

'I wonder if Daddy will bring us presents,' mused Estée.

Adelaide smiled at her daughter, suspecting that any reply she made would stick in her throat.

'I should call Roger,' said Adelaide, looking down at Rosemary who was on all fours under the table picking up food scraps from beneath the children's dining chairs.

'Save it for tomorrow,' said Rosemary, blowing a rogue curl from her face.

Sia returned with a large plate of watermelon that the children fell upon before she set it down on the table.

'Okay, Charlie,' said Rosemary, standing, 'just a couple of pieces and then we have to head home for a bath.'

Charlie, crunching loudly, gave no indication that she had heard her mother.

AFTER several failed attempts and choruses of wailing from three children, Rosemary and Charlie prepared to leave. Adelaide leant down to help Charlie with her coat and beanie, while Rosemary extracted the rest of their belongings from the tangle at the front door. Adelaide pulled Charlie's beanie down over her eyes and asked, 'Is that good? Did I do it right?'

'No!' giggled Charlie.

'How about now?' asked Adelaide, pulling it down farther before correcting it and kissing the little girl on the cheek.

She stood and looked at Rosemary. 'Thank you, Rosie,' she said, her eyes intent and serious.

Rosemary drew her into a firm embrace and whispered in her ear, 'You're my hero,' before ushering her daughter out into the cold night air.

'Okay, you guys, head upstairs and start getting undressed for your bath time please,' said Adelaide.

'I don't want bath time,' whined Darcy.

'We have a bath every night, you grub,' said Adelaide, tickling his ribs.

He giggled and the twins trudged upstairs, leaving Adelaide and her mother at the foot of the stairs.

'I was thinking I'd head home tomorrow afternoon,' said Sia, carefully.

Adelaide had grown so used to her mother's presence that she was momentarily taken aback by the statement.

'Yes, of course. I mean you're welcome to stay longer, but… Well, maybe you can come back for another stay soon.'

'I'd like that,' said Sia and turned to walk away.

'I couldn't have done this without you, Mum,' Adelaide called after her.

'Of course you could, but I'm happy to have helped,' said Sia, over her shoulder.

THAT night, Adelaide lay in bed fantasising about sleep. She wondered if she should go rummaging around for sleeping tablets but decided that the next-day brain fog would do nothing to help her plight. She listened to the whipping wind and heard the exact moment when fat drops of rain began to patter against the roof. She stared into the inky darkness until an unexpected flash partially lit up the room. Lightning? No, the light had come from her phone, switched to silent, resting on her bedside table. She rolled onto her side, reached for her charging phone and squinted into the screen.

Joy burst within her at the sight of Alec's name. It was such a surprising feeling, in stark contrast to how she felt a moment earlier, that it almost knocked the breath out of her. She had forgotten her body could produce the chemicals that caused such a feeling. She paused, savouring the moment until curiosity got the better of her and she swiped open the text.

"Hello friend (we are friends, right?), Just wanted to check on you. Xena told me she spoke to you, said you were being very courageous... which doesn't surprise me at all. We miss you here. We are sending our prayers and love."

Adelaide felt jubilation and sadness collide in sparky explosions inside her. She didn't feel courageous, and she certainly didn't feel heroic, as Rosemary had said she was. She felt small and battle-worn and strangely embarrassed when she thought of Ivy's daughter contesting the will. The whole situation gave Adelaide a sordid feeling, like she was some tacky character in a daytime drama trying to cheat the virtuous daughter out of what was rightfully hers. She vanquished the image and re-read Alec's message, her index finger hovering over the keypad as she waited for her sluggish brain to concoct a suitable response. But what could she say? "You are the happy thought that gets me through each day. When I am feeling the craziest, I worry that you are a figment of my imagination." She emitted an audible snigger, disturbing the silence of the otherwise peaceful house. *Well, what would be so wrong with that?* she mused. Emboldened by the anonymity of the night, she typed out her thoughts. *Trouble the darkness*, she recalled, feeling both amused by and detached from her own recklessness. She stared at the two glowing sentences, mesmerised. She would never send it of course. She reached for the delete button with her thumb but under shot it because her phone was laying almost flat, still tethered to the charger cord. The block of words turned blue, signifying their successful dispatch to Alec's eyes on the other side of the world. Adelaide sprang up, yanking her phone from the charger, her mouth thrust open comically.

34

SUNSHINE spliced in through a gap in the curtains as Adelaide woke feeling groggy and disoriented. She listened for her children but heard nothing. Perhaps they were still sleeping? The brightness of the light suggested that it was late in the morning. *What time is it?* She looked at her bedside clock and saw the white charger cord hanging limply over the side. Realisation hit her as the events of last night came back in quick succession, like a flipbook animation. The confessional text, mistakenly sent to Alec, the vigil she had held, unblinking as she tried to coax a reply from her screen using telekinesis. She must have fallen asleep while holding her phone. She searched frantically through the froth of her bed covers, locating it between two pillows. The screen lit up, obedient to her touch, revealing a single text from Joe. Adelaide fell back onto her bed with a groan.

"I'll finish work early and be over around 4:00. I've got an Airbnb from next week, so there's room for the kids to stay with me. I want joint custody—not negotiable."

Adelaide's stomach felt scooped out. The last thing she wanted was for her and Joe to enter a legal battle for their children, like a pair of mangy seagulls fighting over a chip. But the idea of only having her children with her half the time was soul-splitting. She supposed that Joe felt the same way. The riddle of this conundrum had her chasing her tail since the moment she realised she could not stay married to Joe. Secretly, she had hoped that Joe would be satisfied with partial custody, but she knew deep down that she was fooling herself. Joe could live without her but not without the twins. She replied to Joe, saying that this was fine and attached a link to one of the many parenting websites she had consulted, about how to navigate divorce with children.

Adelaide heard the front door open and close. She walked to the top of the stairs and saw her mother, pink-cheeked from the cold, returning from dropping the twins off at kindergarten.

'Oh, you're up,' said Sia, hanging her coat on the stand.

'You let me sleep?'

'You needed it.'

Adelaide smiled down at her mother.

'I'll make coffee while you get ready for work,' she said.

WHEN Adelaide arrived at Retrograde, Celeste was in the middle of a consultation with one of their real estate clients. Adelaide greeted the two women, made brief small talk, and headed upstairs to the office. A short time later, she heard the front door buzzer sound, followed by slow footsteps ascending the stairs. She walked to the top of the stairs and saw Roger clutching the handrail with both hands, making his way up.

'Roger!'

She rushed down to help him scale the last few steps, holding his elbow for support. Once at the top, he stood breathing hard, his pale eyes watery, whether with emotion or age, Adelaide couldn't say for sure.

'Hello, dear,' he said, sufficiently regaining his breath.

She helped him to sit.

'Can I get you anything? A tea?' asked Adelaide, protective of this frail, sweet man.

'No, no, I'm fine,' said Roger, waving a crooked hand.

Adelaide seated herself in the chair opposite him. *What must it be like for him to be here,* she wondered, her eyes involuntarily flicking back towards the stairs.

'I've come to talk to you about Amy,' he said carefully.

'Ah,' said Adelaide, leaning back in her chair.

'I'm very disappointed. Embarrassed even, by her behaviour. It's just that—if I can speak frankly, dear—she's always been jealous of you.'

'Jealous? Of me?'

'Ivy and Amy have never really seen eye to eye. They clashed so much when Amy was growing up. I think Ivy felt that Amy was ashamed of her, she always seemed to be standing in judgment of her, which reminded Ivy of her own mother. They even look alike,' said Roger, shaking his head.

Pulling out a large white handkerchief from his jacket pocket, he blotted his eyes and replaced it.

'And I suppose Amy felt as though her mother was never interested in her. Which wasn't true,' he added, thrusting a palm out. 'And then you came along and you just... gelled.'

Roger laced his knobbly fingers together to emphasise his words.

Adelaide looked down at her lap and nodded.

'Perhaps if you could talk to Amy,' said Roger, tentatively.

Adelaide straightened. What would she even say to Amy? *I'm sorry you think your mum loved me more than you, but she's dead now so you have to move on.*

Adelaide placed a hand on Roger's bony knee. 'If you think it would help, I will,' she said.

Roger extracted a scrap of paper from inside his jacket and pressed it into Adelaide's palm as Celeste arrived at the top of the stairs. He made a move to stand but didn't have sufficient momentum to extricate himself from the low armchair. Adelaide stood quickly and helped him up.

'I'll walk you out,' she offered.

'WHAT was all that about?' Celeste asked from her desk when Adelaide returned.

Adelaide slumped down into the chair opposite. 'Ivy's daughter is contesting the will.'

Celeste's eyes darted around as if following the trajectory of a fly.

'It means she's disputing it. She's saying that Ivy wasn't of sound mind when she left me this place,' Adelaide explained.

'Shut up!' said Celeste, throwing herself back in her chair.

'Roger wants me to call her,' said Adelaide, looking at his loopy scrawl on the scrap of paper.

'Yikes,' concluded Celeste.

WHEN Celeste left in search of lunch, Adelaide dialled Amy's number. The sound of the ringtone played like Chopin's Death March in her ears. The tune stopped and Adelaide heard a muffled voice imploring somebody to, 'Turn that thing down for a second, it won't kill you!'

'Hello, Amy speaking.'

'Hi, Amy, it's Adelaide Jones here.'

There was a long pause, followed by the sound of a closing door.

'Hello, Adelaide,' said Amy, coolly.

'Your dad thought it would be a good idea if we spoke,' Adelaide began.

'Oh?' she said, feigning innocence.

'About your contesting Ivy's will.'

'What's there to talk about?'

'You don't really believe that your mum was not of sound mind, do you?'

'Well, what other explanation could there be, Adelaide?'

Amy said her name as though it were something unsavoury.

'Honestly? I think Ivy knew you'd have no desire to run Retrograde. Frankly, I'm surprised that you do.'

'Who said I'm going to run it?' said Amy, as if Adelaide were the stupidest person on the planet.

'Then, why do you want it? Just to sell everything off and shut up shop?'

'As if I'd run Retrograde! I'd rather set a match to all that stinking old shit. How you convince people to buy that stuff is beyond me,' Amy scoffed.

Adelaide felt slapped, rendering her momentarily speechless.

Celeste returned with two plastic salad bowls and mouthed the word 'what?' in response to Adelaide's stunned expression.

'Your mother worked for decades building up this business, doesn't that mean anything to you? Don't you want to see her legacy live on?'

'That's right. *My* mother,' spat Amy.

If being the primary carer of two pre-schoolers had taught Adelaide anything, it was when to cut her losses. No good could come of this line of conversation.

'Well, I'm sorry you feel that way. For what it's worth, your mother loved you. I'm sorry if you feel like my relationship with her somehow detracted from that.'

'See you in court,' said Amy, snidely.

Adelaide slumped back in her chair, feeling like she had run a marathon. She looked up at Celeste, frozen to the spot, still clutching lunch.

'That sounded like a total drainer,' said Celeste, finding her voice.

'You can say that again,' agreed Adelaide.

Celeste put the salads down on the desk, sat opposite Adelaide and opened the lid of her own brimming container. The plastic groaned and the sound shot pins into Adelaide's already tender temples. She was no longer hungry.

Celeste crunched loudly. 'So, what did she say? Was it super awkward?'

'It really was. The poor woman thinks Ivy left Retrograde to me because she loved me and not her.'

'Psycho,' said Celeste, elongating the word in a sing-song tone, her mouth displaying a veritable garden bed of super greens.

'She's not psycho, she's just sad and angry and misguided. Maybe she thinks getting this place will prove she's won over me, I don't know. I find myself in a competition I never entered, for a prize I never actually wanted.'

Adelaide looked down at her unopened salad, hoping to be appetised. Instead, her eyes were distracted by the sudden illumination of her phone sitting beside it. A text from Alec. Adelaide's body jolted as she grabbed for her phone.

'Um, hello? Jumpy much?' teased Celeste, running a finger around the rim of her empty container and popping it into her mouth.

Adelaide laughed self-consciously.

'It's from a... friend... in Greece, who I've been waiting to hear from,' she said, purposely omitting the word "him" from her explanation.

Celeste pointed a shiny index finger at her and squinted, a smile curling her lips. 'Something happened over there and I'm going to find out what it was,' she said, gathering her rubbish and heading towards the kitchenette.

Adelaide steeled herself for the possibility that Alec's text would be reprimanding, or worse, indifferent. She opened the text and one word jumped out and slapped her in the face: "ruined". She took a deep breath and read.

"I used to be able to tell myself that my feelings for you were just daydreams. But now, I'm afraid you've ruined that, Adele. You have shown me that reality can be better than dreams so now I have nowhere to retreat to. The question is, when can I see you again to prove I'm not a figment of your imagination?"

Adelaide, realising she had been holding her breath, exhaled luxuriously.

THE smell of lemons and roast chicken greeted Adelaide when she opened the front door. She walked into the kitchen and found her mother ladling soup into two neat rows of plastic takeaway containers from a huge saucepan on the stove.

'What's all this?' asked Adelaide, grinning.

'*Avgolemono*,' said Sia, shrugging.

Her mother must have cooked all day.

Sia wiped her hands on her apron and rearranged the contents of Adelaide's freezer to make room for the stockpile.

'I spoke to Ivy's daughter today,' said Adelaide.

'Oh?'

'She seems pretty determined to get the business,' said Adelaide, leaning back against the bench.

'Well…' said Sia.

'Well?'

Adelaide knew that her mother's "wells" were laced with meaning.

'Well, sweetheart, how would you feel if I left my house to Louise from across the road and not to you?' Sia challenged.

Adelaide felt defensive, although she couldn't exactly say why.

'Well, does Louise like the house more than I do? Do I think the house is a pile of dirt?' Adelaide asked, her voice sounding snarkier than she had intended.

Sia didn't bother to reply, choosing instead to focus on her task. After placing the last container in the freezer, she made her way to the sink to retrieve a dishcloth that she took to the soup-speckled benchtop. She seemed to be grappling with something, deciding how to proceed.

'Spit it out, Mum,' said Adelaide, surprised to be channelling her teenage self.

Sia straightened and looked her dead in the eye. 'Okay,' she said, throwing the dishcloth onto the bench. 'You haven't made a single decision in your whole adult life.'

Adelaide flinched, regretting starting this conversation.

Sia went on, 'You started off so promising. All that study! No one in our family ever even went to university before and here you are getting a PhD in something I couldn't make heads nor tails of. I couldn't wait to see what you were going to make of your life. I knew it would be something more than someone like me could imagine. And then you got pregnant, to that absolute lump of a man who—to add insult to injury—you idolised!'

Adelaide stood rooted to the spot, trying to process the avalanche of words that crashed down on her.

Sia paused and adjusted her tone.

'Obviously I adore the twins. They are a blessing and a miracle, and I thank God every day for them. But now you have the chance to take charge of your own life and instead of doing that, you're going to step into Ivy's. That furniture store was her dream, not yours.'

Sia paused and narrowed her gaze upon Adelaide.

'So, my question for you is this: What is your dream, sweetheart?'

EPILOGUE

SEA spray kissed Adelaide's upturned face as the warm Mediterranean wind whipped through the tails of the scarf tied around her head, making them flutter at her nape. She checked her phone for any word from Alec but there still wasn't any service on the open sea. She breathed in deeply, enjoying the warm glow of nervous anticipation that travelled in an electrifying current up and down her sternum. The two years since she had been here had passed in an exhilarating blur.

Following her split from Joe, the twins had been her primary concern and Adelaide was relieved to find that Joe was as committed to helping them through their divorce as she was. In some strange, abstract way, apart from creating their two miraculous children, their division of one life into two was their greatest achievement, a validation of their entire relationship, their swansong.

At first, Adelaide found the alternate weeks without the twins heart-wrenching, especially in the evenings. The house was so quiet that she sometimes wanted to scream, just to break the unbearable silence. That's when she started reaching out to her old contacts: professors, gallery curators and fellow students from her university days.

One of her former professors, Janeen Winters, had left teaching to embark upon an ambitious project to document what she described as "endangered" textile techniques. When she heard of Adelaide's seedling of an idea to partner folk-artisans with ethical-designers, she was utterly enthused. 'We can form a kind of conservation society!' she quipped. And so Dxtrs was born.

It was Celeste's idea to start a crowdfunding campaign to finance the company, and the two women once again worked side by side after the liquidation of Retrograde by Ivy's daughter. The most remarkable contribution of all however came from Joe, who convinced the new board of Grasp Digital to build the platform, which now formed the foundation of Dxtrs, as a charitable donation. Adelaide supposed his generosity was the product of being in love and happy. Joe had met Sharon at a mentorship program that paired successful entrepreneurs with those aspiring to take the next step with their businesses. She was the owner operator of a nail salon, looking to expand to multiple locations. Just yesterday, in Bali, they had married, with Estée, Darcy and Sharon's teenage son Bryce looking on.

Adelaide's phone vibrated to life in her dress pocket and she hastened to retrieve it. A cluster of texts from various people beeped into existence as the ferry drew nearer to Ikaria. Business updates from Janeen, poorly framed and slightly out of focus pictures sent by Joe's mother from the wedding, and a brief text from Alec.

"Won't be able to make it, stuck at the hotel. I've sent a colleague, I will see you tonight."

Disappointment fizzed through her body, despite her best efforts to deter it. It was completely reasonable that Alec would need to work, and it was only a few more hours until she would meet him for dinner. Still, when the ferry docked at the port, Adelaide made no rush to disembark. She shuffled along with the last of the passengers, staring at her espadrilles and taking care to keep a firm hold on her suitcase. She craned towards the car park, looking for the familiar shape of the Ilios Choros Kombi van but could barely see anything past the throng of holidaymakers. As her shoes touched the concrete of the pier, an almighty roar erupted just ahead of her.

It took Adelaide a moment to register that the small crowd was assembled for her. Xena and Alessia waved their arms and whistled as Xena's mother and aunt clapped their hands. Penny stood smiling, balancing a chubby baby boy on her left hip, an ash-haired man smiling sheepishly at her side.

At their centre Alec stood, his arms outstretched, the wind ruffling the bottom of his white shirt to reveal glimpses of his tanned stomach. His hair blew in the breeze and, as he swept it up from his eyes, Adelaide could have sworn he transformed into the teenage boy she had fallen for more than two decades prior. His smile was broad, his eyes sparkling mischievously.

Adelaide stopped on the spot and hung her head to laugh. She stood there a moment shaking her head at the silly sweetness of this gesture of friendship. Abandoning her suitcase and handbag on the dock she made the last few steps at a jog and was scooped off the ground by Alec who had run to meet her. He buried his face in her neck and breathed in deeply before setting her down, shielding her from their friends' gazes with his body. He looked down at her and she came alive. She lifted herself up on the tips of her toes and kissed him deeply, savouring the delicious taste of possibility.

ACKNOWLEDGEMENTS

The first person I must thank is Torie Miller. If it wasn't for her slightly unnerving ability to ask the exact question I didn't know needed answering, I wouldn't have figured out that I needed to write, just write, like, immediately.

To my husband, Paul Rabinovich, who didn't laugh out loud when I told him I would *try* to write a novel, and who commemorated the first 10,000 words with prosecco and Rare Earth's *I just want to celebrate*.

To Marion Osmond, whose conviction in my eventual authordom bordered on the terrifying. To Lisa Kelly, whose encouragement could be felt from all the way across the pond. To Vicky Hanlon, whose technical knowledge of writing awes and mystifies me. To Peter Gaitanis, David Bowley and Russell Freeman, who provided invaluable feedback and encouragement during drafting of my contemporary women's fiction novel, though they are neither women nor contemporary.

To Elysia Todd, Fin MacDonald and Karl Phillips, for treating me as though I am the source of sunlight. To my mother, Lisa Freeman, who thinks I'm the greatest author in history, living or dead, and my father, Bryan Freeman, who doesn't. To Davie, for making me a mother, and to Edie, for making me a writer.

Thank you to the countless friends who enthusiastically volunteered to read drafts of this novel and for the kind emails that followed. To Carolyn Martinez, from Hawkeye Publishing, for comments in the margins like 'Holy shit! I'm totally sucked into this story!'

And, finally, to you, the reader. Thanks for taking a chance on a debut author, and for accompanying Adelaide on her journey. I hope you found what you needed in these pages—I loved every minute of creating them for you.

.

ABOUT THE AUTHOR

From her little teak desk in Northcote, Victoria, Anne writes contemporary fiction about women who are stuck in life and the extraordinary ways they shake themselves loose. They're always engaging and sometimes funny with reluctant adventures, sexy escapades and friendships that uplift.

A former award-winning milliner, promotional model, wanderluster, television extra, accessories designer, vintage market organiser, sales and marketing maven and creator of human life – Anne now chalks up her kaleidoscopic past to research and character development.

In stolen moments, she undertakes a Bachelor of Creative Writing at Deakin University.

Returning to Adelaide is her first novel.

Book reviews can make or break a book. If you liked what you read today, please do consider posting a review on Goodreads or your favourite forum.

Returning to Adelaide is available at www.hawkeyebooks.com.au and all good bookstores and libraries.